Iz the Apocalypse

Iz the Apocalypse

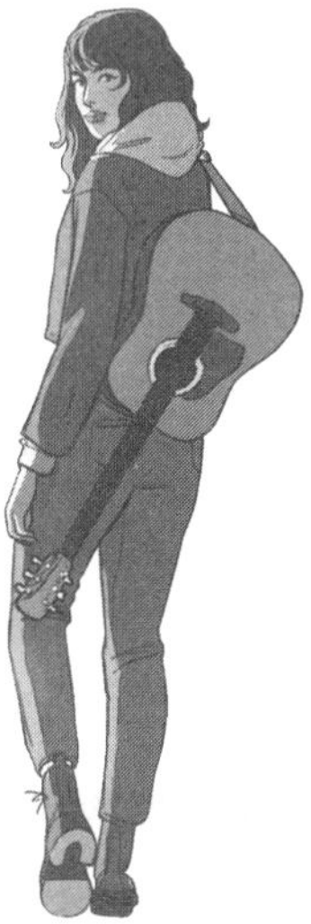

Susan Currie

Common Deer Press

Published by Common Deer Press Incorporated.

Published in 2023 by Common Deer Press
1745 Rockland Ave.
Victoria, BC
V8S 1W6

Library and Archives Canada Cataloguing in Publication

Title: Iz the apocalypse / Susan Currie.
Names: Currie, Susan, 1967- author.
Identifiers: Canadiana (print) 20230159079 |
Canadiana (ebook) 20230159087 | ISBN 9781988761848 (softcover) |
ISBN 9781988761862 (EPUB)
Classification: LCC PS8555.U743 I99 2023 | DDC jC813/.6—dc23

Cover Illustration: Bex Glendining
Book Design: David Moratto

Printed in Canada
www.commondeerpress.com

This book is dedicated to three people:
to Rachel, who was singing before she could talk;
to John, my brilliant and beloved life partner;
and to Heather Cooke, passionate supporter of all things Métier.

"Art is chaos taking shape."

—Pablo Picasso

Chapter One

The opening chord of the music exploded in Dennison Hall, shattering the silence.

And Iz Beaufort, sitting there in the audience, suddenly burst into tears like a complete idiot.

"Shut up," she was whispering furiously to herself.

But as the music gained momentum, she found herself getting more stupidly worked up, not less.

It was the way the chord *looked*.

All charcoal grey and black, streaked through with sullen blue, with flashes of slicing silver. It was like some multi-storey building that loomed and morphed in Iz's head.

Meanwhile, Audra Allen started kicking the back of her chair, saying, "Hey new kid, some of us are trying to watch the *show*."

Which was a joke, because Audra Allen had been going around telling everyone how boring this concert was going to be.

"Sorry," Iz muttered.

She hunched down in her chair, crossed her arms furiously and protectively, trying to get the music out of her head. But the trouble was, Iz and music were totally complicated. It was like some relationship in which they were always fighting or making up or ghosting each other.

Mostly ghosting for the last two years, actually.

That was when she'd shoved her guitar under the bed and vowed not to play it again. It was right after she'd been in a really bad foster home, where playing the guitar had led to horrible things she mostly tried not to think about now. It had been a survival thing, hiding it away, going undercover, pulling a kind of fog around herself, and trying not to stand out.

And she'd mostly succeeded.

But here in Dennison Hall, at the most unlikely of moments, this extraordinary chord was smashing doors open in her head. Memories were spilling out.

She was thinking about the curve of her guitar under her arm.

She was thinking about placing her fingers on the frets in places that were *homes*.

She was thinking about the way she could pick out one melody line, then add others and see them like threads she was twisting together into some complex piece of weaving.

"Hey! New girl!"

Iz swung around.

Audra was smirking at her, and the other kids were doing that thing where you pretend not to laugh but you also want the person to know you are pretending not to laugh.

"Everything . . . okay?" Audra said.

"It's great," Iz said tersely.

"'Cause we're getting a little worried back here."

"Sorry about that," Iz said.

She twisted back around to the front, ignoring their giggles.

Audra Allen had picked Iz out on the first day Iz arrived at the school. Audra, like so many other bullies, had kind of sensed that something was not quite normal about Iz. And, restless and bored, hunting around for something to dominate, Audra had settled on her, because she had known Iz wouldn't fight back.

She was right on all counts.

Iz was absolutely no good at normal. Other people didn't seem to get all tangled up like she did when they listened to music. They didn't seem to picture it as a kind of structure with additions and passages you could go down. Nor, as far as she could tell, did they spend all their time fighting with themselves, wrestling between rebellion and fear and a weird kind of frustrated grief.

Applause exploded over the auditorium.

Iz raised her head then.

The musicians dropped their arms and grinned at the audience. They turned and slapped hands together, laughed, threw an arm around each other's shoulders. Released from the focus and precision of that wild performance, they were now loose-limbed and utterly cheerful.

And she realized with surprise—

They were scarcely older than she was.

They were kids.

A man strode onto the stage, amid the applause. He was tall, with a mop of black hair. He moved easily, like he was completely comfortable in himself.

When he spoke, his voice drifted out mildly, as if he was strolling around some flower show.

"Good afternoon! I am Dr. Aaron Perlinger, and this is Manifesto, from The Métier School. Let me introduce them. From the left—Becky, Ahmed, Rina, Jasleen, Kwame, Teo, Will, Bijan, LaRoyce."

Applause burst out again while the performers shuffled around grinning somewhat self-consciously now.

Dr. Perlinger continued, "Everything is written and performed by these extraordinary young musicians. But that is not the most important thing about them. They *support* each other. They *build* each other. They hold each other up."

"It all comes from you, Dr. P," said one of the girls onstage. She was standing beside a large instrument that looked like an overgrown violin. "That's what makes Manifesto what it is."

"Ha! I just walk alongside you all, Jasleen," he said. "I just encourage what's there already."

Iz was staring, trying to make sense of this conversation. Who were these kids who could write something as endlessly powerful and complicated and multifaceted as that chord? And who was this man who directed them and spoke about how they all looked after one another? Why did they beam at him like they loved him?

A pain erupted in her out of nowhere, so strong she was bent over with it. It was a woken-up, broken kind of longing. Because she had the strongest feeling suddenly that if she tried to explain herself to these kids, to this man, they might *actually understand.*

Dr. Perlinger said, "That piece you just heard was called 'Post-Punk Beethoven.' It's the creation of Ahmed and Will and Kwame here. Tell us about it?"

He ushered three boys to the front, who were shuffling around and bashful but with eyes like intelligent arrows.

They started talking at top speed, filling in each other's thoughts.

"Yeah, we were kind of riffing on the idea of *rebellion*."

"And post-punk is like rebellion on top of the original rebellion of punk. Joy Division, Talking Heads, The Cure—"

"Then there's Beethoven. He ushered in a whole new era by basically blowing up the rules for how you write music—"

"So we kind of mashed them up together, like rebellion on top of rebellion on top of rebellion!"

Rebellion on rebellion on rebellion.

She had seen that in their music—piled-up strata that were all about refusing to accept the way things were and fighting against what held you back.

Maybe that was why she had burst into tears.

Because it had been like seeing her own complicated self looking back at her.

All at once, she wondered—what would *her* life have been like, if Dominion Children's Care hadn't spiraled her through twenty-six foster homes and fourteen schools? What if she had not learned to be afraid of writing songs and playing her guitar because of what had happened in That Place? What if there had been a group like Manifesto for her to join, and a leader like Dr. Perlinger to walk beside her and bring out of her what was already there?

For the first time in ages, she longed to actually take out her guitar. She longed to play alongside them.

It was like that chord was the Big Bang or something.

The universe inside Iz was suddenly expanding outward at an unthinkable speed.

Chapter Two

When Iz entered Pat's house after school, Pat and Britnee were sitting in the living room, surrounded by mountains of fabric and sequins. They were laughing and cutting and gluing.

Pat looked up with a gentle, unseamed face, like the moon on a clear night. "Hi, honey. School good?"

Britnee held up a ruffled thing. "Butter dish holder!"

Britnee was Pat's daughter. She was marrying Vance in only a few months. Pat and Britnee spent most of their time working on wedding favours and phoning people to sort out issues. Vance spent most of his time being silent.

Iz found herself saying, "We had our field trip today. It was these kids from this place called The Métier School. They auditioned to get into it."

"That's the one downtown," Britnee said in her husky, luxurious voice. "Fancy schmancy international high school for music. My friend tried out but didn't get in."

"Probably dodged a bullet." Pat peacefully bit off a seam.

"Oh, totally. She said later she would have hated it."

"Why?" Iz said.

"Just, you know, places like that can be a little full of themselves. A little too-too." Britnee folded a blue ribbon like an accordion between her fingers and deftly pinned it.

"Right." Iz shifted from foot to foot. She wasn't planning to say anything more, but somehow heard her voice talking anyway. "How . . . how did she audition?"

Britnee flicked her lashes up at Iz and asked humorously, "Why, are you going to try out?"

"Ha! No!" Iz flushed.

Pat smiled kindly at her. "Oh, hon, can you even imagine?"

Iz swallowed, pushed everything down. "Yeah, that would be crazy. Well, I've got a lot of homework. Think I'll go upstairs and get started."

"Take a snack, Iz. There are cookies. Chocolate chip. I made them this afternoon."

"Thanks, I will!"

Iz grabbed three cookies from the plate on the counter, then backtracked through the living room and up the stairs, past the portraits of Pat and Britnee beaming on a cruise ship, on a beach, in a restaurant.

She entered her bedroom, closed the door softly. Then she sat down on the floor and peered under the bed.

"There you are," she whispered.

It had been living under beds for the last two years.

It looked lonely, rootless, like it had been starved for affection. She pulled it toward her, pushing aside crumpled papers and food she kept on hand just in case. Then she opened the lid, lifted the guitar out at last, and simply held it against her chest. She rocked it, like an abandoned child.

"Remember when I found you? In the dumpster. And you didn't have any strings, till I made a deal with that guy. He stole them from his brother, and I did his math worksheets for a month."

No one would want her to do their assignments now.

It flashed into her head then, a sudden clear memory of back when she'd been eager to go to school each day, when she'd been creative, optimistic, curious about things. That had been before everything had happened in That Place. Before the things that Iz was not going to think about right now.

She crossed her legs and drew the guitar into position. Ran her hand along its curved side. Played a cluster of notes, tuned it, played again, head practically resting on its comforting wood. At last, her fingers picked out a series of darting fragments, like someone escaping.

Her old notebook was in the guitar case too. She drew it out and flipped through the pages, looking at all the songs she had written.

Then she turned to a blank page and stared at it.

After getting out of That Place, she had not ever written songs again. Melodies and ideas had slowed in her mind, like sap that had been chilled. But now, for the first time in ages, a new tune was gnawing at her, and rebellious words were forming themselves.

Slowly at first, and then more quickly, she scribbled. She went back and crossed some words out, added others. Then she created a little meandering guitar line that played against her voice, looping above and below. She could picture it in her mind—two bright strings flying together and apart.

Softly, under her breath so Pat and Britnee wouldn't hear it, Iz sang.

My compass is not the same as yours
I will not walk the roads you choose for me
You say my road's not there at all
Although it seems to me that it is all I see
You say my compass is lost like me
But I'm running from you
And I am
A joyful refugee

As she played and sang, Iz felt like she had joined some kind of living current. She was filled with it, urged on by it.

She had no idea how much time had passed when she finally let her hands drop. It was only then that she decided for sure what she needed to do.

Iz opened her door and looked up and down the hallway. No one was there. Finally she crept across the hall and right through the open door opposite her own room. Her heart was pounding.

The walls in the room were dotted with photos of Britnee in each grade at school, at first dressed up in frilled outfits like a doll and later wearing trendy designer clothes.

But none of that mattered. The important thing was the heavy laptop computer sitting on the little table by the window. It looked like it was a thousand years old, but maybe it would still work.

Iz inched into the desk chair, pressed the ON button. At first nothing happened. But then, grudgingly, the laptop began making resentful waking-up noises. After what seemed like forever, a logo appeared, followed by a desktop view of several icons.

Iz fumbled around until she found her way online.

Then she typed quickly into the address bar.

The Métier School.

First the screen was black, and then words appeared: *A new vision of musicianship.* Then a picture gradually emerged—young people running down a rocky hill with energy and purpose and rawness. With a shock, she realized she was staring into the faces of the kids in Manifesto. It dissolved into other photos. Rehearsal halls. Orchestras. Choirs.

Her eyes flicked ravenously through the list of links, till she saw it.

Auditions.

She slammed her finger down on the mouse.

"Iz?"

Britnee's voice was soft, but Iz leapt out of the chair, twisted in the air so she landed facing Britnee like a cornered animal.

"Ha!" Iz said. "I'm sorry! I should have asked."

Britnee gazed at her with pale-blue eyes. "Oh, baby, I'm sure my mom doesn't care if you use the computer. At least someone's using it! But what are you doing?"

"I—" Iz said. "I just was doing some homework."

"What homework? Need help?"

Her mind raced. "No, thanks, I-I think I know what to do. It's for music. We have to write a report about the concert today. I was just looking up the website of that school."

Britnee gazed at Iz a bit more with those uncanny eyes which seemed to be cataloguing everything about Iz. Finally she said, "Cool."

They smiled at each other.

"I, uh, so," Iz said. How did you politely tell someone to go away?

Britnee turned and walked to the door. As she was heading into the hallway, she said, "Hey, if you have any trouble figuring that old thing out, just call me. I had to use it all through school because Mom was too technophobic to upgrade to something decent."

"Okay," Iz said.

Britnee drifted down the hallway, leaving the door open as if Iz might get into some kind of criminal activity if she wasn't watched closely.

Iz sat there all rustled and confused, wondering what on earth was wrong with herself.

She couldn't audition for The Métier School. Pat and Britnee had laughed out loud at the idea—with good reason. After all, Iz had been in twenty-six homes and fourteen schools by the age of fourteen, always arriving in classrooms that were in the middle of things and leaving before anything was completed. Her knowledge was all fragmented and piecemeal.

Also, she'd never had music lessons.

And then there was the fact that she hadn't even written anything or sung or played her guitar in two years.

But she stared again at the faces of Manifesto. They looked so confident, so happy. Everything in her yearned to be with them.

And suddenly she knew she was going to audition whether Pat and Britnee thought it was stupid or not. And she wasn't going to tell them—not until after, and only if she got in.

Her eyes raced over the instructions on the screen. There was an online form to fill out. That was easy enough. And she had to attach a transcript and two letters of reference.

It didn't take long for her to learn that a transcript was a list of all of your school grades, and a letter of reference was something an adult wrote to tell people how great you were. Which sounded simple, except that Iz's grades were terrible and no adults knew her well enough to say anything particularly enthusiastic.

She sat there feeling completely discouraged for a few minutes, until something hit her.

It was so audacious that all she could do was sit there and let out a low, appalled whistle.

"Hey," Britnee said from the door.

Iz's heart practically flung itself out of her chest.

"H-hey!"

"I don't think the printer's hooked up. This cord should work."

"Oh! Good! Thanks!"

Hastily, Iz clicked the registration form closed, as Britnee leaned behind the laptop and fiddled with the cord. She turned on the printer and it made chugging noises. "Okay, I think it's good, if you need it. How are you submitting your work?"

"Uh," Iz stammered. "I'm not sure. They didn't say."

"Just print it off then. That's the safest."

"Perfect!" Iz said tensely.

"Let me know if there's anything else."

"I will!"

Britnee stepped lightly back into the hall, leaving the door open again.

Iz let out a long, slow breath.

She thought again of that outrageous thing.

What if—

What if you created a school that didn't exist?

Her brain started to race. She could probably find examples of transcripts online and create her own, with the kinds of marks that she *might* have gotten if everything in her whole life had been different. She could write letters of reference from teachers at that imaginary school—Compass Community School—who would have known her since she was very young.

It shouldn't be so hard. Iz hadn't really had much experience with computers in any of the foster homes—too scared to ask, and nobody ever offered—but at school she had learned how to create documents and how to insert images. She knew how to upload things.

And obviously she could create a fake address and phone number, and fake email addresses for her fake parents, when she filled in the registration form.

It was all pretty basic.

It was also completely illegal and wrong.

And she had not felt so alive in ages.

Chapter Three

Phil's Music Store was empty except for a mother and kid looking at trumpets, and a tall young man who was helping them.

And Iz.

She was holding Pat's phone in her shaking hand. She was going to take photos of books. Then she'd send them to the new email address she'd set up for herself last night (surprisingly easy to do). After that, she'd make hard copies using the printer Britnee had set up.

Because she had an audition scheduled for December 2nd at 11:15 am—three weeks from now.

When Iz had taken the phone out of Pat's bedside table, her heart had been pounding so hard, she was sure Pat and Britnee would be able to hear it. *You could be kicked out for stealing. You could go to juvenile detention.*

But Iz was counting on nobody noticing it was missing. She'd overheard Britnee saying to Pat, "What's the point of having a phone when you just keep it in your bedroom drawer?"

"It just has too many bells and whistles," Pat had said.

"Mommy! It's the best phone out there! People lined up around the block for this version. And anyway, I could *help* you."

"Can I help you?"

Iz jumped. The young man had slipped in behind her.

"Uh—no, just browsing," Iz said, flushing.

"Let me know if you need anything." He headed back to the counter, waving goodbye to the mom and kid.

Iz drifted along behind the shelves. What she needed was something completely simple, for someone who didn't even know how to read notes. Because that was her. Everything she did was by listening and then picturing all of the sounds in her head.

Then she saw it—*Theory for Beginners.*

She grinned. That was exactly what she needed.

The first chapter was entitled "What Are Notes Anyway?" It showed lines with circles on them, similar to what she had occasionally seen at school in music classes. But she'd never really paid attention to what was happening because there was no point. She'd be gone before long.

Iz centred the phone on the page and took a picture.

Then she flipped the page, clicked again.

She had gotten through eleven pages when the young man spoke directly behind Iz.

"You know, you are actually supposed to buy the books."

Iz whipped around, then stood there numbly because she hadn't thought through what she'd do if she got caught.

"Taking a theory course?" His face wasn't all that disapproving. More curious.

She shrugged, half-nodded, wary.

"Who's your teacher? Some of them have arrangements with the store."

"Connor McHugh," Iz said immediately. That was the author's name on the book.

The young man frowned. "I'll look him up in the system."

Not surprisingly, he returned shaking his head. "He's not in there. Sorry about that. I can't offer you a discount."

"That's okay," Iz said, feeling tense and cornered. Without thinking she added, "I don't have any money anyway."

Flushing, she began to walk to the door.

"Hey," he said.

She turned.

The young man regarded her for a long minute.

"So you just came in to take pictures of things."

"Yeah. I—I just wanted to learn about rudiments of theory. And—" She consulted the crumpled papers in her hand. "A vocalise and contrasting songs from two musical time periods, and scales and arpeggios."

"Voca*leeze*," he said, but not unkindly. Gently, actually.

"Voca*leeze*."

He regarded her. "That's a very specific list."

"Yeah. It doesn't matter. I'm sorry. I'm going to go."

Iz began to feel claustrophobic with him staring at her.

She tried to blink away the tears that were suddenly blurring everything, but they fell down her cheeks anyway. All she could do was swipe at them, furious and embarrassed and confused and defiant all at once.

The young man said softly, "What if you tell me who you are and why you need to take pictures of these things today?"

Iz could only shake uselessly and mutinously at him.

He held out his hand. "I'm Jamaal Wickerson. And you are?"

She mumbled, "Iz Beaufort."

"Hey." His head was on one side, regarding her. "Hey, come sit down."

He led her over to one of the couches. Iz followed numbly. Now that she'd been exposed, she was weirdly frozen—unable to speak or to run either. Her eyes rambled desperately around the room, trying to avoid his gaze.

Jamaal smiled at her, very patiently and carefully, as if she was a wild animal he was trying to tame. "So I'm a music student at the university, working on my doctorate. I'm also a teaching assistant there, and I have a band, and I write music, and I work here part time. How about you?"

His face was friendly and open as he waited.

When she didn't answer, he continued kindly. "You know, when I was a kid, I had this teacher at school. She taught me music for free. I owe everything to her, actually."

There was a silence.

"Want to play me something?" he said.

Iz looked down at her old guitar case, and back up at Jamaal.

Finally she took out the guitar, held it in her arms, placed her fingers on the strings, and strummed gently. She closed her eyes, shut everything out.

The song she'd written last night came into her head then.

You say no road is even there at all
Although it seems to me that it is all I see

There were two melodies she started to explore on the guitar—one that sought to fly and one stuck in earth. They circled, in a standoff. But the very power of their battle fuelled them, and somehow they rose up, still wrestling, with the world laid out below.

When the song ended, she let the last chord linger in the air.

Finally, she opened her eyes.

Jamaal was looking intently at her, intelligent eyebrows drawn.

She took a breath, smeared tears with her fist, glared down at the guitar. Her voice started spurting out words she had not expected to be saying.

"I have an audition for The Métier School on December 2nd. I don't know anything. I can't even read music."

Jamaal exhaled very softly and slowly. He nodded, as if he actually got what she was saying. Then he asked, "What are the entrance requirements?"

Iz actually glanced at him then and saw that he was genuinely interested. She took another shuddering breath and let it out slowly. Should she?

A second later, she found herself passing him the wrinkled audition papers.

Jamaal's eyes flicked back and forth across the pages.

"Okay. I can help with this. Let's find some vocal repertoire. I've got an idea—"

Then he took off amid the bookshelves. He was gone a long time. When he came back, he spread out several books on the couch beside Iz.

"Take a picture of this page, and this one ..."

Over the next hour, she did as he directed. Occasionally, someone would come into the store and Jamaal would disappear to help them out. Then he would be back, often with another book.

Sometime during the hour, they migrated to the piano. There, Jamaal played and sang all kinds of songs—some lyrical, some like intricate puzzles, and one that seemed deranged and panting, like it was running for its life.

"What's that?" she said.

"'The Erlking.' By Franz Schubert."

She said softly, "It sounds like being scared of someone."

"Ha!" Jamaal grinned. "Funny you should say that. It's about this evil demon guy who's chasing a father and son through a forest. He wants to catch the son. The son knows he's there but the dad doesn't believe it."

"What ... what happens?"

"Oh," Jamaal said cheerfully, "the demon gets the kid. The kid dies."

Iz's insides clenched. And for a minute she couldn't figure out why. Then she realized. She'd tried to tell people there was a demon in That Place. They hadn't listened either.

She said softly, "Can you play that one again?"

It was much later that she noticed the sky was darkening outside the shop window.

"I think I have to go."

Jamaal nodded. "You get all the photos you wanted?"

"Except in here." Iz held out the *Theory for Beginners* book.

"Tell you what, that one's on the house. I'm going to buy it for you. It's my good luck gift for your audition." His eyes were warm.

Iz frowned, completely confused. She wanted to ask him why he was being so helpful and kind. In her experience, people were not often like that.

As if Jamaal guessed what was going through her mind, he said, "Mrs. Daskalov. She was my school teacher. I'd hang around after class and she'd show me stuff on the piano. And she taught me guitar—we used hers." He regarded Iz. "I wouldn't be defending my PhD in a few weeks without her."

"Well, but still, I can't—"

"Think of it this way," Jamaal said matter-of-factly. "It's like a chain of giving. She didn't have to help me, but she did. Maybe she saw something in me, who knows? And maybe I'm seeing something in you, so I want to help *you*. Then, maybe one day, you'll be blown away by some incredible young musician who could use a hand. And you'll pass it on. And maybe they will pass it on too, to someone else we can't even imagine. Maybe a century from now, someone will be passing on the giving from today. All connected."

"Thank you," Iz said, in a barely there voice.

He smiled at her. "No thanks needed. Just come back if you have questions. I work on Tuesday and Thursday nights. And definitely tell me how the audition goes."

"I will," she said, lying.

You always moved on—whether they made you or you did it yourself.

Then she was waving goodbye, and sprinting back toward Pat's house, as the sky darkened.

As she ran, Pat's phone abruptly burst into a metallic jig. Words flashed on the screen: *Baby Brit*.

For a minute, Iz couldn't figure out what was going on. Then the awful truth dawned on her—Britnee was calling the phone.

They'd figured out it was missing. Britnee was trying to locate it.

With unsteady fingers, she selected all of the photos and sent them to her new email. She deleted them from Pat's phone. She wiped it with her sleeve to get the fingerprints off and shoved it in her pocket.

When Iz opened the door to Pat's house, Britnee's voice was blaring like an exasperated trombone: "I just hope you didn't leave it anywhere public."

"I can't even remember if I've ever even taken it out of the house, but I might have."

"Mom! Someone could have stolen your identity! They could be racking up huge bills on it. We have to call the provider."

"I hate that thing!" Pat said fervently.

Iz silently took out one of Pat's purses from the closet, slipped the phone into the front pocket—then put it back on the shelf.

"Iz! Are you there?" Britnee padded out, golden eyebrows drawn together.

Iz swung around.

"Yeah. Sorry I'm late. Uh … there was a school club. Singing. Like in a choir." Her voice was faltering.

Britnee said slowly, "I wanted to show Mom how to use her phone today, and it was missing from where it usually is. You didn't happen to see it, did you?"

"Her … phone?" Iz said, blinking. "No. I haven't seen it."

The way Britnee was looking at her, Iz could tell she was not quite convinced.

A weird part of her felt almost indignant. Why assume that the foster kid had stolen the phone?

Even though she *had*.

"I, uh … I have studying to do."

She crept upstairs, opened her email, and sent all the photos to the printer. Then she stood by the door, listening for feet on the stairs and willing the ancient machine to hurry up.

At last, the final paper yawned its way out. Iz snatched up the papers, remembered to shut down her email, and raced silently back into her own room.

She shut the door.

She half kneeled in front of the bed.

She spread the papers out in piles.

"The Erlking"
"Where'er you walk"
"Vocalise in G minor"
The Romantic period
The Baroque period

It felt good to just look at everything. It felt like making a plan. It felt like starting an adventure.

More than anything else, it felt like not sitting back—not allowing other people to decide what would happen next.

At that moment, someone shouted something downstairs. Then she heard footsteps coming upstairs and along the hallway.

"Iz. Can I come in?"

Britnee was knocking and opening the door at the same time.

"Sure. Everything okay?" Iz said tensely, jumping up and shielding Britnee's view of the papers on the bed.

"Hon, I wanted to tell you, we just found the phone. It was in one of Mom's purses."

"I, uh, okay, good," Iz said, feeling completely numb.

There was an awkward pause.

"And I just wanted to say, you are such a good kid. And you have such a bright future ahead of you. You just work so hard. Baby, sky is the limit for you, seriously."

Britnee was trying to make up for thinking Iz had stolen the phone. It was all so condescending and humiliating. But obviously, Iz had no business feeling resentful.

"Thanks," she said tightly.

Chapter Four

Over the next while, she slipped into a weird double life.

During the day, she was the usual Iz, who didn't make eye contact with anyone and kept to herself. She went to school and tried not to be noticed. At Pat's house, she listened to the two of them talk about rosettes for the wedding trellises and sympathized when Britnee complained that Vance was hardly involved in anything.

But at night, when Iz closed the door to her room, she turned into that wild, woken-up other person.

She pored over all of the pages Jamaal had found for her, listening urgently in her head to the melodies he had sung and played. She figured out how to sing them herself, going over and over each part till she had it all figured out.

And she started to construct accompaniments for her songs on the guitar—arcs and phrases that seemed to fit the melody and the words.

Like in "Where'er you walk."

It was about a girl who was so beautiful that nature actually rearranged itself to make life easier for her. So Iz experimented with creating several melodic guitar lines that bent gracefully around each other as if they were branches twisting themselves into a swing for the girl.

"Vocalise in G minor" felt a bit sneaky and furtive, so she built fleeting clusters of rapid notes on the guitar that were like someone darting around. She had four tunes going at once and she could see them in her mind, the notes creeping guiltily sideways, up and down.

Mostly, she was able to keep the two sides of her life separate. But sometimes they blended in her head. The Erlking thundered through the forest while she was trying to work on a math assignment. Or she started hearing a scale in her head as she climbed to the second floor of the school.

And sometimes everything spilled right out.

Like one day at her locker, when a voice sang derisively, "Hey. Why are you always *humming*? Like, are you not right in the head?"

Iz whirled around, dropping the crumpled papers in her hand—notes about the Baroque and Romantic musical periods. She crouched down, grabbed them up.

Audra Allen stood there, surrounded by the little gaggle of girls that followed her around.

"Are you, like, trying to be a mosquito? Because I don't want to hurt your feelings, but you kind of sound like one."

The others giggled.

Iz flushed.

Think of scales.

And arpeggios. Like skip-counting up a staircase by twos and threes.

She'd been practising them obsessively for the last few days, exactly as Jamaal had demonstrated them. She could *see* them laid out, like a blueprint.

"Are you going to cry again?" Audra said. "Like at the concert? Music makes you emotional, huh?"

Forcing her voice not to shake, Iz said, "You don't know anything about me."

"Duh," said Audra Allen. "Obviously. You've only been here for two weeks. I'm not psychic. But I do know you had yourself a little meltdown at the concert. Quite the drama. Does that happen every time you hear music? If so, you should really get it looked at."

Her voice was light, almost dancing around Iz like some kind of poisonous moth.

"What do you even care?" Iz said, clutching her papers in a chokehold.

"Well, I mean, it's going to hold you back in life, isn't it? 'Cause that's just not normal. It's not *balanced*," Audra said.

Iz stood there, rage simmering, trying to hold it back.

Then a memory shot into her head—*that chord*. She thought of the boys who had written it.

She said in a kind of strangled voice, "What does *balanced* even mean?"

"Uh," Audra said, "if you have to ask, I'm pretty sure you're not there yet."

Suddenly, Iz was stepping forward. Without even planning to, she pushed Audra hard. The other girl stumbled backward and into a teacher passing by.

The teacher almost tripped. She turned, like a slow-moving storm front. "What's going on?"

Audra's voice was filled with outrage. "She's crazy. She just shoved me for nothing."

"Is that right?" The teacher was looking right at Iz now.

"Sh-she insulted me," Iz said, flooding with anxiety.

"What did she say?"

"She made fun of me for humming."

As Iz spoke the words, she could hear how stupid they sounded.

Sure enough, the teacher said, "That hardly seems like a reason to shove someone."

"Yeah. Violence is never the answer," said Audra.

"Are you new?" the teacher said, looking down at Iz.

"Uh, kind of."

"What grade?"

"Eighth." Though it should have been ninth, if not for that year they'd kept her back.

And it *would* be ninth, if she got into The Métier School.

"And where were you before?"

Iz sighed. Then she gazed off into the middle distance and recited the whole list of schools, all fourteen of them. And when she looked back at the teacher, she pretty much knew what would come next.

Sure enough, the teacher's face changed. "That's a lot of schools."

"It sure is," Iz said, not meeting her eyes.

The teacher then said, much more gently, "It can be hard settling in to a new place. There are ways we can help. I think I know a club you'd really like."

Iz didn't answer because she knew what was coming next. It had happened at school after school.

It would be some kind of self-esteem-building thing. Or it would be a collaborative group project. Or it would be a games club that only thinly masked the fact that they thought you needed help in improving your terrible social skills.

"Come with me," the teacher said. "I want to introduce you to Mrs. Deagle, who runs the Great Expectations Club."

"Oh," Iz said. "That sounds cool."

"It *is,*" the teacher said. "They kind of help to keep morale high around here. They do a lot of inspirational things. Like posters and displays and announcements. I think you could really help them."

"Sure," Iz said in a monotone.

But as she followed behind the teacher, she was surprised to notice she wasn't as bothered as usual by being pigeon-holed into yet another group for difficult kids falling through the cracks.

Maybe it had to do with the fact that she was laying her escape route, piece by piece.

Maybe it had to do with the ribbons of brightly coloured sound that curled and swirled through her brain, lighting it up with the promise of being anything but *balanced.*

Chapter Five

The teacher in the hallway ended up talking to Iz's home room teacher, Mr. Bains.

And Mr. Bains was extremely excited at the idea of Iz going to the Great Expectations Club.

Over the next few weeks, Iz played along. After lunch each day, she trotted out in the direction of the club. Then she circled around and hung out in the washroom until the end of the break, flipping through all the papers on which she'd scribbled information about the Classical and Romantic periods, arpeggios, and scales.

Everything was working well. That is, until the Thursday before Iz's audition, when Audra Allen came trooping into the washroom with a group of girls.

Iz hid in a stall. From there, she could hear Audra saying, "There is literally nothing to do around this place."

Someone else said, "Here. I stole it from my dad."

Then there was laughing and silence. The smoke from a cigarette began to curl around the room.

After several minutes, Iz heard the washroom door bang open.

A teacher's voice rang out. "Girls! Are you smoking in here?"

"No!" Audra said.

A cigarette sailed over the door of the stall Iz was hiding in. It landed on the floor, smoke rising. Iz reached down, grabbed the cigarette, and threw it in the toilet, where it sizzled loudly.

"Who's in there?" the teacher said then.

Iz was silent.

"I said, who's there?"

Finally, Iz unlatched the door.

She saw Audra break into a smile at seeing who it was.

"Were you smoking?" the teacher said.

"No."

The teacher looked in past Iz and saw the cigarette floating in the toilet. "Well, what's that?"

"It's not mine," Iz said.

"Really?" said the teacher. "Whose is it then?"

Iz locked eyes with Audra.

"Hey," Audra said. "Aren't you supposed to be in the Great Expectations Club?"

Iz swallowed. "I'm just about to go there."

The teacher eyed Iz. "No, I think you need to come with me."

Then Pat got called and Iz ended up with an in-school suspension for a day for smoking on school premises.

Which should have bothered her a lot more than it did.

But actually, once she was over the shock and unfairness of it, she felt like the suspension was a piece of luck. Because tomorrow was the day before her audition. And now she'd be able to spend it going over and over her notes, sitting in whatever punishment chamber she got put in.

The following morning, Iz went without complaint to the Responsibility Room, where students had to go when they needed to think about being more responsible. She settled at one of the tables and spread out her school assignments in front of her.

Then, for the rest of the day, she pretended to jot down important things while actually studying everything for the audition.

The history stuff, the theory stuff, "Where'er you walk," and the vocalise—those were all more or less as good as she could make them.

But she was still not quite satisfied with "The Erlking."

For weeks, she had been trying to create the perfect guitar accompaniment to suit the nightmarish story of the demon chasing the father and child. But she continued to have a mental block about writing it. Maybe it was because monsters got to call all the shots. Maybe it was because children cried in terror while adults who were supposed to represent safety were utterly clueless.

Whatever the problem was, Iz wrestled it for most of the day. But everything she came up with still sounded like some feeble and cowardly person tiptoeing around a volcano without having the courage to explore what was inside it.

At the end of the afternoon, the teacher in the Responsibility Room said, "You've really worked hard today. I'm going to tell the principal that."

"Thanks," Iz said humbly.

"Let's not see you in here again, okay?"

"Okay."

Then she gathered her things and fled the building.

When she entered Pat's house, the first thing she heard was Britnee's languid voice in the kitchen, all saturated with annoyance.

"—Asked him four times already and he said they were almost done—"

"He's a man, dear. They are going to drag their feet."

"But how hard is it to say you love someone? Unless, I mean, he *doesn't* love me. I thought he did, but maybe I was wrong."

"Oh, baby, he loves you."

Iz closed the front door softly so they wouldn't hear her. Then she tiptoed upstairs and settled on the bed with her guitar. Her fingers began to walk through the story of "The Erlking" again and again, still trying to hit on exactly the right formula to convey the nightmare of it.

Much later, the doorbell rang.

She heard Britnee answer it.

"Good. Come in. You're going to write them right now at the kitchen table."

Vance rumbled something in response.

There was a long silence then.

Iz sat there bent over her guitar, frozen, waiting. She was certain it wasn't over.

Sure enough, Britnee's voice spat out like gunfire. "What's that word supposed to even *mean?*"

And then—

"Babe, I don't understand why you're dragging your feet here. Here. Give me the pen."

Iz crouched by the bed, burying her head in her knees and covering her ears. She rocked back and forth.

Frantically, she tried to push Britnee and Vance out of her mind. She imagined she was the girl in "Where'er you walk," who was worshipped by all of nature. Iz tried to picture waving wildflowers twisting their faces warmly in her direction. Manifesto was walking with her there, laughing and pointing things out. It was a world of golden light where her way was made smooth.

Slam!

Iz jumped and started shaking uncontrollably. She waited, tensely, for what would come next.

But as the silence went on and on, dread started filling up inside her.

Had they killed each other?

She could almost hear thundering hooves, could almost feel the Erlking gaining ground.

Pat tapped at her door. "Hey, hon." She opened it, leaned her head around, saw Iz cowering. "Aw, baby. It's okay. It's just a lover's spat."

Iz crammed her papers into a pile and sat on them. She nodded rapidly.

Pat went on, "Britnee's helping Vance with his vows, that's all. Poor boy has been stuck. Are you hungry? Let's get some squares. I made them this afternoon. Follow me, baby. I'll show you everything's okay."

Pat led the way into the kitchen, loudly saying, "Come on in Iz, there's nothing to worry about. Poor Iz was scared you were fighting."

Iz could tell that Pat was using her as a way to ease the tension.

Britnee and Vance were sitting beside each other at the kitchen table. Britnee was gripping the pen while Vance watched. The whole kitchen seemed to be saturated with a combination of viciousness and heaviness.

Britnee said immediately, "Oh no, hon. We're having creative differences but we're not *fighting.*"

"Vance, can I get you some coffee?" Pat sounded all blurting and anxious.

Vance mumbled something in a way that reminded Iz of a cake that had collapsed.

"Sure, I'll make you some coffee," Pat said. "Iz, can you get the squares from the fridge?"

Iz opened the fridge door like a robot while they all watched.

Then panic started rising in her. Memories of That Place were bubbling up—people standing right over her.

Suddenly she couldn't breathe.

She muttered, "Sorry, I just forgot something. I-I'll be right back."

She took the stairs two at a time and closed the door to her bedroom. She put a chair against it, trembling.

The claustrophobia ballooned until she couldn't contain it all.

Iz grabbed her guitar. She ripped her hand across the strings, thundered out furious, ugly chords. Swiped and struck and smashed.

It was like an exorcism.

And somehow, through that act of self-preservation, of holding the panic at bay, a weird thing happened.

Pat's little bedroom dissolved into a forest, and Iz was begging her horse to go faster and faster. The demon was getting closer with every passing second.

She slammed out discordant phrases that were harsh and angular, bloody and psychopathic. They manipulated and controlled. They let you take the blame for smoking, they harassed you about writing your wedding vows all wrong, and they made you feel doubtful and ashamed and guilty and scared about the very things that lay at the heart of who you were.

She was thundering back at every cruel bully in the universe.

And she'd found the accompaniment for "The Erlking."

Chapter Six

The next morning, on the day of the audition, snow fell for the first time in earnest, all swirling and chaotic. It echoed what was going on inside Iz. She was full of madness, potential, disaster.

"I'm supposed to meet my friend at the library. We have to do music homework," she said to Pat, hovering by the doorway to the living room, guitar in hand.

Some foster mothers grilled you. *What friend? What homework? How long will you be?* But Pat kept gluing beads on candle holders. "Sure, honey. Have a good time."

"Thanks, I will."

As soon as Iz stepped off the snow-covered porch, she began to run, scarf flying behind her like a superhero's cape. Her feet were cold—she should have worn boots—but she wasn't going back now.

Just as she got to the bus stop, the bus rumbled up through the slush, exactly when the online schedule had said it would appear. She handed over money Pat had given her for school lunches.

The whole trip took over an hour, with the bus swooping through the swirling snowflakes like some ride at a carnival. She transferred downtown, which turned out to be easier than she'd expected.

When her stop finally came, she gathered everything up, made her way to the door, and climbed down the steps onto the slushy sidewalk.

The driving snow made it hard to make out the shapes of the

shops around her. Then she saw the outline of a building that brooded over everything, bulging with additions that must have been put on over the course of many years. Maybe it had been a church once or a fire hall, at least a century before.

As Iz walked closer, she saw the sign:

The Métier School
Building a new vision of musicianship

This was it.

Kids were walking up the steps with adults who were probably their parents. Iz closed her eyes, took a deep breath, tried to build up her courage. Then she got a better grip on her guitar, crossed the street, and climbed those steps too.

Inside, people were milling around in a confusing mob. She could hear snippets of conversation amid the whines and squawks of instruments being tuned.

"Don't forget to say you like all the time periods equally."

"Come here, have another look at your study notes."

"Do you remember what to tell them about the Bach?"

Iz joined a line that was snaking up to a front desk. She shuffled forward, her eyes darting around the room as she took everything in.

"Your name, please?" said the lady when Iz reached the front.

"Isabelle. Isabelle Beaufort."

The lady scanned the list. "Here you are!"

She typed rapidly, then took a paper off the printer. "You'll hand this to the panel. Your audition will be in about ten minutes. We have practice rooms available if you'd like to warm up."

Iz took a deep breath. "No thanks. I'm fine."

"Good luck!" said the lady.

Iz found an empty chair and sank into it. She tuned her guitar, resting her head on its top. She closed her eyes, shutting out everything except total determination.

It felt like only a few minutes had gone by when a voice broke into her thoughts. "Isabelle Beaufort? You're next. Are you ready?"

Iz jumped up, heart exploding.

"Huh! Yes!"

"Down that hallway, first door on the left. Good luck!"

"Th-thanks."

She walked along a hall covered in wooden carvings. She stopped in front of a huge door that looked like it weighed a thousand pounds.

Finally, she pushed it open.

"Hello!" A chorus of voices greeted her.

Several people were seated at a long table. Behind them, tall windows revealed the cityscape—bare branches that scratched against the flat December sky, scarcely visible through the unending, dizzying movement of driving snow.

"Hello," she said, thinking how tiny her voice sounded. She handed her paper to the person in front of her.

Then she saw him. Second from the right. Dr. Aaron Perlinger. Legs sprawled out easily under the table. Big feet. Red sweater. Shock of dark hair. Intelligent eyes watching her.

It felt completely unreal.

The lady said, "Tell us a bit about yourself!"

Iz took another involuntary deep breath. "I'm fourteen. I-I love music. I've been singing for a long time."

"Fourteen. You look older," said the woman. Everyone murmured an agreement.

"I feel older," said Iz. "Ha ha, like a hundred sometimes." Then she wanted to kick herself. What a stupid response!

But it made Dr. Aaron Perlinger look up with a little smile. "And what training have you done in the last hundred years to get ready for today?"

"I-I've been studying scales and arpeggios and vocalises and different songs."

"Who is your teacher?"

"Um . . . Jamaal. Jamaal Wickerson." Her face began to beat red. She hadn't seen him since that day in the music store, but he still felt like the only real music teacher she had ever had.

They all nodded at each other with interest.

"He is in the Wickerson Trio, yes?" someone said.

"Uh, yes. I think so."

"How long have you studied with him?"

"Oh," Iz said, waving one shaking arm. "A long time."

With a sinking heart, she realized she sounded like she couldn't put words together at all. This was not how she'd imagined it in her head.

"What songs will you be singing?"

"Ah … um," Iz said, fumbling wildly in her backpack. "'Where'er you walk' by Handel and 'The Erlking' by Schubert."

The pages were stuck in the seam of the backpack, and she had to yank them out.

"Do you want to see the music?"

"No, no, that's fine."

She shoved them back in again.

"'The Erlking,'" said Dr. Perlinger. "That's very ambitious! Tell us why you chose it."

She looked up at the tall windows above his head, at the chaotic snowflakes that were smothering out the world—like the fog had smothered her for two years after That Place.

"It made me think of how it feels—how it must feel—to be a kid at the mercy of something that nobody else thinks is there."

She crossed her arms, put her head down, tried to find just the right way to say it.

"I mean, I-I thought about how scary it is for the son, trying to get his dad to understand that the Erlking is hiding in the shadows and is going to steal the boy away, trying to tell his dad that everything is way more dangerous than he thinks. And meanwhile, the real terror, the nightmare, is that even if his dad *did* listen, he wouldn't be able to stop it."

She added, softly, "The boy is completely on his own. He's facing something that no adult can fix. He is completely lost."

There was silence in the room.

"An *absolutely* evocative description. Let's start with that one," said Dr. Perlinger, his eyes sparkling. "Did you bring an accompanist or will you be accompanying yourself?"

"I-I'm accompanying myself."

He gestured to the grand piano with an inviting smile. "Take it away."

"Oh! No, no, I'm using my guitar."

"Guitar?" One of the examiners was frowning at her now. "You won't be playing Schubert's accompaniment?"

"I wrote my own," she said in a low voice.

She suddenly knew she'd made a mistake. She closed her eyes. Maybe she would just stand there as long as needed, until they called for people to take her away.

Then someone cleared his throat, someone out there in the darkness, not seen but felt.

She heard a voice say, "Isabelle."

When she opened her eyes, Dr. Perlinger was smiling at her. His dark eyes were kind, as if he guessed the turmoil in her.

"I am *very* curious about your accompaniment. Whenever you're ready," he said.

Iz gulped and nodded. She took a last breath, hissed it out softly.

Then she flexed her fingers, placed them on the frets, readied her left hand. Paused. Squeezed her eyes shut. Attacked the strings.

***

When at last her hands dropped and she found herself panting, the panel surprised her by applauding. Iz bobbed her head, unsure how to respond.

A silence fell.

"Well, well, what an extraordinary performance," said Dr. Perlinger. He was smiling quite broadly.

"Thanks," Iz said tightly.

The first lady said, "You have a very good natural voice. It has potential."

A man said, “Not much technique yet. But with more time, more training, who knows?”

The other woman said, “You chose to sing in English rather than German. Can you tell us about that choice?”

“I—uh ...” Iz said, blushing. “What?”

“The original is in German, of course.”

“Oh!”

Her thoughts raced. “I just, you know, I was *rethinking* it. Trying to tell it in my own way.”

Please, let Dr. Perlinger not decide that she was a complete idiot.

He said slowly, “Well, the Schubert accompaniment is so well known, such a duet really with the singer, that I couldn't imagine what you were planning to do. I hoped it wouldn't just be dull strummed chords, but nothing could have been further from the truth. What a tour de force! Tell me about how you came up with it!”

Iz let out the breath she didn't know she had been holding.

Her brain scrambled over the fabric of the music, trying to find a thread to pull that would reveal everything. “I wanted the guitar to be a kind of shadow world, so a lot of the time it's deep underneath the singer, two or three low tunes going like this.” She demonstrated, playing them out. “But sometimes the guitar rises up, crashes against the voice as if the shadow world, the nightmare world, is breaking into the real world.”

Her voice shook but she kept going.

“I gave the Erlking his own tune. It goes like this.” Her fingers flew over the six-note theme. “And I put it in all over. It's backward and upside down against when the dad is talking, because the dad doesn't understand.”

Dr. Perlinger was nodding, waiting for more.

“And when the son shouts to the father, I put that tune against this screaming sound on the guitar. I wanted it to be like the guitar and the voice were both freaking out, kind of. The Erlking is going in for the kill and the boy is terrified.”

Then Dr. Perlinger rested his nose on his clasped hands, slouched down in his chair with his pointy shoes sticking straight up. He looked like he was considering all parts of what she was saying.

Stupidly, she just began to babble, even though everything was suddenly warning her to stop and think about what she was saying.

"I-I can see things in my head and play them. It's almost, you know, kind of like drawing pictures with the sounds." She took a huge breath. "I mean, I could—I could create something right now about the picture I have of you."

"Really?" Dr. Perlinger said. He shot upright, all attention. "We have time, yes?" He beamed around at the rest of the jury.

"Uh," Iz said, panicking. She could actually feel the colour leaving her face.

Idiot! Why did you say that?

But now he was sitting there expecting something.

So—

She allowed her mind to drift.

She pictured him standing on the stage at Dennison Hall, commandingly tall and misleadingly mild, with Manifesto standing around him. She remembered the way they spoke so lovingly of how he helped to draw out what was inside them.

The longing in her was immense, almost too much to bear.

So she began to pluck gently, to build a melody on the guitar that on its surface undulated like an unbothered ocean.

"This is how you seem right now when we're talking—calm."

She began a second tune below the first. It darted down, down into the depths, met with two other tunes manipulated by all of her fingers. They played, chased like fish, letting off sparks of brilliance.

"But underneath is where something else is happening. Something creative and surprising that not everyone gets to see, but maybe your students do, and ... and—"

Now she had five different melodies charging around each other, some above the water and some below. Swimming fish and flying fish, separate but about to be part of the same melody, strong and enduring like the ocean and atmosphere themselves.

The melody exploded then with joyful chords that joined the

world above and below, like dolphins leaping, like fireworks that dove under the waves.

"And this," said Iz, "is when you are leading Manifesto and the ideas are turning into sounds, and everyone—the whole world—has come together to perform or to listen, like a big circle or something. I just—it would be the greatest joy to be *part* of that. It's all I want—to walk with you and to learn and to be part of Manifesto. It would be everything."

She let the chords build and build.

As the tears poured down her face.

Chapter Seven

She kept checking her email all that evening and the next day, but there was nothing.

Her brain cruelly filled up the time by telling her all the ways the audition had been a disaster. She'd made a million mistakes in the theory. She'd forgotten where to breathe in the vocalise. She'd mixed up who Schubert and Handel were. And what had possessed her to write him a *song*? That had not been part of the plan at all.

Monday morning came still without any word at all.

When Iz got to school, Mr. Bains took her aside and said very kindly, "So I know things were a bit tough on Thursday. And I missed having you in class on Friday."

"Yeah," Iz said cautiously.

"Also," Mr. Bains said even more gently, "it sounds like you haven't quite made it to the Great Expectations Club yet?"

Iz's skin prickled.

"Do I have to?" she said.

"No, you don't have to do anything. But you might like it, being part of a group. It's good to feel connected." Then he added, "It might help with stress too. With solving problems. Handling arguments."

Iz sighed.

"How about trying it out today?" Mr. Bains said. "I could walk you there."

Iz caught Audra watching the conversation. Suddenly she wanted to end it as quickly as possible.

"Uh, no, I can get there myself."

So at lunchtime, deliberately fifteen minutes late, she pushed open the door of the classroom where the Great Expectations Club was meeting.

A bright voice rang out.

"Isabelle! Come on in!"

Glancing around the circle, she recognized a few kids from her classes: the guy who sat at the back in Math and carved things in the desk, the girl who had been kicked out of Science for swearing, and the mousy kid who crouched in his desk in English class, never said a word, and looked like he wanted to disappear into the floor.

Everyone was clearly as unwilling to be in that room as she was.

She sat down in a chair, stared up at the ceiling and crossed her arms.

"So Isabelle, if you want, you could share something about yourself."

"Uh, sure. I've been here about five or six weeks." She took in a tired breath, then sighed loudly. "Probably be gone pretty soon. I'm in foster care. They move me a lot. That's it, really."

The teacher said warmly, "Well, Iz, you might remember that I'm Mrs. Deagle. And I want you to know that we are happy you're here. And we would like to get to know you better. This is going to be a safe space."

"Great," Iz said.

"We are just in the middle of planning our display case for the front foyer," Mrs. Deagle said. "It's to inspire the school to strive toward their goals, to succeed despite the odds. So if you have any ideas, just spitball them."

The Great Expectations Club felt completely cruel in that moment. Iz had *tried* to succeed despite the odds. With every passing minute, though, she was becoming increasingly convinced of all the ways her audition had been a pathetic failure.

She said, "Yeah. I have an idea."

"Great! Tell us!"

"We could show, like, the destruction of the world. We could have explosions, buildings that've collapsed, cars all crashed, the oceans dried up, fires in the forests, people and animals lying everywhere."

Mrs. Deagle was frowning, looking confused. "Um, I don't think—"

"Then," Iz continued, "we could say, 'It can only go up from here.'"

There was a short silence.

Mrs. Deagle said mildly, after a minute, "I think we can *maybe* come up with something a little more positive."

"You do?" Iz said.

Her freshly broken heart was suddenly jagged, raw, bleeding.

"Maybe *you* should be making this empowering display case then. Maybe you could put in some, you know, teddy bears holding a sign saying, 'Bear to dream,' or flowers all holding each other's leaves with a speech balloon that says, 'We're blooming powerful,' or-or a flying saucer that says, 'Success is not an alien concept.'"

"Those are all very good," the other teacher—whoever she was—said, starting to jot them onto the whiteboard.

"No, they're not."

"Relax," one of the other kids said, like Iz was some kind of a mutant.

"I am *never* relaxed," Iz said.

She stood up abruptly, shoving her chair back. It collided with a table of art supplies. They all clattered onto the floor—brushes and markers and paint.

Someone clapped. The swearing Science girl held up her phone to record whatever was coming next.

"Oh! Sorry!"

Iz started trying to pick it all up. Both of the teachers were immediately doing the same thing right in front of her and behind her.

She could feel breath on her neck. Claustrophobia started rising.

She needed to get away. Now.

Things got blurry. In her confusion, she pushed one of the teachers. The teacher lost her balance and tumbled into another table.

More materials fell to the ground. People were laughing and cheering now.

Iz stumbled to the door. She ripped it open.

She slammed it behind her so hard that the glass shattered.

About half an hour later, Pat arrived in the principal's office. Her usually serene face was pink and strained. "Baby! What happened?"

Iz shrugged and shook her head.

Then she sat there watching Pat and the principal forming words at each other while the secretaries glowered and slammed things around like Iz was complicating their whole lives by taking up space in the office. After that, she and Pat walked out to the car because Iz was suspended again for a day. This time it was an at-home suspension.

As they pulled out of the parking lot, Pat said gently, "Did those teachers say something to make you feel mad, hon?"

"No."

"No? Then why did you shove them and break the door?"

"I just . . . got a little stressed. I didn't like the Great Expectations Club that much. I didn't like being put in it."

Pat drove quietly for a while. Then she said, "Did you try telling them that?"

"Not really."

"When Brit was little," Pat said, eyes anxiously on the traffic, "she used to have the cutest saying. She came up with it on her own. 'Nobody gets to decide but me.' You get to decide what you want for yourself. That's what it means."

"Ah. Right."

"And if they don't listen, you keep going till you find someone who will. You use your words. You make them take you seriously."

"Okay."

"But no violence," Pat said earnestly. "That's not you. That's not the Iz I know."

Never mind that she had only known Iz for around six weeks.

When they got home, Iz went upstairs and lay on her bed. She gazed at the ceiling, traced a water stain on the wall.

She was starting to feel guilty as well as embarrassed.

And angry. She was tired of being controlled by memories that exploded in her head without being invited. What she *wanted* was the future, not the past.

She squeezed her eyes shut. She imagined that chord. She pictured it shooting across the landscape of her life like some kind of sonic vibration that could sweep away old pains, make space for possibilities, rewrite everything.

If she wished hard enough—if she could somehow turn her longing into a kind of magic, a powerful reshaping of the universe inside her head—

Nobody gets to decide but me.

Finally, she swung her feet over the side of the bed and stood up.

She snuck across the hall to the computer room yet again. She sat down in the desk chair in front of the ancient laptop, took a deep and focused breath, and opened her inbox.

Ping! A new email came in at that moment.

It was entitled *Trying to get hold of you.*

It was from Dr. Perlinger.

Iz sat there, staring. She was completely scared to open it.

"Ahh," she said, grabbing her hair. She jammed her hand down on the mouse and clicked on the email before she could think twice.

> *Hello Isabelle,*
>
> *I hope you are doing well. The phone number on your application appears to be out of service. Is there a new number where I could reach you? I'd like to have a word whenever you have a moment.*
>
> *Yours,*
> *Aaron Perlinger.*

"What?" Iz said out loud.

Why would he want to have a word?

Wild electricity coursed through her. Hope was back, at the end of this horrible day.

She sat there hugging herself, getting up the courage to write a note back.

Finally she typed quickly.

> *Dear Dr. Perlinger,*
>
> *Thank you for your email. I'm sorry you couldn't get through. The phone is broken and they're working on it. Is there a number where I could call you?*
>
> *Sincerely,*
> *Iz Beaufort*

Then she was practically bouncing around the room, waiting, waiting, waiting. Finally the mail pinged. And there it was, Dr. Perlinger's *phone number.*

She snuck the hall phone into her bedroom, punched the buttons with fingers that kept making mistakes. It rang twice.

"Hello?"

"Y-yes, yes, this is Isabelle Beaufort. Iz, I mean. Or you can call me Isabelle, that's okay too. Hi, uh, Dr. Perlinger!"

She sounded all blustery and idiotic. She started trembling so hard that the phone was pummeling her ear like a boat bashing against a dock in the wind.

"Hello, Iz! How are you? Looking forward to the holidays?"

"Y-yes. How are you?"

"I am doing very well!" Dr. Perlinger said. "I'm delivering good news. I couldn't resist telling you in person. The email will follow later today with all of those boring administrative details. But Iz, you're coming to us! You're ours! Welcome to Métier."

"What?" Iz said, and burst into silent tears.

Dr. Perlinger kept talking, oblivious. "Iz, I've never seen an audition quite like yours before. Technique can be learned, but your performances were really quite astonishing and original. You roared like a lion!"

She barely recognized the shuddering words coming out. "It's the only thing I want on the *whole planet.* It's … it's like the air I want to breathe."

Dr. Perlinger's voice was warm. "I completely understand. I can't wait for us to work together. I'm thinking we should dig into Schubert really, since you were so drawn to 'The Erlking.'"

Iz blurted out, "Oh, yeah, I love 'The Erlking.'"

She sounded like such an idiot.

"Your transcripts were excellent too," Dr. Perlinger said. "And the letters of reference were outstanding. Your teachers obviously adore you. You're going to fit into Métier beautifully."

"Huh!" Iz said. "I'm so glad."

"Well, I won't keep you. I just very selfishly wanted to be the first to say welcome. Now it remains for you to receive your email and accept the offer of admission. Let's get on with things!"

"Thank you! Thank you!"

Then she sat there, a mix of excitement and terror.

Chapter Eight

Dear Isabelle,

We are delighted to offer you a place in our first-year class at The Métier School. The competition this round was extremely strong, and we were very impressed with your audition, transcripts, and letters of reference.

Classes for the Winter Term will commence on January 8th. Payment of fees for the first month ($1500) may be made at any time, in person, or at this link up until that date.

We ask you to confirm acceptance at your earliest convenience by replying to this email. Again, we warmly congratulate you and look forward to meeting you.

Sincerely,
Dr. Rebecca Starling
Director
The Métier School

Iz read the letter about three times. The blood was draining out of her face.

She went to the website and clicked everywhere in a panic. And there it was: *Monthly fee—$1500.*

How had she missed it?

"You can solve this," Iz whispered desperately.

Maybe Dominion Children's Care would pay it now that she had gotten in on her own. Except she had made up the transcripts and reference letters. That was probably a crime for sure. And Dominion Children's Care would tell The Métier School, and The Métier School would take away their offer of admission.

At last, she stumbled downstairs, her head dizzy, to where Pat and Britnee were looking at a huge colour-coded spreadsheet on the dining room table. Britnee was saying, "I just think it's worth getting the bulk discount on the glasses."

"Hey!" Iz said, trying to sound nonchalant.

"Hey," Britnee said meaningfully. "Sounds like you had another exciting day."

Iz ignored this. "If a foster kid got into, like, a school where you had to pay fees, how would that get paid?"

Britnee's eyes widened. "How would it get *paid*?" She looked at Pat doubtfully. "Does Dominion Children's Care pay for private schools?"

Pat shook her head slowly. "Oh … I don't think so. Not when there's a public option."

"What if," Iz said, tensely, "what if it was a really special school? Like, if it was hard to get in there and a kid did it? Would they pay for it then?"

"Where's this coming from, baby?" Pat gazed at her placidly.

"Huh! Nowhere," Iz said. She tried one last time. "But what about a foster parent then? Would a foster parent ever pay for something like that?"

Pat said reflectively, "Maybe if they were rich." She waved her hand over the spreadsheet for Britnee's wedding and burst into laughter, like she was going to have to go to a homeless shelter later that evening.

"Is it because you're suspended for the second time and you don't want to go back after tomorrow? You'd rather go to a private school?" Britnee's eyes were laughing, but not especially cruelly. They were more conspiratorial, like *of course* Iz wanted to avoid going back to that place.

"Uh, I guess. Something like that."

"Well, I hate to tell you, but private schools don't usually take kids who get suspended. So you'd be better off trying a little harder in the school where you are."

Britnee sounded so lofty. Iz had to sit on her clenched fists.

And in that moment, she decided a couple of things.

She was definitely going to go to The Métier School.

And she was going to have to do it on her own.

Chapter Nine

The next day, while she was suspended, and while Britnee and Pat were interviewing DJs in the living room, Iz crept all over the house, looking for her binder.

The binder had been made by a foster mother at some point, and it followed Iz from home to home. She had flipped through it once when nobody was around. It was divided neatly into different subjects—medical records, monthly reports, authorization forms, and other things Iz couldn't remember.

Most importantly, it had a section all about finances.

Sure, she wasn't supposed to touch her bank account—it was for when she aged out of Dominion Children's Care—but it was technically her money, and this was an emergency. And since foster parents were supposed to be making deposits into her account regularly, Iz figured there might be thousands of dollars in there by now.

The binder was nowhere to be found in the bedrooms or the computer room or the dining room or the kitchen. She couldn't check the living room because Britnee and Pat and the DJs were in there.

So Iz crept finally down to the last place she could think of—the basement.

And almost immediately she recognized it on a shelf, standing out with its pink flower decorations. Heart beating, she sat down on a plastic tub and opened it in her lap.

Sure enough, there was a section called "Financial." Iz turned to it and almost right away saw what she was looking for. Her bank account number, branch, and transit information. A bank card, neatly inside a baggie that was stapled to the page.

And a password.

Iz took the pages out of the binder and stuffed them in her pocket.

"Iz? I thought I saw you go by. What are you doing down there?"

Pat was at the top of the stairs.

"Uh . . ." Her brain raced, as she shoved the binder back onto the shelf. "I was . . . I was just exploring."

Pat came down a couple of steps, looking completely puzzled. "You were *exploring*?"

"Yeah. I guess I was getting bored. I think I don't ever want to be suspended again."

Pat let out a long sigh. "Well, I'm glad to hear *that*. But it's dirty and dusty down here. Come on up, baby."

"Okay," Iz said humbly. She had what she needed, anyway.

The next morning, she phoned the school absence line. "Isabelle Beaufort is ill and will not be attending classes today." Then she left the house as usual.

But when she reached the corner, she went the opposite way, to the nearest bank she'd found online. In her backpack was the pin and bank card.

About three hours later, she ran up the stone steps of The Métier School, guitar case gripped in her hand. She yanked open the main doors, hopped up the little step into the foyer and sprinted along the hallway into the main reception area. It was completely deserted.

"Can I help you?"

There was a lady behind the counter and she was smiling. She was wearing a little name tag that read, *Ellen Harvey, Administration*.

"I'm Isabelle Beaufort. I'm accepting the offer. I'm going to be a student here this term. This is my money. It's fifteen hundred. It's all there. You can count it." She could tell she was babbling and forced herself to calm down.

She'd gone to four different bank machines to withdraw it all, so she wouldn't attract any attention to what she was doing. And now she only had fourteen dollars left in her account. So much for the thousands of dollars she'd expected. It turned out that twelve years in Dominion Children's Care didn't pay as well as she'd thought.

Ellen Harvey looked inside the envelope at the thick wad of bills, eyebrows raised.

Iz felt panic rising.

She blurted, "It's a long story, but my parents once got hacked really badly and now they kind of like to pay things in cash. I hope that's okay. If you want to contact my mom, her email's on the form."

She was losing track of how many new email addresses she'd made.

Ellen Harvey said, smiling. "Cash is just fine. No worries. Let's look up your information."

Iz waited an eternity, trying not to hyperventilate, while the lady frowned at the computer.

"Here you are!"

"Oh, good! Thank you!" Her voice sounded ridiculously loud in her ears.

Then she watched, slightly feeling like she was out of her body, as the lady counted the money, put papers on the counter, and talked to her about deposits and receipts.

And she kept telling herself it wasn't stealing if it was your own money.

Ellen Harvey said, "Will either of your parents be accompanying you on the first day?"

Iz thought quickly. "No, probably not. My parents work a lot."

"No worries." Ellen Harvey bundled up the papers and handed them to Iz. "That is it! First day is on the eighth. And congratulations, Isabelle. You're going to love it here. The Métier School is really wonderful."

"I know," Iz said softly. She couldn't help adding, "And Manifesto—I can't wait to meet them."

Ellen Harvey laughed out loud, like something was funny. "They are pretty remarkable, that's for sure."

Out on the street, Iz wanted to jump and caper, screaming. But she couldn't just yet. There was more to do.

She began walking in search of exactly the right place. At last, after three full blocks in one direction and two in another, she found herself in a neighbourhood filled with elegant bistros and boutique shops.

She stopped in front of a restaurant called Festa, then lifted out her guitar from its case, tuned it in the icy morning air, and ran her hand across the strings. The sound was like a stream of water charging down a mountainside, all crisp and pure.

Everywhere around her was a swirl of activity. Cars, buses, people walking. Snowflakes tumbling over everything. Well, she was about to enter it herself. She existed! She was part of this messy day, this chaotic world. Now, on this young, new day, she was finally renouncing Dominion Children's Care and entering into her own life.

Iz began with a driving bass line that was automobiles charging through slush. She added in flashing rhythms that represented human movement—people rushing, pausing before shops, slipping forward again.

It was like a hymn, a battle cry of gratitude.

Over top of it all, at last, she added her own voice. At first she sang just a triumphant, wordless melody. Then, gradually, bits of ideas whispered to her. She thought about patterns and weaving. She imagined that everything around her was like fabric on a loom, made up of words and melodies and noises and actions. She pictured herself woven in there too, part of the messiness and movement. Finally the song constructed itself:

Wouldn't it be something
In this woven world of wonder
If our little lives were threads
And we were passing through a loom
Building up a pattern
That the naked eye can't see
Don't know where it starts and ends

I only know that we
Are weavers in
This wild, interwoven world

She sang the melody over and over, improvising words, crying thanks until her fist was strumming an anthem and her voice was untamed birds strung out against the sky, yelling their free intention, glad and proud.

Clink!

Coins jingled into the guitar case. Iz blinked, startled out of her song, and looked down at them. A bunch of bills were fluttering there too! Several people were reading the lunch menu for the restaurant. As she watched, some of them slipped inside.

"Hey! You!" A man stood in the doorway of the restaurant, holding the door half open. He had a thick shock of grey hair. His eyebrows crowded over his nose like furious caterpillars. "You can't stay there. You're blocking the door."

"Oh, sorry." Iz stepped through the snow to the left. "Is that better?"

The man rubbed his nose and the caterpillars started fighting for territory on his forehead. "No, it's not better. You're still standing in front of the window. You're losing me business."

Something drew itself up inside her. She was so tired of being pushed down, told off, made small, controlled.

"A bunch of people stopped to listen to me and read the menu and then they went into your restaurant. I would say I'm *gaining* you business. Watch this."

A couple was walking along just then. Iz began to strum, hoping she could pull off this outrageous bluff.

"I've been working on a love song," she said to the grey-haired man. "Not about a person, more about the *idea* of love, and love is all mixed up with music. Basically, it's like a love song to music."

The man was frowning at her as if she had a second head and it was talking nonsense.

Iz began to sing, dragging words out in the luxurious way Britnee spoke, fingers coaxing the melody from the strings. Slowly she constructed a love song to the afternoon, to the couple.

At first she thought they would walk on. But then the woman stopped her partner with a hand on his arm. As Iz kept playing and singing, the woman smiled and fumbled in her purse and brought out a bill. Iz was pretty sure it was ten dollars! The woman gently placed it in the guitar case and Iz nodded to her in gratitude.

Meanwhile, her partner was gazing at the menu posted outside the restaurant. "This looks nice," he said softly, putting his arm around the woman.

"Are you open yet?" she asked.

"Of course, of course!" The thick-eyebrowed man was all smiles now, welcoming. He held the door for them and they walked inside.

"I guess I didn't lose you those customers." Iz held his gaze, daring him to look away.

Finally he shook his head and made a sound that could have been disgust or amusement, part snort and part bark. "Just don't stand in front of the window."

But there was something in the not-quite-smiling wrinkles around his eyes or the quivering downturn of his mouth that suggested he wasn't so angry.

"If I show up again," Iz said daringly, "you should give me a regular pay cheque."

"Ha! You should be so lucky." He went back inside and closed the door.

Chapter Ten

On the last day before the Christmas holidays, Iz blew the hair dryer on her face so it was hot when Pat checked it.

"I kind of feel awful," Iz said.

"Oh, baby, yes, you're burning up."

"I don't know if I can go to school."

"No, no, you need to stay home. I'll call the office."

Pat bustled around, getting Iz orange juice and an extra quilt. Then, looking slightly worried and doubtful, she said, "We have a cake tasting at eleven o'clock. And then we were going to do lunch afterward and check out bridesmaid dresses. Will you be okay on your own, baby?"

"Of course! I'm fourteen," Iz said weakly.

She lay there in the bed, listening to them getting ready to go, willing them to hurry. Finally, the door closed and the garage door rumbled up. Pat's car started. Iz heard the wheels crunching over the snow in the driveway. Then there was only silence.

Iz lay there awhile longer to be sure that they were really gone. Then she took the hall phone into her room. She dialed the number quickly before she could lose her nerve.

"Headway Public School."

The secretary's voice was crisp, clipped. From what Iz had seen of that office, everyone always seemed to be worked up, unfriendly, and resentfully in the middle of a crisis. She hoped she could make that work to her advantage.

"Yes, hello," she said, trying to deepen her voice and make it sound adult. "My name is Claudia Smith and I'm Isabelle Beaufort's caseworker. I'm calling to let you know that Isabelle is being withdrawn effective immediately. She's moving to a new district."

She'd looked it up on Pat's computer—*how to withdraw your child from school.* Supposedly you could just tell them that your child was leaving. At least, that was the case in the one district she'd read about before Britnee had interrupted her.

"Ah!" the secretary said explosively, like this was the last thing she needed. "Okay. Wait just one moment while I bring up her file."

Iz could hear typing.

The secretary exhaled loudly. "So then I'll just need you to fill out the withdrawal paperwork. Will you be coming into the office today, or should we email it to you?"

Withdrawal paperwork?

Iz started improvising, trying not to panic.

"Um . . . unfortunately, my schedule today is full with meetings, so if you could send it, that would be great."

Then, with a horrible jolt, she realized she hadn't made a fake email for Claudia.

She blurted, half forgetting to sound calm and mature, "And actually, I'm just getting a call on the other line. So could I call you back in a second with my email address?"

The secretary said, "We'll just use the one on file."

"Oh!" Iz said, brain feeling like it was splitting in two. "No, that one is actually old! Sorry, I have a new one."

She waited, not breathing, to see if the secretary would tell her to put the real social worker on the phone immediately.

But at that moment she heard voices raised in the background. And the secretary said hastily, like she needed to leave the conversation right away, "Okay, I'll wait for your call then."

"Thanks, talk to you soon," Iz said. She hung up.

Then she ran into Pat's computer room and hurled herself into the chair. She quickly made an email address entitled DCC.Claudia .Smith@gmail.com.

After that, she called the school again.

The phone rang and rang before the secretary picked it up.

Iz's hands were in fists while she gave Claudia's new email address. She waited to be told that it was totally fake.

"Fine. I'll email the form to you," the secretary said in a huffy rush.

Iz sat in front of the computer then, waiting and waiting. Finally an email pinged into her inbox. She opened the attachment.

Request for Withdrawal from Headway Public School.

Trying to stay calm, she began to type.

Everything was fine until she got to the part asking for the address of the new school. Which obviously didn't exist.

Iz raked her hands through her hair, trying to think. Should she put in something fake? But what if someone looked it up and discovered there was nothing there? She couldn't put in the address of a real school, either, because she couldn't risk Headway trying to get in touch.

At last she wrote, "Isabelle will be attending a school out of the district. She is not yet enrolled. Once she is settled, the school will contact you if they require information."

Would it be good enough? It was a total gamble. But hopefully the secretary wouldn't think twice. With any luck, she'd be dealing with some erupting office drama and just assume Dominion Children's Care had everything under control.

Iz finished the rest of the form, then sat there, fingers cupped over her nose like she was praying to the universe.

This was risky, risky beyond words.

But it was also the gateway to her future.

Finally she pressed SEND.

Chapter Eleven

On the morning of her first day at The Métier School, Iz wolfed down her breakfast an hour before the usual time.

Pat said, “You’re up so early, baby.”

“Oh, yeah. They started a new guitar club. It’s an hour before school. And it’s going to be every morning. Also, I joined the choir after school, so I’ll be coming home at least an hour late each night. Apparently the teacher likes to go long.”

“That’s intensive.” Pat flipped through the bridal magazine in front of her. “Is it too much for you, kiddo?”

“No!” Iz said. “I’d do twice as much music if they’d let me.”

“Yes, hon, of course you would. Do you want a drive?”

“Oh, no thanks, I kind of like to walk.”

Then Iz crammed in the rest of her breakfast, brushed her teeth, grabbed her backpack and guitar case. She waved goodbye to Pat and headed out into the snowy air.

A little over an hour later, she was climbing the steps of the great, hulking building. The sun was just starting to rise, highlighting its crags and towers. Iz felt like the rest of her life was gleaming there amid the dull red brick.

She put her hand on the doorknob of the great wooden door. At exactly that moment, it burst open, and a tall body slammed into hers. Iz grabbed at the railing and her guitar case bashed against the metal.

"Oops! I'm so sorry! Are you okay?" The boy swung around, catching the door and her. His tone was resonant, like it had more room to vibrate than the average voice.

"I'm fine." With a shock, she recognized him. "Y-you're in Manifesto."

"Ha! Yeah." He grinned at Iz, straightening up. "I was just getting coffee. Should have looked where I was going—"

Iz was about to stammer out something in response.

But just then, the clasps on her guitar case flew open.

Her beloved instrument tumbled out, hitting the cement steps with an echoing, tuneless, horrible thud. Papers fluttered down the stairs and into the street.

"Ah!" Iz collapsed beside the guitar, picked it up, cradled it, turned it over to look for damage. It seemed okay. She put it tenderly back in the case, heart pounding. Then she got up to run after her papers.

The boy from Manifesto was picking them up too. He held out a wrinkled handful. "No offense, but I think your filing system could use a little work."

"What?"

"Well there's this thing called a binder." He crouched down, picked up more pages. "You punch holes in all your papers and then you put them in there and it keeps everything organized. So your stuff doesn't, you know, go flying down the street."

He was smirking at her. He thought he was funny.

But he wasn't.

Iz stared at him, with incredulity and then dawning fury. This was the last place where she had expected someone to point out all the things that were wrong with her.

She said coldly, "I thought you needed coffee. Don't let me keep you."

"Changed my mind." He held out his hand. "I'm Teo Russo."

"Iz Beaufort," she said, reluctantly shaking it for the least amount of time.

"You're new today, Iz Beaufort," he said.

"Yes, I know. Excuse me, I'm going to go check in now," she said.

She pulled the door open and marched inside, leaving him standing there.

At the counter, Ellen Harvey greeted her warmly. "Good morning, Iz! Welcome to The Métier School! And I see you've met Teo!"

Iz looked wildly up, and there he was. He'd followed her inside.

"We literally just ran into each other," he said blandly.

Mrs. Harvey beamed at them both. "It's really perfect timing."

Iz stared confusedly from one to the other. Perfect timing for what?

As if he guessed what she was thinking, Teo said, "Manifesto is mentoring the new students today."

Mrs. Harvey said, "Since you've already met, I'll team you up together."

Iz fought a wave of intense frustration. She wanted to ask if she could have another mentor, but it seemed like a rude way to start things off.

"Come on, Beaufort," Teo said cheerfully. "I'll give you a tour of the place."

She sighed. Then, reluctantly, she followed him up the staircase and into the main hallway, past a blur of carved wood, warped floors, stained glass, and bodies moving in all directions. She could hear music seeping out of closed doors and through the walls—a violin, flutes, somewhere an orchestra. A girl's voice ran through some kind of impossibly acrobatic vocal exercise.

Teo was meanwhile blathering on. "The layout is a little complicated. Nobody likes to talk about it, but we're still trying to locate a couple of first years from last term."

He pointed out classrooms, lecture halls, a concert hall, and a recording studio. Iz was trying to memorize it all but found herself getting distracted by the way he kept greeting everyone and high-fiving them.

"So what's your specialization anyway, Beaufort?"

"My what?" Iz said.

"What were you accepted for?"

"Oh. Uh, Composition." She still wasn't even sure exactly what that meant, really. "And I play the guitar and I sing."

"Cool. Who are your profs?"

"Um . . . I don't know."

"It's on your *timetable.*"

Iz flushed at how condescending he sounded. She shuffled through the fistful of papers Mrs. Harvey had given her, now keenly aware of how disorganized they were. Which she was sure he was noticing.

Teo's eyes scanned the page. "Okay. Dr. Nguyen for Guitar. Dr. Henderson for Voice. Dr. Williams for Theory and Composition . . . and you have the trio of death teaching Curriculum Studies, which is all that stuff like English, science, geography, history . . ."

On and on he went, listing every class and every professor who would be teaching it. Music History, Ear Training, Music in Contemporary Societies, First Year Ensemble. Iz started to tune out his overly confident voice.

But then he said, "Oh, hey, you've got Dr. Perlinger for Special Projects. Awesome! He's my tutor too."

A little flutter of excitement went through her at the sound of Dr. Perlinger's name. "Tutor?"

"Everyone has a tutor. You meet with them twice a week on a research project. Dr. P is pretty selective about who he takes on, and he hardly ever works with first years." Teo regarded her. "You must be pretty good."

"I am," Iz said sharply. Before she could stop herself, she added, "I'm going to be in Manifesto."

Teo looked astonished, which was gratifying. "Did he put you in there already?"

She flushed. "Uh, no. But I'm *planning* to be in Manifesto. Soon."

He grinned at her then. "Ha ha. Okay then."

"What's that supposed to mean?"

He spread his hands as if to show he didn't intend any harm. "Nothing. Just that it's not easy to get into Manifesto right away. It's not enough to be an amazing musician and writer. You have to tie it all to something original that you have to say, and it has to grow out of academic research. There's a reason they write about Manifesto in music journals all the time. We're totally unique."

Iz despised him even more in that minute.

"Thanks for the pep talk," she said.

"Hey, I'm sure you're an incredible student, considering Dr. P is tutoring you. You'll be in Manifesto in no time. Like, maybe even on Monday. That's when the next auditions are. There's a sign-up sheet by Dr. P's office."

"Good to know," Iz snapped tightly.

It was the first useful thing he'd said.

Chapter Twelve

Teo took her all around the school during the next half hour. Finally, he came to a stop in front of a door labelled R. Nguyen.

"So! Today's Day One on your timetable, which means your guitar lesson starts in three minutes. You going to be all right, Beaufort?"

"I'm fine," she said tersely. "Thanks."

"Hey, any time. Let me know if you need anything."

He swaggered away at last, and she stood there with her brain all disoriented and frustrated and confused.

For weeks now she had been imagining that Manifesto was going to welcome her into their midst like a long-lost sibling because they'd immediately see the ways that she was like them. But after a half hour with Teo, she wondered if they were all going to be as arrogant and condescending as he was.

If so, this whole thing had been a terrible mistake.

She stood there seething for a while. But at last, she told herself that she'd auditioned and made it in to Métier. She belonged here as much as he did. And what did she care about the opinion of some too-tall fool with more ego than he knew what to do with?

At last she knocked on Dr. Nguyen's door.

The door swung open to reveal a man who was smiling broadly.

"Come in! Come in! You must be Isabelle! Welcome to Métier! How's it going so far?"

He projected a kind of funny, nervous, quick-witted, self-deprecating energy.

"Uh ... great. Great!" She forced herself to sound energetic and enthusiastic and positive. But she was also bracing herself because she knew *exactly* the conversation they were about to have. And it would not be good.

"Sit, sit. Let me get my guitar, and you can get yours out too ..."

He picked up a gleaming, richly-coloured guitar from behind the couch, which was covered in papers and books.

Iz unclipped the clasps, opened the lid, pulled out her old friend.

Dr. Nguyen nodded, eyes darting back and forth across it. "Why have you strung it like that?"

Yep. That was the question. She'd been expecting it.

"Ah, ha," Iz said. "It's a long story."

She watched confusion, disbelief, and curiosity flutter across Dr. Nguyen's face so quickly they were almost gone before they were there.

"Hey, play me something," Dr. Nguyen said. "I just want to see."

Iz squeezed her eyes shut as she sang and played a bit of her new song, "Interwoven World."

When she opened her eyes again, Dr. Nguyen was staring.

"I know," she said in a low voice.

"That's really interesting. Your strings are all out of order, plus you've tuned them to a bunch of unique pitches ... How did that happen? I mean, any teacher would have—" He stopped himself. "So I guess, my first question is, have you *had* lessons before?"

Her face flushed.

She thought about lying, but he would find out the truth anyway. At last she said in a low voice, "No."

"Okay. Okay." He was clearly fascinated. "So how did it get strung this way? I mean, did it come to you like this?"

"Um, I kind of put it together." She flushed. "I found the guitar without strings on it. Then I got some strings and I just, you know, put them on."

Be careful, be careful.

She couldn't exactly tell him that she'd been a seven-year-old foster kid who had decided, in a freewheeling and independent way, to tune the out-of-order strings to the pattern she heard in her head. She couldn't explain that she'd decided to keep them that way, even after learning that they were wrong, because they were *hers* and hardly anything else was.

Embarrassment washed over her.

"No. Way. Amazing," Dr. Nguyen said.

He seemed to wrestle with how to put the next thing.

"So, here's what I think. Your guitar is in a long, proud history of stringed instruments through the centuries that are maybe not in the central canon these days. Viols, chordophones, vielles, tromba marinas, you name it."

He paused.

"And it's marvellous. And I get that it's second nature to you to play like this. But to go forward, we need to get accustomed to the traditional order of the strings." He smiled at her kindly. "And it's going to drive you crazy relearning everything."

Tears were blurring her vision.

"Okay," she said softly.

"May I?" He gestured to her beloved guitar.

"Uh . . . right now?"

A tear plopped on her hand.

How was she going to speak?

Dr. Nguyen froze. He seemed to size up what was going on. Very gently he said, "Change of plans. Let's use my guitar for this lesson. Put your baby away. We won't touch her today."

Iz let out a long breath, all mixed up inside.

"Okay," she muttered.

The rest of the morning got worse.

She discovered in her private voice class that she did not sing properly at all. She sang from the throat, but apparently she should be making sounds from the back of her cheekbones or something.

Also, she was not able to stand loosely and tighten her diaphragm. And when Dr. Henderson did actually coax something out of her that she said was a step in the right direction, the smooth and relaxed sound felt a bit like a betrayal of who Iz was. Jagged was her first language.

That cold little thought crept into her mind again: *you don't belong here.*

Then there was Theory and Composition. They played some kind of game, and it was all about parallel fifths and plagal cadences and enharmonic changes and accidentals versus key signatures. And she realized that, while she might feel comfortable and confident in her own small sphere of writing, she was not anywhere near the skills or knowledge of the other students.

Meanwhile, she kept having flashes of That Place in her head the whole time.

At lunch, she made her way to the cafeteria, her stomach so tight she doubted she would even be able to eat anything. She kind of wanted to just storm out and run back to Pat's place. At the same time she was angry with herself for feeling that way.

When she walked in, a voice shouted, "Hey, Beaufort! Over here!"

It was Teo Russo, grinning and waving, at the centre of a group of people. She stood there frozen, trying to figure out what to do. The last thing she wanted was to talk to him again.

But he kept yelling, as if he could summon her by sheer noise. "Beaufort! Come and join us!"

She let out a huge, exasperated sigh. Finally, holding herself rigidly, she walked over.

And as she got closer, she realized that everyone sitting at the table with Teo was in Manifesto.

An electric shock ran through her.

She was face to face with the reason why she had done everything so far.

"Hey," she said, trying to be calm and cool, losing all feeling in her face.

"Everyone, this is Iz, my student mentee," Teo said easily. "Iz, this is Ahmed, there's Kwame, and Jasleen, and Rina, Will . . ."

"H-hi!" Iz was nodding and smiling jerkily, trying not to look like an idiot. Everything in her wanted to say something memorable and incredible, to convince them she was really remarkable. But the Iz who had sat dreaming of Manifesto in her bedroom did not actually seem to be related to the real Iz standing here tongue-tied.

"Have a seat, Iz," said a boy with kind eyes. "I'm Bijan."

"I'm LaRoyce. How was your first morning?" another boy said, with a loose ease that seemed like a gift.

"Uh, good." Iz fell into the chair they offered.

"What did you have?"

"G-guitar. Voice. Theory and Composition."

"She has Nguyen and Henny," Teo said helpfully, from where he was lounging across the table.

"Did she tell you to resonate behind your cheekbones?" LaRoyce said.

"Ha, yeah." She could seemingly only speak in single-syllable words now. "I, uh, I saw you all at—"

She was interrupted by a squealing sound.

Kwame had blown up a balloon and was now letting air out of it slowly so that it was squeaking an impossibly high note.

Will opened his mouth and emitted a loud falsetto that matched the balloon's squeal exactly.

Jasleen whipped out her phone. "Wait! Do it again!"

Kwame blew up the balloon once more and created an even smaller opening for the air to escape. The sound climbed higher. Everyone in Manifesto began to try to match it.

"Send me that," Ahmed said to Jasleen.

Iz stared.

"We're slightly obnoxious," LaRoyce said apologetically to Iz.

"Hey, Beaufort," Teo said. "*You* give it a try."

She crossed her arms tightly. "Yeah, no."

"Come on!" Then he turned to the table and said, "Iz is going to audition on Monday."

"Hey! That's great!"

"What are you going to perform?"

"Huh," Iz found herself saying. She had no idea yet. "Uh, you know, maybe one of my songs."

Jasleen was nodding. "Good, but try to link it to something academic."

"That's what *I* said," Teo was sprawled all over the place like the entire earth was his personal birthright. "Dr. P wants you to say something original that's connected to research."

Ahmed added, "Like Will's audition—remember that? He mashed up the invasion of Dieppe with a heavy metal compilation of Debussy's etudes, arguing that they all represented pushing human endurance to its utmost."

"And Becky's project—coding meets twelve tone series—" Rina slapped a girl's back affectionately.

Kwame said to Teo, "And of course a little hint of 'Che gelida manina' stuck in cement . . ."

"In Napoli," Teo said with a grin.

Iz stared from face to face, understanding nothing they were saying.

"If you want," Jasleen said to her kindly, "I could send you some examples, if you give me your info."

Then she was holding out her phone to Iz while everyone watched. And out of nowhere, Iz felt the same overwhelming claustrophobia as she had in the Great Expectations Club when she was stuck under the table with the teachers. If she wasn't careful, she would do something weird and violent like she had done then.

"Hey!" she said, shooting to her feet. "I just forgot, I have an appointment thing. Uh . . . I have to go."

She gathered up her things and slammed the chair back.

Most of the cafeteria turned to look.

"It was good to meet you," Jasleen called after her.

Everyone else at the table chimed in too.

Out in the hallway, Iz wanted to yell at herself.

What kind of loser moved heaven and earth to be somewhere, and then, as soon as she got there, ran away from it?

A loser named Iz, that was who.

She went along the hallway until she found a row of practice rooms.

Then she slipped inside one and stuck her head in her hands. She sat like that, furious with herself. Her stomach was growling, but she did not have the stupid nerve to go back into that cafeteria again.

When the bell pealed out to signal the end of lunch, Iz raked her hands through her hair. She squeezed her skull as hard as she could, trying to mask the anxiety with physical pain. She just wanted to go home.

But finally she riffled through the papers till she found her timetable.

Curriculum Studies, that was next. The English and math and stuff.

She stumbled out of the practice room, clutching the map they'd given her. Then she went in the completely wrong direction, turned herself around, and took about three corners the wrong way before she found Lecture Hall C at last.

She pushed open the heavy door and was hit with a wall of noise. It seemed like a hundred other kids were finding their seats.

After a little while, three teachers came out to the podium.

The trio of pain, that's what Teo Russo had called them.

"Welcome to the second term of First Year Curriculum Studies," one of them said. "I'm Dr. Elizabeth Maynard. For those who are just joining us, these are the subjects that some of you will be tempted to consider to be of lesser importance than your music courses. That would be a mistake."

Another said, "And I am Dr. Gordon Park. Let's not forget, The Métier School is a *high school.* If you don't keep up your marks here, you will be removed from the program."

"That said," said the third, "we do things a little differently in here than in your average high school. You'll find we integrate subjects together. A lot of what you will do is project based, individualized. No two of you will have the exact same program, because you will be exploring and synthesizing your learning in your own way—within the larger expectations of the curriculum, of course. And I am Dr. Harpreet Gill."

"Does that sound intimidating?" said Dr. Maynard. "It should. You'll work harder in here than you would out there in a regular school."

Dr. Gill added, "But I think you'll find it matters more to you because you are making your own meaning out of it."

Iz sat there thinking about her horrible marks and how she had only half listened to anything for the last few years. These teachers were going to figure all of that out in about two minutes.

She moaned out loud, then clapped her hand over her mouth apologetically. "Sorry," she whispered, not meeting anyone's eyes.

Other kids grinned at her, like they understood where she was coming from. But really they had no idea.

At the end of the day, she stood by her locker, staring into it, trying to figure out what had just happened. And the answer was, she had expected herself to be different—better somehow—once she got to The Métier School. But the only thing she'd changed was her location. She was still a messed-up powder keg.

Finally, she gathered up her stuff, slammed the door shut, and left.

Without signing up for a Manifesto audition.

Chapter Thirteen

Iz slipped into Pat's house an hour or so later, clutching her useless guitar.

"Hey, baby!" Pat came out into the hall, smiling, holding purple gauze in one hand and ribbon in the other. "How was the guitar club this morning?" Then her face changed. "Everything okay?"

Iz flushed, alarmed. "Uh, great."

"Are you coming down with something again?" Pat felt her forehead.

Iz resisted the urge to flinch. "No, I'm just tired. First day back, you know. I think I'd like to just head upstairs and crash for a while."

Pat stared at her concernedly again for a minute. Iz waited, hardly breathing.

Then Pat smiled. "Sure, baby. You go rest. I'll call you for dinner."

Iz climbed the stairs slowly, feeing like she was trying to crest Mount Everest. She hardly had the muscle power to do it.

She heard Britnee saying, "Let's put the full payment down on both trellises. Live big!"

Iz closed the door to her room, put her guitar down on the floor, and fell onto the bed. Then she lay there with her eyes closed and tried to make the wobbly feeling in her stomach go away.

She was such a fool to honestly think she could just waltz into The Métier School and take the place by storm.

Part of her brain whispered, *You don't have to go back.*

It was true. She had an escape route. She could call the old school and tell them that Iz Beaufort was returning. She could probably fill out papers online to enroll herself just as easily as she had completed the withdrawal stuff. Then she could just show up there tomorrow morning, and nothing would have changed. This whole thing could be a ridiculous, unlikely dream that would recede in her mind.

Iz swung herself off the bed. She snuck out into the hall, picked up the phone from its cradle and brought it back into her room.

She grabbed her notebook and started flipping through it, looking for where she had written down the old school's number.

As she turned over page after page, she saw all the songs she had written over the years.

"Cloud Princess" was about one home she'd lived in, where the foster kids ate in the basement on holidays. Up above, a floor away, the family's daughter had been like some charmed creature in the sky.

"Mirror" told about how Iz felt like she was a reflection without actually existing herself.

"The Star Who Fell"—it was the last song she had written, a kind of a fable about how a celestial thing got sucked into a black hole. She'd scribbled it down as the darkness of That Place closed around her, as her own light began to be muffled under the need to be cautious, watchful. As she stopped being a free thing in her own mind.

For the first time since *waking up*, for the first time since *that chord,* Iz thought of the experience of writing each of the songs. She could see each place in her mind, all the different foster homes, each with a reason why she couldn't stay there.

Because of the accident, I just can't look after you.
Our family is moving.
My real daughter is finding it tough having you here.
I am just realizing I don't have the time and energy.
The teacher keeps calling about you from school.
You're eating more than I expected.
You're refusing to eat.
We're getting divorced.
You argue too much.

You never talk.
My father died and I am finding it hard to cope.
You are a strange and kind of creepy child.
I lost my job and we're downsizing.
I'm not sure what you're thinking most of the time.
There is friction between you and the other foster kids.
We have decided we will not be fostering children anymore.
It's hard for me to look after you now that I am ill.
You'll be better served in another home.
You are too messy.
You keep asking for things.
Fostering isn't quite what I thought it was going to be.
This is a temporary placement.
It's just not clicking.

She remembered feeling like she was going to explode if she didn't get her thoughts down on paper and build them into notes and phrases. Writing songs had been a way of focusing that frustration and rage into something that wasn't violent. It had been a way of trying to make some meaning out of a thing that was basically meaningless.

Looking at all the songs, she felt a weird sense of grief and protectiveness and compassion toward that younger Iz who had been trying to speak the best way she could amid all of the homes and the upheaval. Her voice had been hidden and small and suspicious and broken-hearted. She had concealed it in a notebook. And finally, after That Place, she had silenced it altogether.

Iz flipped the pages over and over.

Right now, this minute, she still wanted to speak.

If she was honest with herself, that was what had upset her so much at The Métier School. When given the chance to have a voice, she had discovered she had exactly nothing to say. In fact, she'd turned out to be exactly what the woman in That Place had told her she was—an arrogant little girl who was all puffed up with delusions of brilliance, who answered back too chirpily, who was nothing but hollow, wasted space inside.

Finally, she grabbed her completely messed-up guitar. She drew it into her lap. She closed her eyes.

She began to let her fingers pluck out the turmoil in her mind, tentative note by note.

It was like her heart was a snarl of twisted melody lines. Her fingers walked through each one, separating, examining. It was meditation. It was hypnosis. Music had always been like that for her—a language and grammar that matched her own thoughts and helped her work things out.

As she played, she let her brain range over the what-ifs.

What if she walked into The Métier School again tomorrow?

What if she went back to another guitar lesson?

What if she went on Pat's computer and looked for a guitar template thing she could print off and use to practise fingerings?

What if, whenever she felt intimidated, she reminded herself about all of her songs and all of the places where she had written them, and she decided not to let that younger Iz down?

What would it feel like?

It would feel scary. It would feel huge. It would feel like more than she could handle.

Her fingers played that out. They played the massiveness of The Métier School in great ringing chords. They played her own lack of any musical background, in frightened shards of sound.

And somehow, her playing honoured all the confusion and fear. Weirdly, it turned the things that were troubled and confused inside her into some sort of bravery. Because anyone who was that scared and who chose to go back to the thing that scared her would definitely be courageous.

When finally she let her hands drop, she sat there alone on her bed, looking at the phone.

So what was she going to do?

Chapter Fourteen

The next morning, as she climbed up those stone steps, Iz told herself that she would handle whatever came her way.

But, when she walked in, she froze.

Hoots and screams were coming from somewhere upstairs. She could hear rhythmic clapping too. People were chanting things. It sounded like a huge fight.

She started shaking.

"Hey, Beaufort!" A voice practically bellowed in her ear, making her jump. "Come and join the par-choir."

There was Teo Russo again, with the same annoyingly confident smile.

"W-what?"

He grinned. "It's parkour but this is Métier, so par-choir. Come on!"

"Uh, no. I have to get ready for class—"

"Beaufort! Come and meet people. I'm your mentor so you should do what I say. If we're lucky, someone'll wipe out like Bijan did last year. It was *spectacular.* It's on YouTube." Then he added, like he was some kind of fount of wisdom, "You're a Métier student now. If you just go off by yourself, you're missing half the experience."

He smirked at her cajolingly, like there was no way she could resist his charms.

Iz let out a long, exasperated breath. It was becoming clear that the only way to get rid of him was to go and see this thing. Finally she said, "Just for a minute."

As she followed Teo up the main staircase to the second floor, the sound of laughter grew louder and her stomach felt tighter.

They entered the cafeteria. Kids stood around the walls, and in the centre was a kind of obstacle course. There were tables lined up, with music stands and chairs and ramps in various configurations. Signs were taped here and there, with instructions that contained what Iz assumed were musical jokes. *Crawl Bach through here* and *Liszt to the Left* and *Vivaldi Vault!*

"We do this every term to welcome the new students," Teo said, grinning down at her. "Technically we're not supposed to, but everyone looks the other way. It's like a rite of passage, the par-choir."

She stared at him in horror. "Well, *I'm* not going through there."

He laughed. "How did I know you were going to say that, Beaufort? Don't worry. Nobody's going to make you do anything you don't want to do."

He led her through the crowd to the front, where she could see everything. Some first-year student was down on his hands and knees, creeping through the Scriabin Scramble.

"Hey! Iz! You going to give it a try?" It was LaRoyce, from Manifesto.

But Teo shook his head immediately. "Beaufort's just watching."

"You sure? It's a cleansing experience."

Applause broke out, as the first-year student staggered triumphantly out of the last part of the course. Everyone was high-fiving him. He looked flushed and energized. He looked like he belonged.

Iz hugged herself tightly, fighting against that claustrophobia again. She tried to remind herself about sitting on her bed last night, playing out her fears, turning them into courage.

But suddenly it felt like too much, having everyone pressed close around her.

She said to Teo, "I have to go."

Then she was shoving out through people, trying to get as far away as possible. She could hear him calling after her, but she ignored it.

Once she was in the safety of the hallway, she leaned against the wall and covered her face. She breathed in and out, calming down.

Finally, she drew out her crumpled timetable and searched for what her first class would be. It was her tutorial with Dr. Perlinger.

Iz's brain whispered immediately, *You're going to disappoint him.*

"Shut up!" she hissed back.

She followed the numbers till she found his office. Then she sat on the bench outside, drawing up her knees. She put her head down and closed her eyes.

After a long while, she heard steps coming up.

"Iz Beaufort. Well, well, well. How was your first day? And how is your second day going so far?" It was Dr. Perlinger's voice.

"Hey!" Iz's head shot up. "It was—it *is*—okay."

Dr. Perlinger was quiet for a long time. Waiting.

And his silence seemed to create a space into which her words spilled, even though she wasn't planning to say anything.

"I mean, I don't know what I'm doing. But other than that, great."

Then she was yelling at herself, inside her head. *Shut up! Shut up!*

A silence fell.

"It is quite all right not to know things before you know them," Dr. Perlinger said mildly at last. "In fact, I believe it's impossible to know things before you know them, according to how we understand the universe at present."

She said in a low voice, "Yeah, well, I'm doing great then."

"Of course you are," Dr. Perlinger said. "Why *should* you know everything? What a loss that would be. A lifetime of curiosity and discovery, over before it began."

He sat down beside her.

"You are a Schubert fan, so here is a piece of Schubert trivia for you. Did you know that he had a beautiful singing voice as a boy, but his family couldn't afford a proper musical education? So they came up with a plan. If he auditioned to be a young singer in the royal church, he could have a *free* education at a place called the Stadtkonvikt, the imperial boarding school."

He paused.

"But Schubert was not at the level he needed to be for the audition. So he had to learn a lot in a short space of time. Oh, it was quite the campaign. His dad instructed him in playing the violin and his brother taught him piano. They found him singing lessons with a choir leader at a church nearby. And he had to work hard on all his other school subjects to achieve a certain academic level in order to be considered."

Iz was silent. But inside, her heart was flopping over. Why was Dr. Perlinger telling her about Schubert scrabbling his way into a music school despite the odds? Had he figured out the truth about her?

Dr. Perlinger said softly, "You would not be here if we did not believe you were superlatively talented. I may be wrong, Iz, but I think you're mainly self-taught. Yes? And that is extraordinary. The rest of it can come. The terminology and the technique."

He slouched, stretched his legs so that his pointy shoes aimed straight up. "Reach out always. Don't muddle along when it's worrying you. And don't compare yourself to others or allow them to determine what you think of yourself. Summon that terrific audition and let it be your strength. You're an original, Iz, and you have original things to say."

Something loosened around her chest at his words, like she could breathe again for the first time in these two overwhelming days. She said softly, "Sometimes, you know, I feel like I'm standing outside in the snow or something, looking in the window while everyone is getting ready for a party." She thought of Pat and Britnee. "Or a wedding."

"A wedding," Dr. Perlinger said thoughtfully and slowly. Then he sat upright suddenly. "*Winterreise*!"

He sounded like he was sneezing.

"What?"

He beamed. "It's a song cycle by your friend Schubert, based on a set of poems by Wilhelm Müller. Literally, it's exactly what you just described. A poor, lonely Wanderer standing outside a window, looking in at people planning a wedding."

"What's a song cycle?"

He waved his hand. "A collection of songs. In this case, all about a poor man whose heart's broken because his Beloved is not getting married to *him*."

"Cheery," Iz said.

"Tell you what," said Dr. Perlinger. "Let's go into my office. Let's have a look at the English translation and we'll listen to it. I think it might catch your interest. Then, this week, at home, listen again, maybe a few times."

"Okay," Iz answered in a little voice. "But—"

"Yes?"

It was humiliating but it needed to be said, because you couldn't predict what Pat or Britnee were going to be doing.

"I don't have, you know, I might not be able to—only if I can get on a computer o-or a phone."

Dr. Perlinger didn't draw in his breath in horror.

He said evenly, "Well, we'll loan you a tablet then. You have Wi-Fi?"

"I—yes, kind of, I think." She would just have to figure out the login information, which hopefully would not be too hard.

If it surprised him that she didn't even know if her home had Wi-Fi, he didn't let on. "I'll get you one with Wi-Fi built in, just in case."

She exhaled a long low breath that seemed to let out some of the stress inside her.

Dr. Perlinger said encouragingly, "Iz Beaufort, have faith. We are going to have *so much fun* this year."

"Okay." She tried to smile in a hopeful and confident way.

Over the next hour, Iz and Dr. Perlinger read through all the lyrics for *Winterreise*.

Then they listened to it in German while looking at a document that compared the German lyrics to the English lyrics.

Dr. Perlinger kept stopping the recording and saying things like, "There! Doesn't the piano remind you of dripping icicles? Schubert is famous for making music *sound* like things—spinning wheels or galloping hooves, for example."

His enthusiasm seemed to get right into her brain and heart. It was like the two of them were embarking on their own winter journey together, right alongside the Wanderer.

And at the end of the hour, when she left Dr. Perlinger's office, she felt better than she had since starting at The Métier School.

She stood there looking at the auditions sign-up sheet that was on his door. Yesterday she hadn't felt like she deserved to be part of Manifesto. But now Dr. Perlinger's voice was in her ears. *It is quite all right not to know things before you know them.*

In a fit of daring, she pulled out a pen.

She wrote her name on the list.

There!

Chapter Fifteen

"You survived your first tutorial with Dr. P?"

She jumped, halfway through packing everything up at the end of the day.

There was Teo Russo again, over at his locker, wrapping a scarf around his neck and zipping up his leather jacket.

Great, they were leaving at the same moment.

"How did you know I had my first tutorial?" she said shortly.

He grinned in that superior way. "Photographic memory. I saw your timetable, remember?"

"Oh."

"And Curriculum Studies, how brutal is that? Did they say you were going to get kicked out if you didn't put, like, three thousand percent effort into their class?"

"Uh, yeah. Maybe." The stress started building in her, just thinking about it all. Defiantly she added, "It was better today, though."

That was true. After the main lecture, everyone had been sent to small group tutorials, and the teaching assistant had started breaking down the details of their first project—a mix of science, English, and math—and it had actually sort of fit the way her brain worked.

"Yeah," he said, "just keep up with the workload in there and you'll be fine."

He sounded like he was a king or something, throwing a couple of coins in her direction.

She blurted out, "Great. Thanks. Well, see you. I have to go."

She edged along the hallway away from him. He fell in beside her, his backpack over one shoulder. She went faster, but his long legs easily kept up.

It was really annoying. She needed to shake him before heading over to that restaurant because if he saw she was singing in the streets to make the $1500 she needed for next month, he would probably spread it all over the school. Which would be deadly.

"What are you going to study with Dr. P?" Teo asked.

He was so nosy. Iz let out a loud sigh. "*Winterreise.*"

"Ah!" Teo said brightly. "Fremd bin ich eingezogen, fremd zieh' ich wieder aus."

"What?"

"'As a stranger I arrived, as a stranger I shall leave.' It's the opening lines of 'Gute Nacht,' you know, the first song in *Winterreise.*" He looked completely delighted with himself for being so full of encyclopedic brilliance.

Iz stiffened, suddenly feeling totally inferior again. And his words pierced right through to the truth of it. She *was* a stranger. She'd always been one, in fact, even to herself, in every home.

But then she thought of last night, of sitting on her bed figuring out who she was by playing her guitar till she worked the knots out of her mind. She thought of Dr. Perlinger telling her it would be boring to know everything.

She said loftily, "I actually prefer song number five, 'The Linden Tree.'"

He laughed. "Oh, yeah, the one where he used to hang out with his Beloved at the tree but now it's all leafless and frozen, just like his sad, sad life. That guy just could not catch a break, am I right?"

They were going down the main staircase now, and even though she kept speeding up, he was holding steady beside her.

He said cheerfully, "So you'll be glad to know there were no major injuries from the par-choir."

"Awesome."

"But you know what would be cool? Some kind of obstacle

course based on *Winterreise*. You know, the Hurdy Gurdy Hustle, The Charcoal Burner Chase. Maybe we should do *that* next time."

He just would not shut up. Iz let out a long sigh, trying to contain her frustration.

Finally, as they reached the bottom of the stairs, she turned on him. "So, it's been a thrill talking to you. But I've got to run. I mean, 'as a stranger I shall leave.'"

Then, she took off like she was trying to outrace the Erlking.

Once she was outside, she pelted through the snow, not looking back. She took three different corners and ran along unfamiliar streets. If he *was* following, she was determined to lose him.

Finally, panting, she arrived again at that restaurant, Festa.

Deliberately, even defiantly, she set down her guitar case, opened it, took out her guitar.

Then, she leaned close to the window, read the menu posted outside, committed it to memory. Cozze in padella. Caprese di Bufala. Spaghetti alla vodka. Gnocchi con pera e Gorgonzola. It sounded exotic and delicious, and the smells wafting out the front door made her stomach grumble.

After that, Iz began deliberately to turn the menu into a kind of ongoing song, slow and low, like steam curling out of great bubbling pots in a kitchen.

Soon he would come out and notice.

He had to.

Wouldn't it be bella
To have cozze in padella?
Or maybe you'd go lala
For caprese di Bufala
Imported from Campania . . .

It took a long time, over half an hour more, till she couldn't feel her ears because her hood kept blowing off and she'd stopped trying to keep it up. But at last the grey-haired man opened the door and leaned out into the cold night, wiping his hands on his apron, looking busy and like he didn't have time for her.

"You knocked over my plant," he said.

She fought to find that gutsy voice from the other day. "I've been writing music about your whole menu, and I talked like twelve different people into going into the restaurant. Listen."

Then she started to sing—joined all those little songs together for him so he could see what an asset she might be to his establishment.

When she was done, he asked, "How old are you?"

"That's a personal question," Iz said.

"Sixteen?"

"Something like that. I'm actually older than I look."

"Where's your papa? Does he know you're out here doing this on a cold night? There could be anybody walking along here."

"Then," she said daringly, testing the waters, "you should let me sing inside. You should give me a pay cheque."

But he was shaking his head at her, turning to go back into the warm interior. "You're a weird kid, you know that?"

Instantly she dialed it back. "Or, you know, I'd settle for something warm. Soup. Actually, I would love soup. Soup would be amazing. Do you have any soup?"

She twinkled at him.

"Ha, is that what you would love?" The man waved his hand dismissively at her, went back inside, and closed the door.

But a little while later, a woman appeared with a large cup and spoon. She was thin, with short grey hair. Her eyes had kind shadows around them.

"It's minestrone," she said. "Come under the awning. You must be freezing."

Iz gratefully accepted the cup. She dipped the spoon in with numb fingers. When the warm soup hit her tongue, she exclaimed aloud, "This is delicious!"

"Thanks. I made it. I'm the chef."

"Do you make all of the things on that menu?"

"Yes. Not on my own though. We have sous chefs too."

"Well, I don't actually know what sous chefs are, but my compliments to you and to them."

More people came by to read the menu.

"You should eat here," Iz told them. "The soup is really, really good. This is the chef. She is amazing."

There was a small smile curling on the chef's mouth.

Chapter Sixteen

When Iz got home, Pat and Britnee were researching honeymoon packages while Vance sat and watched silently.

"I like this place in Cancun," Pat said. "We could go on the lazy river."

"But this one in the Dominican, they have a chocolate fountain in the buffet. And there are twelve bars. And you get unlimited free lessons in water sports."

"Hey," Iz said, leaning into the living room.

"Hi, baby!" Pat said. "How was your day?"

"Better."

"I made squares! Help yourself."

Iz went into the kitchen and collected a couple of squares and a glass of milk, relieved Pat seemed too distracted with wedding stuff to realize how late it was.

From the living room, she heard Britnee say, "And here's one with a butler service."

"A butler service!" Pat's voice sounded reverent.

Iz took her food upstairs and closed the door to her room. She dumped the bills and coins from tonight onto the bed. Painstakingly, she counted it out.

Thirty-one dollars and sixty-five cents.

Then she sat there a long time, trying to keep from panicking. At this rate, she would not have anywhere near enough to pay her

February fees. Métier would be finished, just as she and Dr. Perlinger were embarking on this *Winterreise* journey together.

Britnee laughed loudly downstairs, husky and delighted about something. Maybe about a free helicopter ride. Or some champagne waterfall.

Iz's jaw tightened and her stomach felt sick. Pat and Britnee existed in a totally different universe. Everything was so easy for them.

If only Iz could make money like that! But she was not an adult who could just go out and get a job. She was not like Pat, who must make a *lot* if she could afford butler services.

Iz sat there imagining how rich Pat must be.

Wondering.

Finally she drew out her new tablet from Dr. Perlinger. She typed into the search bar, *How much do foster parents make?*

Up came an immediate answer.

Caregivers receive approximately $3500 per month. It covers the child's expenses, as well as the caregiver's allowance.

Then Iz sat there with her eyes wide open. That felt like a lot.

She wondered what "child's expenses" Pat was paying for. Iz hadn't gotten any new clothes in quite a while. And as for food, she'd eaten lots of Pat's meals and squares and cookies, of course, but had they been worth 3500 dollars a month?

Well, it was easy enough to figure out. Iz flipped to a new page in her notebook. She started writing down everything she could remember eating in the last month. Then she used Dr. Perlinger's iPad to look up every single food on the list and how much it cost.

When she had finally finished, she added it all up. And that was when disbelief and even a whiff of fury bubbled up in her.

Pat was basically a decent person, but she was not spending very much on Iz at all, as far as Iz could tell.

And the less you spent on a foster kid, the more you pocketed as a caregiver.

The more Iz thought about it, the angrier she became. It was almost like stealing.

Then her brain began to circle an idea curiously, like a dog sniffing a fortress trying to find the way in.

Technically, a chunk of Pat's money belonged to Iz.

Immediately, Iz whispered, "No."

Because that idea led to a place that would be really, really bad. It would be *way* worse than anything she had done so far. It was the kind of thing they sent you to jail for.

Pushing the thought away, she typed *Winterreise* into the search engine of her new tablet. She curled up on the bed with her eyes closed, shutting out everything except the piano and the singer. She listened for the dripping icicles Dr. Perlinger had pointed out. She rode over the arc of the despairing and slightly maddened melodies that the Wanderer was singing.

And every so often, she leaned over and scribbled things in her notebook.

Sounds like being strangled.

He's maybe going crazy.

The music is a skeleton—dried out and bleached.

His home is literally nowhere.

But even amid these captivating ideas, her brain kept returning to the same thought, ever more fully formed.

You are entitled to some of Pat's money.

"Shut up!" Iz told herself.

Desperately, she searched for a website that would tell her the right order of the strings. Then she practised putting her fingers where they needed to go for the exercise Dr. Nguyen had given her, even though the strings on her guitar were still all in the wrong places. She did it over and over until her muscles began to understand it.

Her brain kept spurting things out at her, though. And its voice was getting louder.

Pat would probably not even notice.

She said she's scared of banks.

I bet she doesn't ever look at her bank account.

And you can probably do it all online, if you can figure out her number and login and password—which maybe you can get from her cheque book or her bank card or something—

"Shut up," Iz hissed to her brain. "Shut up!"

She was terrified and guilty and ashamed.

Still, a minute later, she slipped out of her room and stood at the top of the stairs, weighing it out.

From the living room, she heard Britnee say, "Vance, take a stand. Which one should we sign up for? The parasailing or the scuba?"

A little curling simmer of rage drifted through Iz all over again.

She slipped down the stairs, crept into the front hallway and began quietly to open the closet door where she'd seen Pat put her purse earlier.

Pat called out, "Iz? Is that you, honey?"

"Ha!" Iz said, jumping.

"Come here and settle an argument, baby."

She shuffled to the living room.

"For Brit and Vance's honeymoon, which one do you like better at this resort? The jungle view or the ocean view?"

"Uh …" Iz said, keeping her face completely neutral. "Probably the ocean, I guess."

"That's what Brit thought. But then I was thinking you're more likely to see monkeys in the jungle view."

"Yeah … true," Iz said. "Maybe jungle view then."

Britnee rolled her eyes at Iz. "You're as bad as Vance. Pick a lane!"

"This property looks like a treehouse," Pat said, poring over a page.

Their attention shifted away from Iz. She backed out of the room. Then she tiptoed back to the hallway closet, where Pat's purse was. Silently, she opened the closet door, grabbed the purse, and lifted out Pat's wallet.

Her brain was stammering and spluttering: *horrible, horrible, horrible.*

She worked quickly—ripped a cheque out of the cheque book, took pictures of Pat's bank card and credit card with her tablet.

But she froze when Britnee said loudly, "Wait a minute! We kept the brochure from the Easter trip last year! It's in the hall drawer I think."

Panicking, Iz squeezed into the closet and pulled the door closed. She scarcely dared to breathe.

Through a crack, she could see Britnee come into the hallway, open a drawer in the cabinet, and thumb through pamphlets. She drew out something at last.

"Found it!"

Humming, she half ran back into the living room.

Iz waited for a while in the darkness before opening the closet and stepping shakily out again. Then she ran up the stairs to her room. She closed the door securely and sank down into a kind of fetal position.

She couldn't do this.

But there was a sudden explosion of laughter downstairs. It sounded satisfied and fortunate, like Pat and Britnee had been showered with good wishes by some helpful fairy.

Then, Iz felt like she was falling away from the earth, from everything good.

She drew Dr. Perlinger's tablet toward her. She typed the name of Pat's bank into Google. And a second later, she was looking at the login page.

Her heart was sprinting like it was being chased.

Hands shaking, she peered at the cheque she'd taken from Pat's purse. Sure enough, there was a bank account number on there. She typed it in.

Then the second box lit up. PASSWORD.

Iz breathed out slowly, thinking. Finally she typed in *Britnee123* to see what would happen.

The webpage thought about it for a minute. Then the screen went blank. After that, a page came up that said things like Balance, Transfers, Payments, Credit Card.

She was in.

Chapter Seventeen

It was gnawing at her, what she had done to Pat. But she tried to look straight ahead, like someone on a tightrope. Thinking about falling would make her fall. Thinking about how precarious this whole thing was would invite disaster.

So she tuned it all out and put her sights onto the next big challenge.

Her Manifesto audition on Monday.

Anxiously, desperately, she spent her evenings writing and scribbling things out again, plucking pointless melodies on her guitar. Each thing seemed inadequate, babyish.

She kept imagining what Teo Russo would say about them.

Not bad, Beaufort, but it's not exactly good. Could you try to make it a little more academic?

She began to despair of coming up with anything. But then, on Friday morning, something happened in her guitar lesson that gave her an idea.

Dr. Nguyen said suddenly, "Hey. Do you know how to transpose? Can you start the exercise on G?"

Iz closed her eyes. She plucked the G, and then kind of measured between the notes to figure out the rest of the melody. It was a bit laborious, because she was doing two kinds of translating at once—working out the tune in a totally different alphabet, and also figuring out the fingerings on an unfamiliar set of strings.

She said at last, wonderingly, "It's . . . relationships. It doesn't matter where you start."

"Exactly! The circle of fifths—it's like a big family tree, right?"

That had been like a door opening.

She'd gone home that night and pored over the circle of fifths, the great chart that mapped out how each key was related to each other key. She'd memorized it. Then she'd listened to *Winterreise* over and over, picking out where the melodies were going into the relative major or the tonic minor or modulating into something else altogether.

It was like building up a huge roadmap through the whole song cycle.

Which was when she'd started imagining different ways that Schubert could have planned his route.

And once she had begun thinking about that, fireworks started exploding in her head.

Most of the weekend, she wrote and rewrote in a kind of fury. Then she practised in an intense, low voice so Pat wouldn't hear.

And she tried to remind herself about how fear could turn into courage.

Monday came quickly.

Iz sat impatiently through classes until the bell finally rang. Then she ran to the lecture hall where auditions would be taking place.

It took her a minute to get up the courage to enter. At last, she pushed the door open and strode into the lecture hall.

A familiar voice rang out. "Hey, Beaufort! Over here!"

There he was, sitting near the front and waving cheerfully at her, like some puppy's out-of-control tail.

She fought the urge to turn and run out of there.

But now Bijan was standing up to let her through the aisle so she could sit in the empty chair that was annoyingly beside Teo. "Good luck, Iz. You're going to be great."

That was when she realized everyone sitting in that row was in Manifesto.

Manifesto would be watching her audition.

Iz stood there in a kind of shock for a second. Then she shuffled past Bijan to sit in the empty chair.

LaRoyce leaned around others to see her. "What are you performing, Iz?"

"I bet she won't tell you," Teo said with fake-sad resonance. "Right, Beaufort? So secretive. So ungrateful. After I took her all around the school on the first day and everything."

Iz arranged her guitar at her feet, ignoring him. He would not sabotage her today, however much he tried.

"I even warned her about the missing first years."

Rina snorted.

Iz hissed at him, half under her breath, "If you don't mind, I'd just like to have a couple of minutes of quiet."

"Quiet," Teo Russo said, nodding immediately, eyes sparkling as if she was amusing. "Quiet is my forte. I did it for two years once."

Then he shut right up. He took out his phone and bent his floppy-haired head over it, shutting her out. And his silence was even louder and more irritating than his voice.

Finally, Dr. Perlinger came barging into the room and speed-walked down the stairs to the stage, greeting people affably as he went. "Sorry I'm late! Technical difficulties!"

For the next five minutes, he called out names and organized the order of auditions.

Then, he smiled right down at the members of Manifesto. He spoke directly to them. "Every audition, here you all are. And you always cheer the loudest."

He looked up at everyone else in the room.

"When I formed Manifesto, I envisioned a group in which the standard would be high for musicality, composition, academics, and technicality—but even higher for *humanity.* This group embodies the notion that none of us operates alone. We inspire each other. We look after each other. We encourage each other. We are all interconnected."

His words echoed what he had said at that concert at Dennison Hall. A thrill ran through Iz at the thought that she was really sitting here, listening to him at The Métier School.

Dr. Perlinger went on, "So when each of you comes up here to audition, know that whatever you offer will be greeted warmly. And on that note, shall we begin? Iz Beaufort, would you like to start us off?"

She nodded, leapt anxiously to her feet. Everyone in Manifesto stood up to let her through. Someone patted her on the back. Kind Bijan smiled encouragingly.

She stumbled to the front and sat down on the stool that was there. She put her guitar in position and looked down at its unique strings.

She took a deep breath.

When her voice came out, it was stupidly shaky and small. "I'm … I'm going to play my own version of 'The Linden Tree' from *Winterreise*. I wanted to explore how the Wanderer is kind of trapped between the past and present, so I created a guitar accompaniment that goes through a series of modulations that represent a kind of net he can't escape from. You could think of them as almost time periods—the sad present and the happy past—that are crashing against each other like ice smashing against ice."

And then, unnervingly and deliberately, Teo whooped.

Iz jumped and glared. He was trying to distract her, but he wouldn't succeed.

She focused her attention inward, bringing all of her fierce desire to bear on what she was about to do. She breathed in the Wanderer for a few minutes, closed her eyes to see him better. Then she *became him*, all frozen in a purgatory of no hope for the future and lost hope in the past.

***

When her hands fell at last, she held her breath for what seemed like forever, hardly knowing if she could handle hearing what Dr. Perlinger had to say.

But he smiled at her from where he sat and said, "Lovely!"

"R-really?"

"Most definitely," Dr. Perlinger said.

"Oh!" Iz said.

Relief flooded her. Then a kind of joy bubbled up.

Bathed in this triumphant feeling, she threaded her way back into the row. She heard Teo saying annoyingly to Ahmed, "I taught her everything she knows."

And she didn't even care.

Because she was going to be in Manifesto.

Chapter Eighteen

There was a paper on Dr. Perlinger's door.

"Thank you to everyone. No new admissions this round. Next auditions in May."

Iz kept staring but the words weren't sinking in.

Maybe this was the wrong sheet she was looking at.

But it definitely said "Manifesto Auditions" at the top.

"Iz, I saw. I'm sorry. I thought your audition was really brilliant. I loved the clashing in the lower voices—like water churning under the ice."

It was generous Bijan, walking past with LaRoyce and Kwame.

"Try again next round," Kwame said. "You've got the kernel of something so cool there. Don't give up."

The kernel.

Kernels were babies. Kernels weren't full-grown. Kernels didn't even know how to grow unless they were in the right circumstances.

Iz gasped out something and stumbled away from the door.

At that moment, a familiar voice, resonant and rich, laughed out loud somewhere along the hallway.

She could not bear to see him at this minute. On impulse, she opened the first practice room door she could find and hurried inside. She closed the door just in time, before Teo could see her. Then she crouched down on the black piano bench, and the tears came fully, like a waterfall of anguish.

Not good enough.

She wept against her guitar, bashed out wild chords like huge violent strikes against a universe that had just put her in her place yet again.

Horribly, her first class of the morning was with Dr. Perlinger.

When she got there and was seated in his office, she could barely look at him. She was torn between anger and shame as fresh as it ever had been in That Place. She was dangerously close to tears.

They sat like that for a few minutes, and then Dr. Perlinger spoke kindly. "I know you must be disappointed, how much it means to you to be in Manifesto."

Iz muttered, "You said my entrance audition roared like a lion."

"Oh, it did!" He leaned forward across the desk, speaking quietly. "And it got you into this place, where you most certainly belong, exactly as you are."

It exploded out of her: "Then why didn't I get into Manifesto?"

Dr. Perlinger nodded slowly, eyes crinkling at her. "Let's put it this way. It is no small feat to start as a lion. But even lions have to grow and change, adapt, get a sense of the landscape and make it their own. Even lions have to *learn*."

The tears were filling up her eyes now so she couldn't see him, which was just as well.

Dr. Perlinger said gently, "Your 'Linden Tree' was an evocative and compelling arrangement—there's no doubt about that. Original and stark. You completely captured his stasis."

Iz waited.

"But it isn't *your* work. It's Schubert's. Even if you brought your own accompaniment to it."

"So I was supposed to write something of my own," Iz said bitterly. "I could have done that. I have lots of original songs. I should have sung one of those."

Dr. Perlinger laughed a little at her frustration, but very gently.

"Imagine this," he said. "You take *Winterreise* as your starting point. But you interrogate it a little. You ask yourself, what's missing?

What could have happened if events or beliefs or choices hadn't happened as they did? You look for connections between it and other things in music, literature, or maybe the world around you. You bring your own meaning to it, original and academic. You find *something to say* about it, something that moves the conversation forward and invites us into your original perspective."

Iz said slowly, "So it wasn't enough to point out what was already there in 'The Linden Tree.'"

"That," said Dr. Perlinger, "was a wonderful starting point. But now you might want to point out what *wasn't* there. Or what *could* be there."

She shook her head, defeated. "I don't know how to do that."

"Not yet. So—let's start by just talking about *Winterreise* today. You listened to it a few times this week, yes? What are your overall thoughts at this point?"

She shrugged.

But he kept waiting very patiently.

So finally she said, "It feels like the air is slowly being squeezed out of him."

Dr. Perlinger's eyes lit up. "Tell me more about that!"

She tried to gather her thoughts. "The Wanderer is, like, stuck in all this grief. He's trapped. He's running out of breath."

It was how she had felt in That Place, and afterward too, in those years of fog. Like she couldn't properly inhale or exhale, still always mentally steeling herself for some blow she didn't see coming.

"And I don't think he's functioning that well. I mean, he believes a graveyard is an inn, and he tries to get a room there. He sees three suns in the sky. He thinks he's being led on by a will-o'-the-wisp. I don't know—when I was listening to this, I almost wondered if the Wanderer was actually sort of insane. Like, how can you trust what he's saying half the time?"

And she was suddenly thinking about the smiling grown-ups in her life who had kept key information back. Or who had showed up with no notice, like a betrayal, to move her to a new home. Or who had created an unknowable, unreadable, unpredictable environment.

Dr. Perlinger said, "An unreliable narrator. Yes! Go on—tell me more about what you're thinking."

She tried to work it out. "He's furious because his Beloved is marrying some rich guy instead of him. But—how do we know she even wanted to marry the Wanderer in the first place? Maybe the whole thing was just in his mind the whole time. Maybe he was actually a stalker."

"Indeed," Dr. Perlinger said. "And here's another possibility. Maybe she had no choice in what was happening to her. Maybe the law was responsible for her marrying the rich man. Maybe it said she could not marry the Wanderer because he was too poor."

"What kind of stupid law is that?" Iz said.

"It was a harsh government at the time. The Metternich regime. A man couldn't get married if he didn't have enough money."

"Money," Iz said bitterly. "How come it controls *everything?*"

She thought about how Pat made much more money than she was spending on Iz. She thought about how Dominion Children's Care would not pay for a foster child to go to a private school. And then, there was that awful thing she herself had done in Pat's hallway, also in the name of money.

Dr. Perlinger regarded her. "That's an excellent question."

There was a pause.

"Just not a good enough question to get into Manifesto," Iz said bitterly.

Dr. Perlinger smiled at her very kindly.

"You know, you are welcome to audit Manifesto rehearsals. I understand if it's a little painful to do that right away. But sometimes it helps to see what other people are grappling with. Sometimes it's inspiring learning from those around us, you know."

Chapter Nineteen

It took 12 days to get up the courage.

On the one hand, she was terrified of putting herself on display as the failure who wanted to learn how to be less pathetic. On the other hand, a tiny part of herself was like a little fierce scraggly plant fighting to grow up through the pavement.

Finally, she summoned all her bravery and just walked into a Manifesto rehearsal after school.

It was a much smaller room than she'd expected—just an empty space with a grand piano, and chairs, and a whiteboard with manuscript lines. Nothing dramatic. Nothing that said *Manifesto* practised here.

She expected them all to look up with pity and judgment, but nobody was paying any attention to her. Some were sitting on the chairs, heads together, talking quietly. Some were sprawled around the room. Near her were Bijan and LaRoyce, actually lying on the floor, frowning at an iPad.

LaRoyce was saying, "See, on that line, bring in a major sixth, augment it, lean into a major seventh—makes it resonate more with the idea of war escalating."

"Yes. It needs to jar. It needs to knock the listener out of complacency."

"Also, isolate the arghul there."

Ahmed was sitting with Will, saying cheerfully, "Then there's the question of, like, climate change and how it plays against Copland's vision."

And Will was saying, "I hadn't even thought of *that*."

Over in the corner, Teo was hunched over a tablet, with Kwame beside him. They were talking quietly, and then Teo seemed to be drawing a kind of arc in the air.

Dr. Perlinger clapped his hands at that moment. "Come on over here, everyone."

They picked up their chairs and brought them over into an uneven circle by the piano.

Iz slipped into a chair outside of the circle—not close enough to be talked to, but from which she could hear every word.

Dr. Perlinger nodded at her ever so slightly, with a little smile. Iz nodded back, trying to look like this wasn't hard at all.

"I can hear great collaborations happening," Dr. Perlinger said. "Teo, what have you got for us?"

Iz stiffened instinctively at hearing Teo's name.

Teo did not look particularly happy at being called on either. He jumped up as if someone had poked him with something sharp. Then he kind of hurled himself at the piano bench, swirled his fingers on the keys for a minute, and coaxed out a sudden, sweet melody.

Speaking quickly, he said, "Yeah, so this is 'Santa Lucia,' a Neapolitan song. Kwame and I were talking about bringing it into the accompaniment. And now I think it highlights the Artist's physical place as a musician from Napoli—"

Kwame added, "And then you added the Che galida manina—"

"Yes, exactly," Teo said. "I mean, that aria is all about Mimi's eyes being like thieves of his heart, totally establishing her as a kind of object. It fits with how the Artist is forced by her husband into a particular mould. Housewife, mother. She has to leave her art behind. She becomes a set of beautiful eyes instead of, you know, some kind of autonomous creator."

Iz was frowning, trying to follow the darting of Teo's and Kwame's thoughts.

Teo began to play again softly, thrumming almost, like a heartbeat. He was nervous.

And then—he began to sing.

He admired your brilliance then planted you in concrete
Gallantly accused you of stealing his heart
And praised the pretty withering of spirit and art

Iz's mouth fell open, utterly astonished.

His voice—

It was toffee being stretched out.

Sweet, rich, enduring layers folded one upon the other. You could see all the darker and lighter shades, elastic and pure and expansive. It sounded like someone much older, someone with experience of sunlight and shadow, thought and perspective.

His voice was angry, heartbroken about whoever this Artist was, who had seemingly not been able to be herself. *Here*, it was saying. *Know about this. Think about it this way. Feel it this way.* And whatever he had done in his accompaniment—whatever other songs he had brought in—seemed to reinforce that anger, made it sound like the whole world was lamenting this woman's artistic imprisonment.

How could Teo know how it felt to be a captive?

Iz heard a noise escape her throat.

Her vision was so blurry, that she was startled when suddenly Teo was leaning down by her chair. "Beaufort, you all right?"

She didn't even have it in her to say something snarky back. "It was *beautiful.*"

Then she felt stupid.

"Aww, thanks. I'm available for weddings, funerals, bar mitzvahs. Check out my website. Book me through the union. Ha ha." Then, gently, he added, "You sure you're okay, Beaufort?"

"I'm fine," she said, recovering some of her tartness.

She realized that everyone was looking at her now. Nobody seemed at all surprised that she was there. For the first time, Iz wondered if some of them had also once audited rehearsals.

"Hey, Iz," Rina called. "You just gave Russo the best feedback he'll ever get."

LaRoyce added, "It'll totally go to his head."

"But you'll kick me down to size, right, Beaufort?" Teo grinned as he settled at the piano again.

Iz was too shocked to really respond. It was as if she'd just seen him for the first time. And he was completely different than that buffoon who kept waylaying her.

Meanwhile, Dr. Perlinger was smiling a bit, as if he was quite pleased with what had just happened.

Chapter Twenty

After the rehearsal, she headed to Festa.

About twenty minutes after she had started to play, the grey-haired man leaned out the door of the restaurant.

"Hey. The specials are risotto alla pescatora, impepate di cozze, gattò di patate e pancetta, and migliaccio. If you feel like writing one of your songs."

Like he didn't completely mind her being there.

Like maybe he was softening.

"Um," Iz said boldly. "I need a few details. Describe this food of yours."

Then the man sort of glared, before launching into an extended speech about fish with rice that was fried and stirred till it sopped up the broth, peppered mussels, potato pancakes with pancetta and mozzarella and parmigiano, and a kind of lemon cheesecake with liqueur in it.

"Okay, fine," Iz said at last. "But I will be out here starving, just so you know."

The man snorted, waved his hand and went back in.

Iz set up and was just starting to create a song to advertise the dishes he had described when the door opened again.

The man held out a plate. "All the specials. For research purposes."

"For me?" Iz said.

"Nobody else here."

"Thank you!"

Iz leaned against the wall and devoured it.

Later that evening, when she got home, she sat up in her room thinking again about Teo kneeling down by her chair. She remembered his eyes, uncharacteristically wrinkled with worry.

And his words: *Check out my website.*

She was sure he didn't really have one. But, for some strange reason, she typed *Teo Russo* into the search engine on her tablet.

To her surprise, there were a lot of listings. At the top was *teorusso.com.*

She sat there for a long time, trying to decide if she would actually click on it. But finally she jammed her finger down, half cringing.

The website came up right away. There was a black and white photo of him—some professional headshot thing—showing off the contours and shadows of his admittedly not-horrible-looking face. There were links to Instagram photos and YouTube videos. There was a list of performances and competitions he had won. Even TV appearances.

She blushed. Pushed the tablet away. Stared at the ceiling, appalled and guilty. But after a minute, she picked up the tablet and clicked on one of the YouTube links.

He was standing there with some orchestra, dressed in a tuxedo, looking supremely calm and as if he was in exactly the right place. She watched as the orchestra began to play and closed her eyes as his voice spilled into the air again. It was supremely flexible and filled with—she tried to define it—filled with warmth and complicated light and insight and . . . and encouragement somehow. It felt like she wasn't alone. Like someone had her back. Like she could put down everything she was carrying for a second.

Like it was all going to turn out, the sneaking around and hiding and secrets.

What was that song, anyway?

It was familiar. After a minute, she realized that it was "Santa Lucia," one of the tunes he had woven through the piano accompaniment in the Manifesto rehearsal. When she closed her eyes, it reminded her of sun-dappled hills, of water lapping on a shore, of a blue, blue sky overhead.

Iz drew her guitar to her.

As Teo sang and that orchestra played, she began to strum along. She raised her voice with his. She sang harmony around his melody.

There was a knock on the door.

"That's so pretty, baby," Pat said, peeking around the door. "You should record it."

Horrified, Iz shoved the tablet under the covers.

"Th-thanks!"

"Seriously. I bet people would pay a lot of money to listen to that."

"Huh, wouldn't that be amazing?"

"It sure would, hon."

"Well," Iz said glassily. "And now, I think I'd better get back to my homework."

"Oh, of course, baby. You carry on." Pat closed the door gently.

Iz heard her feet drifting away. She waited, heart pounding, until it was silent.

Most of the time, she forced herself not to think about how dangerous it all was, how easily everything could come crashing down. Then something like this happened to show her how careful she needed to be.

Finally she drew out the tablet again.

She sat there for a long time, just looking at Teo's website. It was so … professional. Anyone who looked at that website would want to hire him for a job.

Like maybe that man at Festa.

On impulse, she typed, *How do you make a website?*

Then she sat there for hours, just reading it all.

You could do a really basic one for free, which was pretty much what she could afford. It would let you type in your information, and you could still include video links and photos.

At last, experimenting, she started clicking on things.

First, she made a section called "About Iz." It left out everything to do with Dominion Children's Care, obviously. But she did honestly tell about being a student at The Métier School.

Next, she created a page entitled "Recent Performances." She used her iPad to record herself singing and playing "Santa Lucia," and she uploaded the video to her website.

And finally, she set up the most important part—"Booking information."

When she crawled into bed many hours later, she lay there hugging herself with excitement. Because if the grey-haired man could be convinced to take her seriously, this might just solve the whole money situation.

She could stop taking money from Pat and even pay her back.

Chapter Twenty-One

"So? What did you think of the rehearsal?"

It was the next morning, and Iz and Dr. Perlinger were sitting in his office.

She thought about holding back. She was still upset about not making it into Manifesto. But somehow, looking at his open, curious face, she couldn't.

"It was different than I expected. It was ... it was as much about thinking as performing."

"Grappling with big ideas," Dr. Perlinger said, nodding. "Asking questions. Finding connections. Looking at things in new ways."

"Well," she said softly. "I see why I'm not ready yet. I can't do any of that."

"Nonsense. That's what we're doing together—analyzing, wondering about things."

"So we're kind of like ... Manifesto in training?" She couldn't look at him for fear she would see pity in his face.

But Dr. Perlinger said warmly, "What a wonderful way of putting it."

There was still hope, then.

He added, "So! Have you done any more thinking about that unreliable Wanderer?"

She had mostly spent last night working on her website. Now, she racked her brain for something intelligent to say. But all she could think of was how she was going to go to Festa after school and show the site to the grey-haired man.

"I think," she said almost lightly, "the Beloved's too good for someone that crazy and unstable. She should have dumped him and just gone out and gotten a job."

Then she flushed, hearing how flippant that sounded. How not *academic.*

But Dr. Perlinger looked very interested. "Tell me about that!"

"Uh . . . well, if the Beloved had refused to play by the rules of the time, the whole story of *Winterreise* would have been totally different. I mean, she probably wouldn't have hung around waiting to get married to someone. She'd have gone out and made a life for herself."

Dr. Perlinger said, "I wonder what the ramifications of that might have been, though? Do you think she would have been allowed to just take off like that?"

"It would have totally destroyed her family, I bet," Iz said, considering. "And also the rich man's family, I guess. And maybe the Wanderer too. She's kind of like the glue holding the whole thing together, if you think about it."

"Comes back to our discussion of money," Dr. Perlinger said thoughtfully. "Money and power. A young woman, married off strategically, brings both to a family."

Iz thought suddenly of how many people's jobs depended on Iz being in all those foster homes.

"If the Beloved walks out, they lose all of it," she said.

"Such an interesting idea," Dr. Perlinger said thoughtfully. "*Winterreise* thrown on its head because the Beloved refused to do what she was told."

Iz nodded, her mind starting to race. "And what if she refused because maybe she was this rare and amazing, wild, brilliant little girl? Maybe they slowly stifled her. Maybe she'd had enough."

His eyes lit up. "Now you've completely raised my curiosity. Who *is* that young Beloved?"

She blinked.

It was a good question.

"I think," she said slowly, "she had a lot of potential. Maybe she had to hide a lot of it though. Maybe it came out in secret ways."

There was a pause.

She added, "I mean, how much were young girls allowed to do back then?"

And then—

"How come she never actually talks in this whole thing? I mean, is that normal? For someone not to talk at all?"

Dr. Perlinger said, "Hmm, good question. Is it normal for a woman in a nineteenth century story to not say very much? How can we find out?"

Then they spent the better part of the hour reading about the nineteenth century, which was when *Winterreise* had been written. They learned that women were expected to obey their husbands and their fathers. They could not actually have any money of their own. They were dependent on the men in their family.

Iz said, "So the Beloved's job is to basically not have a life."

He laughed. "Yes, I guess we could put it that way!"

"Can I point out," Iz said, "that your average girl would rather stick a fork in her eye than live like that?"

"Well," he said, "let's remember these stories were mostly written by men."

Iz let out a huff of disgust, like she was trying to blow away every place that made you follow its rules—Dominion Children's Care and That Place and the Great Expectations Club and fourteen schools and twenty-six homes.

"I am *tired* of people telling other people how they should be."

He nodded. "Agreed."

Then he sat up from his slouching position.

"What would she say back to them?" he said.

Iz let out a slow breath, thinking it through.

"She'd say she was angry about being ... being forced into these totally unnatural roles. She'd want to escape. But she'd go back and forth in her head about the rightness and ... and the wrongness of making the choice to throw off what society expected from her. She'd have to weigh it out."

He smiled. "Why don't you do some more thinking this week about that voice of the Beloved? Map out what she might do in protest. And then bring it to me next week."

Iz nodded, her brain racing.

And for the first time since not getting into Manifesto, she actually felt hopeful again.

Chapter Twenty-Two

After school had finished, Iz ran through the snow to Festa, as fierce and wild and hopeful and uncontained as the Beloved who was starting to grow in her mind.

She was going to get a job today.

When she got there and began to set up, her mind raced over how she was going to approach the subject with the grumpy man. Maybe she should just walk in and say, *Here! My website!* Or maybe she should wait till he told her to move and then she would say, *Oh, while I have you, could I interest you in seeing my website?*

Just as she was about to start singing, the chef leaned out through the door.

"There you are! These are for you." She fumbled something from her apron and passed it over. "I made them. So you can still play but keep your hands toasty."

Iz took the little bundle. It was knitted gloves with the fingertips missing. She put them on, tried strumming the guitar, wandered through some chords.

"Thank you! They're … they're *brilliant!*"

The chef said, "Do your parents know where you are?"

"Oh, yes, they know."

The grey-haired woman regarded her steadily. "How old are you?"

"Older than I look," Iz said warily. "People always think I'm younger than I am."

"Do you have a permit?"

"Of course! I mean, I don't have it *on* me or anything."

The woman leaned against the post connected to the green awning. "Can you sing oldies? You know, like 'Someone to Watch Over Me'?"

"Sure! Remind me one more time so I remember how it goes."

Then the woman smiled a little bashfully and opened her mouth to sing.

There's a somebody I'm longin' to see
I hope that he turns out to be
Someone who'll watch over me

After that, Iz smiled back and nodded and began her version. She unrolled the notes like sun-glistening droplets on a lure designed to reel the woman in.

As usual, people dropped money into the guitar case and waited nearby to listen.

The chef said, "I'm Gisele. Gisele Santoro. I own this restaurant with my husband, Vito. He's the one who tells you to go sing somewhere else."

"Yes, I'm familiar with him," Iz said.

"You're very good," Gisele said.

A thrill ran through Iz. *This was the perfect moment.*

"If I . . . if I could prove I'd be, like, an asset—would you let me sing inside sometime? I work hard. I'd play whatever you wanted. I would love to, you know, be employed by you."

Gisele was smiling a little around her eyes, although her face was serious. "What's your name?"

"Iz. Iz Beaufort."

"Iz, tell you what. Take some time and put together a proposal. Something to show to Vito."

The electricity was shooting through her. Casually, so she wouldn't sound too desperate, she said, "Actually, I have a website. Can I show you?"

She dug into her backpack and took out her tablet. She typed on the screen, still wearing Gisele's gloves.

Then, smiling brightly, Iz passed the website over to Gisele.

The chef stood there under the awning while the wind blew around them. Her eyes flicked back and forth for a few minutes.

Then she said, "Come inside where it's warmer while I read this."

Iz followed Gisele, scarcely daring to breathe.

The restaurant's interior was all rich woods and stained glass, with wine bottles on shelves in the walls here and there. Paintings hung everywhere with pictures of an ocean, of winding roads with houses seemingly cut out of cliffs. One was of a mountain with two peaks that overlooked water.

"Have a seat, Iz," Gisele said. "I'm just going to show this to Vito."

Iz sank into a chair.

Then Gisele walked toward the bar. Iz realized that the man was back there, doing something with glasses.

They spoke quietly. She heard Vito say emphatically, "Already told her—"

Gisele interrupted softly. She put the tablet down on the table. The two of them bent over it for a long time. Then Iz heard herself singing "Santa Lucia."

Her heart was pounding now.

When the song finally ended, Vito and Gisele stood there, heads close together, talking. It went on and on.

Then at last, they looked up and over at her.

She waved slightly and gave them a bright little smile.

Vito breathed out in a bull-like fashion. He beckoned to her.

"Hey," she said, racing over.

"Have a seat."

She scrambled onto one of the bar stools.

"So." Vito poured something in a glass and passed it to her across the bar. "It's not alcohol, don't worry. Just a soda."

"Okay."

"Because I can tell you're not old enough to drink."

"Not yet," Iz said, as boldly as she could. "But soon."

"And you want to work for us."

"Yes!"

Vito said ominously, "You're persistent, I'll give you that."

She tried to sound dependable. "I give everything my best. I would work so hard."

He waved at her like he was batting away an insect. "Obviously we need to know a lot more about you if we are even going to consider offering you a job."

"I'm earning money for school fees. Fifteen hundred a month. My parents are doing what they can but I'm trying to help." Her voice grew stronger, more confident. "As you know, I can bring customers into your restaurant. I can sing whatever you want, any style—"

"Back to this school," said Vito. "The one on the website here." He tapped the tablet, glowering.

"The Métier School," Iz said. "But please don't contact them. They don't know I'm singing on the street. I'm not sure they'd like it."

Vito ran his hand over his mouth and chin for a long time, frowning. He said at last, "Tell me this. If I offer you a job—*if* I offer you a job—I want to know right now if there's any problem that's going to show up down the road."

"I don't think there is," Iz said quickly.

"I'm going to want to talk to your dad or mom."

"Oh, sure! Of course!" Iz scribbled down the emails she had created for her fictional parents.

Vito regarded her for a long time.

"So, a couple of evenings a week, for a few hours? Fifteen bucks an hour to start?"

"Um," said Iz, pushing down the sudden euphoria, feeling her face pulsing.

Take it slow. Hold out for what you want.

"I'm sort of in the musician's union. Th-the going rate is fifty dollars an hour."

Actually, the going rate was all over the place, depending on which union you looked at. But she'd settled on fifty as being a kind of middle ground he might actually agree to.

Vito's eyes widened, and he stared at her for the longest minute ever. Then he burst out laughing, like he'd never heard anything so funny in his life.

Iz said defensively, "Look at the business I keep bringing you."

"Fifty an hour!" Vito said when he caught his breath, wiping away tears. "Musician's union!"

Gisele said in a conciliatory way, "Well, why don't you play us something you'd do in the restaurant?"

"Okay." Iz lifted up her guitar, ran her hand along the curves, placed her fingers, closed her eyes.

It had to be perfect. It had to be heartbreaking. It had to make them unable to turn her down.

She began to strum.

And what came out was "The Linden Tree," from *Winterreise.* But this time, she slowed it right down so it sounded like dinner music that might make people want to eat and drink and share together in a beautiful atmosphere.

Before the doorway is a well
A linden tree stands there
Many times I've sought its shade
A place of rest and pleasant dreams

Every sensitive chord, every luxurious key change, every gentle nuance was an incantation, making Vito and Gisele *feel* how her music could enhance everything about their restaurant.

At the end, when she finally looked at them, Gisele was wiping her eyes and Vito wasn't laughing anymore.

There was a long silence.

"I can sing you another if you want," Iz said.

Gisele said, "No, no. That was beautiful. It was just right."

Iz took a deep breath.

Be brave.

"But I can't do it for fifteen dollars an hour—"

"No, no. Union rate." Gisele said it quickly before Vito could jump in.

Vito sighed long and loud.

He growled, "It would be a trial period. That's the best I can offer. See how it goes. Cash only, mind you."

Iz's jaw dropped.

Were they really going to pay her that much money?

"Thank you! Thank you!" She flung herself across the bar and wrapped her arms around him, then jumped back, appalled. "Oh, I'm sorry."

"No worries." Vito looked gruffly embarrassed. "But you have to learn some old standards, sing some of the beautiful songs from Italy, be ready to take requests. And our atmosphere isn't wild. You have to fit into it."

"Yes!" Iz said. "I will!"

"Can you sometimes do just instrumental?"

"Of course!"

"Wait here." Gisele walked through the swinging doors, out of view. A few minutes later, she returned with a plate containing pasta shells in cheese. "Try this. It's cacio e pepe."

Iz took a bite and looked up, astonished. "It's amazing!"

"Iz. Do you get dinner at night?"

"Yes! When I go home. I heat it up."

"You heat it up," Gisele said, looking accusingly at Vito.

"Fine," Vito said, in response to whatever Gisele was not saying out loud. "Of course."

"So we'll feed you," Gisele said, wrinkles everywhere as she smiled with her whole face. "Union rate and dinner."

The purity, the sweetness of that was like the most beautiful of water, life giving and soul nourishing.

Chapter Twenty-Three

The next day at lunchtime, Iz sat in the cafeteria at The Métier School, her head still buzzing with everything that had happened yesterday.

She had landed a real job all on her own, a job that would be able to pay the monthly Métier fees. And she would be starting tonight!

What was more, Pat hadn't even batted an eyelash when Iz told her, "I'm going to start volunteering a few nights a week at the library. If it's okay, I was thinking I'd go there right from school and eat when I get home after. I just want to build up my résumé because when I age out I am going to need a job, and everyone says volunteering experience makes a difference."

Britnee had added humorously, "You know, Mama, people who plan ahead actually are more successful in life. Just saying."

"Yes, yes, baby," Pat had said placidly. "But they are also more stressed."

"Hey! Beaufort! This seat taken?"

Iz jumped and looked up. Her cheeks started beating.

She had not seen Teo since the rehearsal the other night, when he had knelt by her chair.

"Uh . . ." she said, feeling like an idiot. "No."

He bounced there, with all of that extra, coltish energy. "So, can I sit down? You're not going to, you know, throttle me or anything?"

"No promises," Iz said.

Teo flung himself into the chair. He gestured at the tablet she had on the table. "What are you working on?"

Before, she would have told him it was none of his business. But all at once she was remembering the song he had performed in the Manifesto rehearsal and she was hearing that beautiful voice in her head again. A new Teo seemed to be weirdly superimposed on top of the old one.

"I'm trying to figure out what it looks like when you're a nineteenth century woman in a story and you are tired of being fit into some little box of being all beautiful and silent and pious and stuff."

Teo burst out laughing.

Something about his dancing eyes was completely infectious in that moment. Iz found herself half smiling back.

"For Dr P?" he said.

"How did you know?"

"Lucky guess." He leaned forward. "So, what *does* it look like when you're a nineteenth century woman in a story and you don't want to be all beautiful and silent and pious and stuff?"

"No idea yet."

Grinning, he said, "With Dr. Perlinger, you will *always* feel like you have no idea. Right up until something finally hits you and you suddenly have this new perspective, you know?"

His eyes were warm while he spoke. He loved Dr. Perlinger too, just like the rest of them. Who could not adore the teacher who walked beside you and coaxed out of you what was already there?

Then he added, "Hey, Beaufort, I never got a chance to tell you, but I think your 'Linden Tree' arrangement—the one you did for the audition—was really interesting. I liked what you were doing with the clashing major and minor in the accompaniment. And"—he looked right at her, which was kind of startling—"I was sorry you didn't make it in. I know you wanted to. You will, though. You're talented."

There was a short silence.

"You're . . . you're talented too," Iz said awkwardly.

Teo pretended to clutch his heart and fall sideways. "Did you just give me a compliment? Be careful not to strain something, Beaufort."

She watched him flounder around like an idiot. Then, after a minute, she asked curiously, "Who was that about, anyway?"

"Who was what about?"

"The song you did the other night at the Manifesto rehearsal. The Artist was trapped—the man planted her in concrete."

"Oh! That was about my Nonna."

Iz said softly, "What happened to her?"

"She was an opera singer in Italy, but her husband made her give it up. Then she had kids—my dad and my aunts and my uncles. And then they moved here, and then my Nonno passed away, and now she lives with my dad and me."

Iz digested all of this.

"Did she ever … sing again?"

"She sings every day. But, you know, not professionally again." He added softly, "She couldn't break out of it, all the expectations of the time. It kills me. I wish I'd been there. I would have stood up for her. I would have convinced her to fight back. I would have walked her out of there."

Then, as if realizing how intense he'd become, he threw his head back, shook his hair, and grinned. "That would've been impressive, right?"

"Too bad you weren't there," she said.

"Yep," he said. "Too bad."

There was a pause.

"And what about *you*, Beaufort?"

She gulped. "What about me? There's nothing about me."

"Somehow," said Teo, "I highly doubt that. I think you're hiding deadly secrets."

"Ha!"

Panicked energy shot through her. She scraped back her chair. "I-I've got class."

He gave her a little salute, but his eyes were laughing at her as if he knew she was a mess inside.

"See you," she sputtered.

She grabbed her things and ran.

Had he guessed something?
No, he couldn't have.
It had just been Teo being Teo.
Teasing.
But not actually that unkindly.

Chapter Twenty-Four

When she entered the restaurant after school for her first night of work, the first thing she saw was Gisele, standing beside a lectern with a sign that read, "Please wait to be seated."

"Iz! You're right on time." Gisele beamed at her.

Iz said shyly, "Where do you want me to set up?"

"Over here. Is this okay?"

Iz followed Gisele to a little space on the far side of the restaurant, where a stool was sitting next to a microphone.

Iz stared. She had never used a microphone before. But how hard could it be?

Beside the stool was a small table with an empty wine glass sitting on top.

"The glass is for tips," Gisele said hastily. "Nothing else."

"Tips?"

"Of course! People are going to tip you."

"Really?"

"Really. They are going to hear your beautiful voice and they are going to want to thank you."

Iz was struck silent at that.

Gisele put a hand on Iz's shoulder. "Can I get you something before you start? Maybe a little snack? Some bruschetta."

"Uh . . . no thanks. I'm good."

"Water," Gisele said. "You need water. Set up and I'll be right back."

Iz climbed onto the stool and found a rung for each foot. While perched up there, she bent the metal stand sideways so the microphone was right up by her mouth. She blew into it tentatively. Nothing happened.

Finally Vito came sweeping by, and turned it on for her.

"Oh! Thanks!" She blew again.

The sound exploded like a bomb.

"Easy!" he growled.

"Okay. Sorry."

She positioned it a little farther away.

Softly she said, "Hello?"

"Better."

Then Iz lifted her guitar onto her knees. She looked around the mostly empty restaurant.

Inside her head, she was screaming, *I work here!* But outwardly she maintained serene composure. She raised her chin like she had all the dignity in the world. Like she had always performed in places like Festa, with soft lighting and gorgeous aromas.

She began to pluck out a tentative melody like waves. Up and down she went, adding another melody, telling herself, *be calm, be calm.*

Gradually, naturally, it evolved into "Dream of Spring," one of the songs from *Winterreise.* She made it match the beautiful smells of butter and olive oil and garlic, drawn out and languid.

As she plucked the guitar strings, her brain ranged over everything that had happened to bring her to this moment. She remembered paying her fees for Métier on that heady December day when she had first been accepted into the school. Then she'd wandered through the snow, this way and that, until ending up by chance in front of Festa. And Vito had been angry at her for standing in front of the window.

She thought about her long game of showing him how indispensable she could be to his business—writing songs for his menu and drumming up customers. Unbelievably, it had worked. Even now, as she watched, Vito strolled to the front door and propped it open so people on the street could hear her. She coaxed a cajoling tone out of her guitar, trying to talk them into coming in. A minute later, a couple walked up to the lectern.

Iz caught Vito's eye and raised her eyebrows at him as if to say, *Now you see!*

Vito looked away, but she caught the glimmer of a smile.

And in that moment, she truly felt as at peace as she had maybe ever felt.

She closed her eyes and swirled out the most beautiful melodies she could think of. She segued into "Santa Lucia," remembering how she had first heard it in Teo's performance for Manifesto. She meandered into other tunes but returned to "Santa Lucia" over and over again, always slightly different.

Much later, she opened her eyes.

The restaurant was beginning to fill up. Many people were watching her. They were smiling and nodding with respect and appreciation.

"Can you do 'Te Amo'?" An elderly gentleman was leaning down, smiling. "It's our anniversary."

"Can you hum it for me?" Iz said quickly.

He closed his eyes, smiled, and began to sing. Iz listened, then found his key and snuck in a few notes at a time until she was playing underneath his melody. He nodded in delighted surprise. Iz grinned back, then began to hum a harmony to the melody while he sang it all the way through again.

"Bellissimo!" he said once they'd finished the second time. As she started to create instrumental variations on the tune—little hills that bumped up ever higher—he folded something in his hand and slipped it into the wine glass. He nodded his head in thanks, smiled again as if they had always known each other, then made his way back to the table where his wife was waiting.

Iz flicked her eyes over to see what he'd put in there.

It was a fifty-dollar bill.

Her jaw dropped.

Festa was packed later on. Iz played everything she could think of, including more chunks of *Winterreise* in a kind of modern, relaxed dinner-y style that seemed to suit the elegant atmosphere. She learned several traditional Italian songs too. After the first gentleman had sung to her, that seemed to open the way for many others to do the same.

In the middle, Gisele brought out a plate of spaghetti, and Iz sat at a little table to eat it. Then, when she was ready, she climbed back on the stool and began to play again.

It felt like no time at all, but Vito was suddenly there, easing himself into a chair beside her. His face wasn't exactly smiling but the creases looked promising.

"Hey. Not bad tonight. They liked you."

"Am I done?" She glanced around in shock.

"You have school tomorrow morning, right?"

"Yes."

"Then you're done." He counted bills into her hand. "Here you go. Three hours. Union rate. See you tomorrow."

She let out her breath slowly, hardly believing it all was true.

Chapter Twenty-Five

Over the next several weeks, Iz kept attending Manifesto rehearsals.

At first, she just sat and watched. But after awhile, the others began to include her in their conversations scattered around the rehearsal space.

And as time passed, she started to feel less intimidated and more curious. She began to see how they were being sounding boards for each other. They were arguing, suggesting, validating. They were *mentoring* each other. And they didn't find it easy, figuring out how to execute what they could hear in their minds.

Everyone was really kind to her, even though she was still mostly tongue-tied in their presence. They didn't treat her like some failure for not making it in. They made her feel like she was a part of things.

One afternoon, Becky said to her, "We're all going to go watch a new musician after rehearsal today. Want to come?"

Iz felt a surge of excitement at actually being invited to go out with Manifesto. But it quickly turned to regret.

"Sorry. I can't tonight. I have to work."

"Next time!" Becky said.

When Iz got to Festa, she started with a gentle swirl of "Il Sole Mio," kind of drifted from that into "Santa Lucia." Then she explored how to meld the two tunes into a duet and began playing with it as a kind of intellectual exercise.

At that moment, the restaurant door opened.

Manifesto came trooping in.

Iz nearly fell off her stool.

And they in turn all stared back at her, recognition dawning. Then they waved and smiled in excitement.

Becky raced across the restaurant to where Iz was sitting and playing. "So *you're* the cool new musician at Festa? Everyone was saying we should come and hear this amazing girl who'd popped out of nowhere. Iz, I hope you won't be freaked by us sitting there. If you are, we could go."

"Uh, no. It's okay."

"You sure? Really?"

"Y-yes." She was having trouble forming words.

"It sounds beautiful," Becky said encouragingly, then slipped back to the table the group was now sitting at.

Frantically grasping at what to do, Iz began to play "Refugee." She had played it for Jamaal what seemed a thousand years ago. Now she changed the feel so it fit the atmosphere in Festa.

You say my road's not there at all
But it seems to me that it is all I see—

She flicked her eyes up at Manifesto.

Teo Russo was staring like he'd never seen her before.

She looked away immediately, her cheeks beating.

Quickly she launched into "Interwoven World," the song she'd composed that first day after paying her fees. Then she sang them the love song she'd written to the night, to music itself, when she had first begun trying to convince Vito to let her sing in Festa.

Rare song
You vibrate in my heart
So I do not know which of us is singing . . .

Manifesto was the best audience she could ever have asked for. They clapped and whistled and hooted at the end of each song. Slowly,

Iz relaxed. No—she felt like she was uncurling, opening up, like some shoot growing toward a warm sun she'd hardly imagined would be there.

When at last it was time for her break, Gisele brought over some lasagne. Iz was just getting ready to eat when LaRoyce arrived unexpectedly at her table. He lifted up the plate.

"Hey!" Iz said.

"We've got a place for you."

"Sit! Sit!" Teo Russo was pushing out a chair for her. Somehow she'd ended up beside him.

Then he levelled his eyes directly at her. And she noticed with a start that they were all light brown and tawny. Almost golden.

"So!" he said, eyebrows raised.

Just that word, but it was imbued with curiosity, wonder, appreciation. Like he was seeing *her* through a different filter made up of her music.

She started to blush ferociously, for absolutely no good reason.

Kwame was saying, "Is that all your own stuff?"

Then they were all talking at once, and she was stuttering answers. It felt strange at first, then wonderful. Because they were really listening and they really had things to say back.

Teo said, "It's a cool sound, Beaufort. It's, you know, growling and dark and . . . and . . . *reaping*."

She suddenly felt far too hot, as if Vito had turned up the thermostat. She tried to make a self-deprecating joke. "Yeah, all the growling. That must be why my throat is so raw."

With actual concern in his voice, Teo said, "How often do you sing here?"

"Three or four nights a week. But it's fine. I was kidding."

He was frowning. "You don't want to get vocal damage. There are ways to make that same sound without it being all in your throat. Ask Henny. She'll help you."

Iz laughed out loud. "Uh, ha, no. Dr. Henderson wants me to resonate in my nasal cavity and maintain the mask in my head voice with an open throat and support the sound and everything. I don't think she'd be interested in my kind of singing."

"You'd be surprised," Teo said. Then he yelled down the table, "Hey, Ahmed!"

"What?" Ahmed stopped flicking Kwame with his napkin.

"Beaufort doesn't think her style of singing belongs at Métier."

"Three words," Ahmed said. "Post. Punk. Beethoven."

A thrill ran through Iz, remembering that concert at Dennison Hall.

Teo said, "See? Métier grows all kinds of musicians. I'm serious. You should ask for what you want." Then he leaned forward, looking curious. "And what's up with your fingering? I was trying to follow it."

Iz froze for a second. Then she told him about how her guitar strings were all out of order. "And I tuned them to thirds or fifths or octaves."

Teo's eyebrows did a complicated little plunge. "It's cool, but don't you think this might hold you back down the road? How are you going to learn repertoire? What does Nguyen think about it?"

She said quickly, "We use Dr. Nguyen's guitar at lessons, and at home I practise all the fingerings on my guitar, even though it sounds horrible. I should restring it, but somehow I just . . ." She looked down at the battered case on the floor. "It's how I play my own stuff."

He was shaking his head at her. "Beaufort, you are full of surprises."

"Well, so are you," she said, without thinking.

"Me?" He laughed out loud, tossing his hair. "There's nothing surprising about me."

"All that stuff on your website—all those concerts and competitions and things."

"Are you stalking me, Beaufort?"

She practically jumped out of the chair, totally startled. "No! I was just trying to figure out how to make a website."

"So you looked mine up specifically."

She felt like she was cornered.

"Relax," he said, laughing so all of his teeth gleamed. Then he swiped and tapped on his phone, looking devilish. "But that means I get to look *you* up."

Panic shot through her. What exactly had she put in the bio?

"It's not that interesting," she spurted.

"That's for me to decide. Hey! Look at you! Guitarist, songwriter." He read silently. "You started playing at the age of seven?" He put down the phone and stared at her. "Are you telling me you strung this guitar and tuned it to these intervals and taught yourself to play at *seven*?"

Chapter Twenty-Six

When Iz raced into Pat's house that night, her head was filled with the scarcely believable evening that had just passed at Festa.

But Pat called from the dining room, "Iz, could you come in here, hon?"

And Iz froze. Because although Pat's voice was light, something darker lay behind it.

"Uh . . . sure," she said.

Her stomach tightened, as her brain raced over the possibilities.

Had Pat looked at her bank account or at Iz's bank account?

Had Claudia called the school about something random and learned Iz wasn't a student there anymore?

Had the secretary phoned to find out if Dominion Children's Care knew the forwarding address yet of Iz's fake new school out of the district?

Iz started shaking.

She peeked into the dining room, where Pat and Britnee and Vance were sitting in stony silence.

Pat said quickly, "Why don't you show Iz some of the photos? Iz, we're choosing the pics for the display boards at the reception. One board for Brit, one for Vance."

"Oh!" Iz said. Relief coursed through her.

Britnee said huskily, "But somebody didn't bring any family photos at all, except for *this*, and it's just a school picture."

Vance made a strangled kind of noise. Then he got up abruptly, muttered something Iz could not make out, and headed into the washroom.

Iz stared down at the table, where there were many pictures spread out. They all showed Britnee smiling on ski hills or leaping in the air with girlfriends or lounging in chairs on beaches.

And in that minute, something bold stirred inside her. Maybe it was because of the amazing evening she'd just had. Sitting there with Manifesto had given her a weird kind of glimpse into what it was like to speak and have people interested in what you had to say. Suddenly she was tired of accommodating Britnee's point of view.

She said flatly, "Maybe he doesn't *have* any."

"Everyone has at least one family photo," Britnee said.

"I don't."

There was a silence.

"Oh, baby," Pat said. "Of course. Of course."

A lot of expressions fleeted across Britnee's face. "Well, why wouldn't he say something? Sometimes I feel like I'm carrying this whole thing—"

Pat interrupted anxiously, "What about one board instead of two? The story of your relationship! How it started, you know, special moments along the way, funny memories . . ."

Britnee considered this, her eyes like light reflecting through an iceberg.

"Interesting," Britnee said. "Interesting. And . . . we could take some new photos together—funny ones, like I'm looking at bridesmaids' dresses, and he could be all, 'I don't know what I'm doing here! I'm totally out of my depth!'"

"Yes!" Pat exclaimed. "Look at that, we solved it!"

"It's a super happy ending," Iz said.

As soon as the words were out of her mouth, she was aware of how sarcastic they sounded.

"Huh! I'm so glad!" she added hastily, trying to make her voice sincere.

But Britnee had heard it.

Iz's brain did a frightened little flip, as she and Britnee stared at each other for the longest minute ever.

Then Britnee said appraisingly, "I'm so glad you're doing better since getting suspended for the second time, Iz. At least . . . I assume things are going better. We haven't heard a word from the school lately, have we? I guess that's good news."

"Oh, it's good news for sure," Pat said comfortably.

Iz said, "Yeah, I-I'm working hard and I'm getting good marks."

"That's great," Britnee said. She flipped a photo over to read the back. "Like what?"

"Pardon?" Iz said.

"Like what good marks?" Britnee's eyes flicked up at her. "Hey, I'd love to see something you're really proud of."

Iz forced herself to stay calm. She was not going to give Britnee the pleasure of seeing her get flustered.

"Sure. I can get something."

"Awesome!" Britnee said, snapping photos down together on the table as if they were playing cards.

"Right now?"

"Why not?"

"Okay, sure."

Iz walked casually toward the hallway. Then she ran up the stairs to her room. She shuffled in the drawer where she kept all of her assignments hidden underneath sweaters and socks. She grabbed the Curriculum Studies project she'd just gotten back from the teacher, filled with comments for next steps. It was the best she could do with no notice.

Iz shoved the drawer closed, ran down the stairs back to the dining room, and thrust the papers at Britnee. "Here. I just got this back. The teacher said it's good so far. He put in some suggestions for the next part."

Then she stood there filled with fury as Britnee looked it over front and back. Iz practically dared Britnee to say something like, *Wait a minute—your school doesn't use this kind of paper*, or, *I know every teacher at your school, and this guy isn't one of them.*

But at last Britnee passed it to Pat, saying, "I mean, there's no mark. But the feedback is pretty good, I guess."

"Baby, well done," Pat said warmly.

"Thanks."

Britnee couldn't resist one last jab, so Iz would know never to mock anything about the wedding ever again.

"Mama, you should keep a closer tab on Iz's school, though. I mean, she could have been failing and nobody would know." She turned to Iz. "When's the next parent-teacher night, anyway?"

"Uh, I'm not sure."

Britnee said to Pat, "You should find out."

Pat was nodding complacently. "Yes, baby."

At that moment, Vance came back into the room, big and silent and watchful. He slid into his chair again at the table.

Britnee's focus was instantly off Iz.

"Mama had a really good idea, babe. Maybe we don't need your photos after all."

In the thick rumble of his indecipherable reply, Iz fled.

Then she sat on her bed, all tossed amid the emotions of the evening. Her thoughts ran from Teo to Britnee—from being taken seriously to being put in her place. She needed to do a better job of keeping these two worlds apart.

At Pat's house, she needed to be much more quiet, humble. And it was probably unwise to get closer to anyone at school.

Chapter Twenty-Seven

She went to Métier the next day planning to be much more cautious in what she said and did.

But almost right away, Teo was there at her elbow, grinning. "Hey! Beaufort! You got a minute?"

The night before came exploding back into her head. She could feel her face beating red. And it was hard to remember exactly what she was not supposed to do or why.

"Um—sure. I guess."

"We have to go to my locker. But it's bad, I'm warning you."

"Why should I want to go to your locker if it's bad?"

"Not the locker, Beaufort. What's *in* the locker."

"This is quite the invitation," Iz said.

When they reached it, Teo punched in his combination and pulled the door open. He pushed his coat and backpack aside, leaned in, drew out a guitar case, shook his messed-up hair back into perfect place. "Okay, this is not even full size. It's three-quarter. I had it when I was younger, but I outgrew it and it's just been lying around the house."

She stared. "This is for *me*?"

"Well," Teo said. "It's no good to me. And see, this way you can, you know, keep playing music in *your* language and you can learn the *other* language too. You'll be bilingual, Beaufort."

Iz stammered, "I can't just take your guitar. This cost a lot of money."

"Let me introduce you to a word. *Gift.*"

"No, seriously, I can't."

"I want you to have it though."

She finally unzipped the case and took the guitar out. It was a beautiful rich reddish brown. She plucked a string, and it *radiated* somehow.

Her eyes widened. "I love it."

He burst into that broad grin that went right up to his eyes. "Good! So in return, I'm daring you to do something."

She froze.

He laughed at her face. "What do you think I'm going to say?"

"I don't know."

"Just ask Henny to help you learn how to make your own sound in a healthy way. I mean, you're in the coolest school in the world and there's room for every kind of sound here. And I'm your student mentor so technically you should listen to me."

Then he beamed hugely, like he was sure his gleaming teeth could convince her.

Not long ago, she would have thought about how arrogant that was. Now, weirdly, she found herself grinning back.

"Okay," she said. "Maybe."

"Cool. At the rehearsal tonight you can tell me how it went."

"We'll see."

She spoke nonchalantly, but the truth was that she could hardly wait for her guitar lesson.

When she arrived at Dr. Nguyen's office and knocked, she was bouncing up and down, so eager to play that beautiful little guitar.

As soon as Dr. Nguyen opened the door, his eyes went right to it. "What do we have here?"

"My, uh, friend gave it to me," Iz said.

He turned it all over in his hands, making admiring and encouraging sounds.

"Well, look at this! Yes, it is nice. Your friend has good taste. Come on, come on! Sit down! Ready to do some scales?"

"Yes!"

G major, D major, A minor. She was almost forgetting to breathe. Her fingers stepped around the frets, feeling their way. And each string was like the interplay of sunshine and shadow, coming to life.

"Beautiful sound," Dr. Nguyen said encouragingly. "That's some friend."

Iz blinked and nodded. "Y-yes."

She imagined Teo sitting there grinning, completely proud of himself.

When she left the guitar lesson an hour later, she felt like a bird flying triumphantly above everything.

But the euphoria didn't last long. As soon as she entered Dr. Henderson's office, she looked anxiously around at the intimidating diplomas on the walls, the shelves of important books, the gleaming grand piano. She realized there was no place for her own small songs in here. There was no room for making a sound that did not follow the proper method.

Not planning to, she let out a ragged sigh.

"Everything all right?" Dr. Henderson said, looking up from the instructions she was typing about how Iz could practise a particular exercise at home.

"Yes, everything's fine," she said quickly and tightly.

But she imagined Teo crossing his arms.

Now or never, Beaufort.

She gulped, took a deep breath.

"I just—I—you know, I write my own songs." She swallowed hard. "Anyway, this friend, this other person, he was saying I should talk to you about how to sing my own songs so I don't, like, get vocal damage."

Then she winced at the floor, intensely ashamed she was asking for something so out of keeping with the room and the piano and Dr. Henderson herself.

Dr. Henderson closed the laptop immediately.

She rose and sat down on the couch.

"Sing me something of yours."

Iz gulped. Her heart felt like it was going to rip out of her chest.

Then she lifted up her own guitar. Stammering, she whispered, "This is called 'Rare Song.'"

While she played, she absolutely could not look at Dr. Henderson. And when she was done, she clasped the guitar tightly and just sat there.

Dr. Henderson said into the silence, "Your sound—it's a bit like a psychological wound, you know."

"Oh!" Iz said. "Is that . . . bad?"

"Not at all. There is no one *right* sound, Iz. The older I get, the more I think there is hardly any right anything. But there are definitely right methods to make sure you can maintain your instrument. So your friend's correct. I can teach you how to do it safely."

"Really?"

"Of course! Let's start with standing up and relaxing that throat."

And as Iz scrambled to her feet, she imagined Teo looking even more profoundly pleased with himself.

See, Beaufort? You should always listen to me!

She couldn't help but smile.

She was still beaming, when she pushed open the door to the Manifesto rehearsal after school. She was planning to tell him about everything, just as he'd asked.

But what she saw stopped her in her tracks.

As if in slow motion, Teo tripped over a chair awkwardly and spectacularly. He fell right into the lap of Jasleen, who burst out laughing. Everyone howled with approval.

Iz heard Jasleen ask, "What do you want for Christmas, little boy?"

Then she watched as Teo leaned close and said in his most smoldering voice, "You."

Iz froze.

At that moment, he looked up and saw her. He grinned radiantly, jumped up out of Jasleen's lap, and loped over like a stretched-out gazelle.

"Beaufort! How'd it go with the guitar?"

"Fine."

Her brain was suddenly all jumbled up and she had no idea why. There was no good reason for it. He could fall in anyone's lap he wanted.

She turned without even planning to and began climbing the stairs to the exit.

He fell in beside her. "Did you talk to Henny?"

She shrugged, continuing to plough ahead, shoving open the door with one hand and storming through.

Teo trotted in front of her, then started jogging backward along the hallway.

"You're going to bang into a wall," Iz said coldly.

"Everything okay, Beaufort?"

"Everything's fine."

"Good." He frowned. "Because everything doesn't *seem* fine."

She didn't mean to say anything in return. But as she looked at him trying to simmer at her, all magnetically cajoling and sure of his effect on everyone, words shot out of her mouth.

"Stop the eye thing. Save it for someone who cares. Save it for Jasleen."

He looked genuinely puzzled as he kept running backward. "What are you talking about? What eye thing? And what's that about Jasleen?"

Then she felt completely embarrassed, which made her even more furious.

She heard herself snapping, "Please get out of my way. I have to go to work."

He said, "Are you talking about what happened right now? We were just fooling around. It didn't mean anything. What do *you* care anyway? You hate me most of the time."

"I don't care!" She was about to storm off around him but couldn't resist throwing a last barb. "And how do *you* know it didn't mean anything?"

"Um, because I was there."

"You're not the only person in the universe," Iz snapped, realizing she was hardly making any sense. "But you certainly act like—like the world revolves around you and you're some mighty star at the centre. You don't actually care about how anyone *feels,* as long as you're the main focus—all glowing and, I don't know, *celestial.* Anyway, if you'll excuse me, I have to go. Thanks again for the guitar."

She left him standing there looking dumbfounded, with his mouth open.

Which would have been quite satisfying if she wasn't so furious.

Chapter Twenty-Eight

Iz ran to Festa, feet pounding through snow. She slammed into the restaurant. She was so full of confused feelings, she could not breathe. She was exploding inside.

She glowered down at her guitar, trying to think of a single tune that wasn't all barbed and raging. Finally she settled on a threatening version of "Refugee," followed by an infuriated "Santa Lucia." She wanted to rip up the world but would settle for shredding music instead.

After about an hour, Vito ambled by and sat down beside her like a wary bear. "Something wrong?"

"No, everything's great."

"Well, bring it down a couple of notches. You're scaring the waiters."

At that moment, the restaurant door opened.

Teo walked in.

She glared ferociously down at her guitar, but she could still hear their voices.

"Table for one?" Vito asked.

"Yeah. Over there, if possible."

The next thing Iz knew, Vito was setting him up at the table right next to her stool. Then Teo was perusing a menu and ordering iced tea in the slowest and most expansive manner possible.

When the waiter had gone into the kitchen with his drink order, Teo said, "I don't have an eye thing."

She kept plucking away at a little tune, fingers mindlessly carrying it on. Suddenly she was completely unsure about everything everywhere.

He flipped the menu over to the back cover, glanced at it, put it down. Iz got the feeling he'd hardly seen it.

"So," he said at last. "I'm trying to figure this out . . ."

"Actually, I don't want to talk about it."

She was feeling stupider by the minute. After all, the only thing he'd ever done was give her a guitar and some actually pretty good advice about asking Dr. Henderson how to sing right. Nothing more. So why had she gotten completely derailed and weird, like he'd betrayed her or something?

Teo picked up the menu again, stared at it till the waiter brought his drink.

"Are you ready to order?"

"Yeah. Do you have any sfogliatelle?"

"No, sorry."

"Okay, just the iced tea, thanks."

When the waiter was gone, Teo said with a little smile, "Ask me anything."

"What?"

Her fingers kept playing, but her mind was buzzing.

He said, "I think I hurt your feelings, Beaufort. To even the score, you get to ask any question you want, no matter how personal or embarrassing, and I have to answer it."

"That's stupid," Iz said. "Also, I'm working."

Vito came over a minute later.

"Who wants sfogliatelle?"

"Me," Teo said. "Just, a lot of your menu is Napolitano, so I wondered. But it doesn't matter."

"You been to Napoli?"

"My Nonna grew up there. And my dad was born there, but they left when he was a baby."

"Yeah? Where'd your Nonna grow up?"

"San Lorenzo."

"Which street?"

"I think ... Via dei Tribulani ..."

Iz tuned them out, until finally Vito said loudly, "So what you're saying is, your family and mine were practically neighbours."

"But he's leaving," Iz snapped, "as soon as he drinks his iced tea. Because I'm working and I shouldn't be fraternizing with *classmates*."

"Oh, you go to Iz's school?"

"Yeah. I was here last night with that big group. I'm a Voice and Composition major."

"Hey, why don't you sing something?" Vito said. "Something from Napoli. A little Caruso. Iz, you know 'O Sole Mio.'"

"I'm just here for the iced tea," Teo said demurely.

"What, your singing isn't any good?"

"It's okay."

"Actually," Iz said, because she had to be fair, "it is kind of amazing."

"So?" Vito lifted an arm as if to show Teo where the spotlight was.

"Iz?" Teo said.

"Fine." She rolled her eyes.

The next thing she knew, she was plucking out the intro she'd played ninety thousand times over the last while. And Teo was standing there listening to what she was doing, getting ready to start.

When he began to sing, Vito's eyes widened and his mouth dropped open, and Iz would have laughed if the whole situation wasn't so peculiar. Teo's voice stretched along the melody like it was a country road in Italy somewhere, saturated with sunlight and languid peace. She could guarantee that nobody had ever sung like that in Festa before.

When the song was done, the restaurant customers all clapped, and Teo bowed. Then he went back to the table.

"No, no, no," Vito said. "Another. Do another and I will go out in this town and *find* you some sfogliatelle."

Teo shrugged, grinned sheepishly, looked at Iz.

She looked back, deadpan.

"'Dream of Spring?'" he said. "Come on, a little *Winterreise*."

"Whatever."

She gave it a rolling set of strummed chords. He picked up on the mood of her accompaniment and matched it pace for pace, like they were old friends chatting.

When Iz's first break came, Gisele brought out linguine con vongole for both of them and also set down a little plate of pastries made of layers shaped like shells. She patted Teo on the back and said, "We sent out for them. Next time I'll make you some though."

"No way! Thank you!" Teo said, lighting up.

"My pleasure. Enjoy."

They watched silently as Gisele made her way back into the kitchen.

Then Teo said, "*Anything*. Go ahead."

Iz raked her fingers through her hair. She wished she could go back and change everything, make it not have happened. But now Teo was sitting here, and the whole thing was weird.

She said awkwardly, "Fine. Tell me your worst secret of all time."

"Really?"

He looked off at the back wall. There was a long silence.

"Okay," he said. "I stopped talking for a couple of years, believe it or not."

"You?" Iz said.

He laughed out loud. "Yeah, I know, it doesn't seem possible."

"Why did you stop talking?"

Teo started playing with the spoons on the table. He did this for so long that Iz thought he wasn't going to answer after all.

"Remember I said my Nonna lives with us? Well she basically had to move in. Because my dad and I were just not really functioning at the time." He laid one spoon over the other and then flipped the one on the bottom like a catapult. It sailed off the table and landed with a clatter on the floor.

"Oops! Sorry!" He jumped up and retrieved it. Sat down again.

"So, is this where I ask, why were you and your dad not functioning?"

"Ha," Teo said. "Well. So my mom and sisters ..."

Now he had the spoons back to back. He took them between his fingers and began shaking them against each other so they made a clinking noise.

"Yeah, so they died."

Iz was struck silent, unsure what to say next.

Finally Teo went on. "They were out shopping for dresses for my cousin's christening. And some drunk driver ran the red. And so, then I stopped talking. For two years, pretty much. And I got kept back in school."

"Hey!" Iz said. "They kept me back in school too!"

Then she stopped, aghast. It had just come out of her mouth, totally unplanned.

She remembered, for the first time all day, about how she'd decided she wasn't going to tell Teo any more things about herself.

"So what happened to make them keep *you* back? Did you stop talking too?" He was grinning at her.

Iz thought about the chill settling around her in That Place, and then about the fog later on when she'd gotten out. It had crept into her pores, blanketed her mind. She hadn't really cared what happened.

She looked curiously at Teo. Their experiences were not so different. For a dizzy minute, she wished she could tell him everything. To share it, and in so doing, walk out of the prison she'd created for herself. But obviously she couldn't.

"I just moved around a lot," she said regretfully. Guiltily.

Then, to change the subject before he could start asking more things about her, she added, "So how did you start talking again?"

Now he had a spoon in each hand, and he was quietly drumming them on the table.

"This is going to sound stupid and melodramatic or whatever. But it was opera."

She blinked, thinking of when that chord had pierced through the fog and revealed her broken heart to itself.

"It doesn't sound stupid."

He smiled. "Yeah. Nonna kept playing it day and night. She kind of saturated the whole house with it, telling me who was singing and bringing all of these big emotions to life. It sounds weird, but it was like some kind of immersive opera therapy, looking back."

Like "Post-Punk Beethoven," shattering through her grief and rage.

Teo went on, thoughtfully, "I feel like opera is this weird quantum thing, you know? It takes big universal stuff and turns it into a medium that you can *hear.* It gives melody to the air you breathe, or to consciousness, or something."

Iz struggled to find the right thing to say. Finally she stammered, "I-I'm so sorry that happened. And I'm glad Nonna was there."

"Yeah," Teo said.

"You're staying to sing some more, right?" Vito was suddenly there towering over them.

Teo blinked up at him, tawny eyes catching the light. "Sure."

"I'll get you a stool."

Once they had finished eating, they set up side by side. They looked to each other, then started with "The Linden Tree" while customers chatted softly in the warm and nurturing atmosphere. After that, Teo taught her "Con Te Partirò," crooning in an almost confidential undertone until she joined him with chords and a harmony line. Then they sang "Santa Lucia," their voices circling each other. Iz thought about how she'd first sung "Saint Lucia" with his recording, and how this was so much better.

She actually relaxed after awhile. But at the end of the evening, when the music stopped and they were just sitting together, she unexpectedly started feeling weird.

"So!" she said, starting to gather up her things—her backpack and the two guitars. "I . . . I guess I'll see you at school tomorrow."

"How are you getting home? Is someone picking you up?"

"I'm taking the bus."

He said offhandedly, "Yeah, I could help you carry this stuff to the bus stop."

"I got it here. I can get it to the bus stop."

"But there might be aliens."

She flashed a look at him then. His whole face was filled with cajoling laughter.

"Fine," she said, shrugging the backpack onto a shoulder and grabbing a guitar.

He picked up the second guitar. "Lead on, Beaufort."

Vito appeared out of nowhere, gruff and grim. "Here's your pay." Then he handed Teo an envelope. "Something for you too."

"Hey, thanks!"

"Come and sing again. Any time."

Teo said lightly, "If Beaufort's cool with it, I'm there."

A weird little course of adrenalin shot through her. "I don't mind . . . if you want. It was pretty fun, I guess."

His smile was like light bursting out from behind clouds. "Totally fun. See? I'm growing on you, right?"

She felt her cheeks starting to pound. "Yeah, whatever." Then, audaciously, she added, "As long as you stop doing the eye thing."

Teo burst out laughing, throwing his head back. "You and this eye thing! It doesn't exist!"

"You're doing it *right now.*" She gestured at his face, while he flung up his hands in baffled innocence.

Vito frowned at the two of them, back and forth.

He said to Iz, "How are you getting home?"

"The same way as always," Iz said. "The bus. You know that."

"I'm walking her to the bus stop," Teo said.

"I feel like a walk. I'll come along too." Vito's voice was slightly territorial.

Iz looked from one to the other, annoyance and amusement mixed in her. "I'm actually capable of taking the bus. I'm pretty good at it."

"It's a beautiful evening," Vito said, as if his decision was final.

Then she found herself in the slightly entertaining position of tramping through the dancing flakes, flanked on either side by the two of them. Vito had her backpack and Teo had the guitar.

And in the elemental chaos of the snow, it was like she could be in any time or place she wanted. She could almost imagine that Vito was her grandfather and Teo was—well, someone she'd known for a long time or something.

In that peaceful dream place, there was no hiding or lying.

She was herself.

Chapter Twenty-Nine

When Iz got home, she ran up to her room, feeling like she was sailing above her own life as if she was a balloon filled with helium.

She threw herself onto the bed, remembering parts of the day.

The gift of the guitar.

Teo showing up at Festa and saying, "Ask me anything."

Singing together.

Leaning forward at the table talking. *Really* talking.

And learning how they were so similar—they'd both gone into a fog and been woken out of it by music.

It was so precious suddenly, everything to do with Métier.

She couldn't sit still. She jumped off the bed and started pacing around. It was as if Teo had ripped open curtains in her head and she could feel actual, warm sunlight beaming into her brain, transforming into every brilliant colour imaginable.

She wanted to explode. She wanted to create. She wanted to write something that summoned The Métier School right into her room.

But what?

Dr. Perlinger's voice came into her mind. *If the Beloved could speak, what would she say?*

Iz laughed out loud, completely giddy.

The Beloved would say she wanted to be free to walk where she wanted and speak with her own voice and to have everyone know.

She would like to stand in that warm sun. She would like to not care about who was watching.

Iz totally understood.

She wished Teo could just show up at Pat's place and say, *Hey, Beaufort, get your stuff. A bunch of us are meeting downtown.* She longed for Pat to call, *Hurry up, the bus for Métier will be coming in ten minutes. And did you finish your theory homework?*

It was a glorious daydream.

But it was impossible. The only way it could happen was if she revealed everything she had done. And that would bring about the end of her time at The Métier School. It might even mean jail.

The Beloved could do it though.

The Beloved was not afraid to completely rip the world apart when she slammed the door. The Beloved was much braver than Iz.

A thousand ideas started crowding into her head.

She threw herself into her desk chair and spread out her notebook. She set up her tablet at her elbow so she could keep going over and over the lyrics for *Winterreise.*

She spent most of the night scribbling furiously.

In the morning, she wolfed down her breakfast. She could hardly wait to take her work to Dr. Perlinger.

Pat sat opposite, drinking coffee, looking anxious. Iz ignored it, assuming there was a glitch with the lasers for the reception or something.

But then Pat said in a nervous voice, "Hon, Brit had a question from the other night, you know, when we were talking about your school."

Iz blinked.

"Oh . . . yeah?"

Pat looked like she hardly wanted to say it. "Brit asked about your report card. And then I started thinking—and this is totally on me, hon—I started wondering if I saw the one you were supposed to get in January?"

A nasty little feeling fluttered through Iz. "Oh! Huh, I thought I showed it to you."

Pat shook her head, looking very uncomfortable. "No, baby. I don't think so."

"Really?" Iz's brain began to do somersaults. "Um, it's probably in my room somewhere."

Pat nodded. "Of course, hon. So what about if you just get it for me before you head out today?"

"I, uh, I don't know if I have time right now. I'll be late for guitar club—"

Pat levelled her with a kind glance. "Baby. I don't want you to ever be scared to show me your report cards. Nobody's looking for straight A's. We love you just as you are."

"Oh good," Iz said, trying to quell the panic.

"So how about you have a quick look up there now. See what you can find. I promise, I won't be mad, no matter what it says. I'm here to help."

Iz nodded mechanically. She pushed away from the breakfast table.

"Okay," she said.

"That's perfect, baby."

Upstairs, she closed the door to her room and sank down against it, clutching her knees.

Think, think!

She groaned out loud, her brain chugging like a half-dead car. If she couldn't produce a report card, Pat might contact the school to get another one issued. Then she'd learn that Iz had been unenrolled and had transferred to another school. Not long after that, everything would come out—the fact that Claudia had not been the one to call and transfer Iz, or to fill in that online withdrawal form with all those vague answers about where Iz was going.

Then Iz's eyes widened.

Online form.

She scrambled to her feet, opened the door to her room, and ran as lightly as she could into the computer room. She yanked at her hair, waiting for the old machine to boot up.

Finally, she typed, *Blank report card.*

A bunch of empty templates came up, with spaces where you could write marks and a few basic comments. None of them were anything like the ones Iz remembered seeing at the fourteen schools she'd attended. But with luck, Pat might not have paid attention to many report cards in the past. And even if she had, Iz could maybe convince her that they'd changed the format recently.

She chose one at random and printed it. Then she raced back to her room, grabbed a pen and filled it in with a shaking hand. She gave herself a smattering of Bs and Cs. She signed it with a kind of scribble that could be anyone's signature.

She ran back down the stairs.

"Here it is! I know the marks aren't that good. But I'm going to pull them up!"

Pat's eyes flicked across the page while Iz mostly forgot how to breathe.

"This isn't so bad, baby," Pat said at last.

"No?" Relief flooded her. The gamble had paid off.

"It really isn't. Hon, I'm proud of you."

"You-you are?"

"Definitely, baby. You're really nose to the grindstone. Honestly, between you and Brit, I feel like just a huge slacker half the time." Pat laughed comfortably.

"You're not a slacker!" Iz said, washed in huge relief. "You're like the mastermind behind this whole wedding!"

"Oh, no, hon. I'm just the lady with the cheque book," Pat said, with complacent cheer.

Then she smiled warmly at Iz, holding out the report card. "Here, put this back somewhere safe. And you'd better hurry, baby, if you're going to get to your guitar club on time!"

"Okay! Thanks!"

Iz fled, thinking about how close it had been.

And a kind of anger welled up in her.

She was writing all about the Beloved, who was unafraid to shatter the very earth around her in order to escape. But Iz was always hiding and lying and working out plans, always racing ahead and anticipating what someone else was thinking or doing, so she could keep her secrets.

She wanted to step out into the open air.

This was starting to feel like an intolerable half-life.

Chapter Thirty

She was on the bus before she realized she'd brought Teo's guitar but forgotten her own.

Stupid! She had been so rattled!

She sat there panicking at first. How could she show Dr. Perlinger what she had written if she couldn't accompany herself?

Well, she would just have to translate her thinking using Teo's guitar. She had been working on learning those fingerings for a while now. Like he'd said, she was becoming bilingual.

When she finally got off the bus, she had found her excitement again. That window in her mind opened once more and she could feel the warm sunlight illuminating the parts of her brain that had been cold and dark.

She could not wait to get to Dr. Perlinger's office. She didn't even go to her locker first. She just sat outside his door until he came along the hallway.

"Iz Beaufort! Good morning!" he said. "Let me just unlock the door."

"Yeah, I know I'm early. I just—"

He turned to smile at her. "You just?"

It exploded inside her.

"This is going to sound really stupid." The words were fighting each other to get out first. "But, I was thinking, what if the Beloved had her own song cycle? It could be like *Winterreise*, except it is *her* wandering. And, I mean, I thought I could steal some of the images and symbols from *Winterreise*, but sort of, you know, repurpose them. Be, like, a musical scavenger, kind of."

Her words ran out at last. There was a silence while he regarded her.

And for the first time in hours of frenetic writing, she doubted herself.

"Or, you know," she said. "Maybe it's not . . ."

Eyes sparkling, Dr. Perlinger said, "*What if?*"

Joy flooded her.

"Really? So. Okay! Good!"

"Come in!" He held open the door.

As Dr. Perlinger hung up his coat and took off his boots, Iz threw herself into the chair. She flipped through her notebook.

"I started mapping it out. I think I want to do four songs. I've basically figured out what the first three are about. But I don't really know what to do with the fourth one. It's about what happens *after* the Beloved busts out."

He came to sit down beside her.

"Explain," he said, in that way that took her completely seriously and seemed to be sure she was going to say something remarkable.

"Well, the first song is 'Dying.' It's about how the Beloved's earliest life was wild and creative, but she got constrained, hemmed in. They're trying to force her to get married. It's like the death of her creative self."

He nodded.

"And in the second one, 'Waking,' something jars her out of her death. She starts to realize it is impossible for things to stay as they are."

Like that chord in Dennison Hall.

"And next?" he said.

"The next is 'Destruction.' She makes the decision to leave, and it's like hacking through a chrysalis, ripping it to shreds so you can get out. And you know how the Wanderer is in this psycho landscape where things might or might not be totally real? I think she should also go into a kind of dream place, or nightmare place, where breaking the rules actually rewrites the laws of the universe. She explodes her prison, and the world explodes too, kind of."

He looked absolutely fascinated.

"But the fourth," Iz said. "That's where I'm stuck. I mean, when you escape, you're still you. So what do you do with yourself? Where do you go? What's next?"

Dr. Perlinger was smiling and nodding. He said, "Have you done much reading about the Hurdy Gurdy Man yet?"

Iz blinked. "The weird little old guy in the last song who keeps getting barked at by dogs while he's playing the same song on his instrument over and over?"

Dr. Perlinger nodded.

"Well," Iz said, "No offense, but I don't think the Beloved and the Hurdy Gurdy Man should get together in the end. They don't seem like each other's type."

Dr. Perlinger laughed. "No. But there are a lot of theories out there about him. And one or another of those theories might give you some ideas about what to do with song four."

So Iz and Dr. Perlinger began to do a search together. And over the next hour, Iz discovered several things.

Some people thought the Hurdy Gurdy Man represented death.

Some people thought he was the first sign of human friendship for the Wanderer, after he'd been alone so long.

Some people thought he was a weird kind of twin of the Wanderer, called a doppelgänger.

At that last one, Iz sat there frowning.

"So it's kind of like the Wanderer meets *himself* at the end of the song?"

"Exactly," Dr. Perlinger said.

Thinking out loud, Iz said slowly, "He asks if he can go with the Hurdy Gurdy Man and sing songs while the Hurdy Gurdy Man plays that instrument."

Dr. Perlinger waited.

"So maybe," Iz said softly, "It's like, becoming whole again."

Then she sat there thinking about the Beloved.

She imagined that wrecked and shattered landscape. She imagined the silence after the disaster. The yawning question of what might come next.

Maybe, in the stillness, there might be a voice. A song.

A song of childhood.

A song of a wild girl before she was captured.

In that magical middle place where endings and beginnings were happening at once, maybe the Beloved would find the part of herself that had been ripped away. Maybe they would begin to sing together.

Maybe she would be healed.

Iz said softly, "If the Beloved meets her own Doppelgänger—and if it's her younger self . . ."

He regarded her for a long time after that.

"It's like starting over," she said softly.

Then Dr. Perlinger slouched down in his chair, the way he did when something was really whirling around his head.

At last he said, "It is an entirely apocalyptic structure, isn't it?"

Iz frowned. "What does that mean?"

"First the Beloved destroys the world. Then, in the rubble of it, she makes way for something new."

"Ah."

She thought about it for a while.

At last, she nodded. "Yes—that's *exactly it*."

Then, anxiously, she passed him the words she had started to scribble together for the first song.

"So, yeah, this is 'Dying.' It's rough, though. I mean, it's just a basic outline really. It will be much, much better. And I still have to figure out what aspects of Schubert's music I want to weave in—"

He interrupted her, smiling. "Sing it for me."

She nodded, picking up Teo's guitar from the floor. She drew up her legs so she was sitting cross-legged in the chair. She found the new places on the strings. Then, tentatively, she began.

My love is angry with me
And now he is wandering
He says I'm faithless
Like a weathervane
Playing with his heart
Throwing him aside
To be a rich bride
Money before love
No care for his pain

What he doesn't know
Is that they stole my voice
The crows with their talons
Took the little girl I was
And wrapped her round
Spun her like a weathervane
And now they force me to be a rich wife
Even though I was the love of his life
And he wanders now
And judges me

I have a shocking secret though
And it would kill him if he knew
My heart is breaking
Not for him
But for the little girl I was
Who ran in the meadow
Played in the Linden Tree
Saw flowers in the frost
Sang her soul into song

The girl grew up
And when she properly looked the part
They ripped away her very heart
Bound her fast in corsets

And promised her to the highest bid
Separated her from her artist's soul
So she was a half self,
Half forgetting
What it was to be whole

Iz plucked out the last, grieving chord. She let it ring. She placed her arm on top of her guitar.

Dr. Perlinger didn't say anything for a long time.

"Like I said, it's just—" Iz stammered.

"It is good," he said. "It is very good, Iz."

"Really?"

"Excellent. Inexpressibly moving." He nodded, as if partly to himself. "And intelligently conceived. You've woven in the ideas of the weathervane, the crow, the linden tree of course, the frost flowers on the windowpane, all from the original song cycle."

"Ah," Iz said, her eyes blurring. Then the tears spilled over.

Dr. Perlinger handed her a tissue. "This is *exactly* the kind of work we talked about at the beginning," he said softly.

She asked tentatively the thing that was on her mind. "Is ... is this something I could do for a Manifesto audition?"

He regarded her warmly. "It is most definitely on the right track, Iz Beaufort."

Joy started bubbling up in her.

The May auditions.

She would try again.

When the lesson was over, she took off running. She had to. She pelted to Theory and Composition and, after that, to Perspectives in Music.

It was like she was propelled all morning by sheer exhilaration.

As she was racing upstairs to the cafeteria for lunch, she turned a corner and slammed directly into another person. He stumbled and fell against the wall, dropping everything everywhere.

It was Teo.

"Hey, Beaufort! You trying to kill me? That's your secret, right? You're an assassin."

"Sorry!" she said, starting to grab things up and blushing and also trying not to laugh. It was like the first day all over again, except this time she had knocked *him* flying. Audaciously, she added, "I think your filing system could use a little work."

He burst out laughing. "Maybe a binder?"

"We'll start slowly with a paper clip."

She met his eyes and noticed how weirdly large they were, all lit up with amusement. Everything from last night shot back into her mind—sitting with him at the little table, singing with him in that lovely restaurant.

As if he knew what she was thinking, Teo said, "Hey, I was going to say, if you ever want to sing duets again, I could come by Festa sometime."

She was about to answer. But at that moment, a voice started bellowing out opera.

LaRoyce came skateboarding into view, singing at the top of his lungs and maneuvering through people walking in the hallway. They all stopped and pressed against the wall and clapped as he shot past.

He rolled up to Iz and Teo, then stopped, giving a little half-bow.

"And a hearty good morning to you both," he said. "Care for a little spin?"

"But of course," Teo said.

So LaRoyce got off and Teo got on, pushing with one foot to get himself started. Iz and LaRoyce stood there and watched as he began threading his way through the hall, singing richly, "Libiamo, libiamo ne' lieti calici, che la belleza infiora!"

"'Brindisi,'" LaRoyce said wisely.

"What is that?"

"The drinking song from *La Traviata*. Typical Russo—so ostentatious."

Teo circled around and zoomed back, looking enchanted with himself.

He jumped off, sparkled at Iz, and jerked his head at the skateboard.

Her eyes widened. "Oh! Huh! No, I don't know how to—"

"Not a worry," LaRoyce said gallantly. "We'll keep you steady."

Completely out of character, she actually climbed on the thing. Teo stood on one side, and LaRoyce on the other, each taking a hand. They began walking forward while she balanced.

"Sing!" LaRoyce shouted.

"Uh . . . I don't know what to—"

"'Muth,' from *Winterreise*," Teo said.

It meant, *courage*. And suddenly she realized it was exactly right.

Teo launched into the song at the top of his voice. And after a minute, Iz joined in. LaRoyce sang too, on the other side.

I have my trusty staff
I have my cheerful song
We will journey on together

They raced faster and faster while Iz was half singing and half laughing.

She felt like the Beloved. She was fiercely clawing through the net she had created for herself. She was rewriting natural laws, overturning the universe.

For a split second, she imagined kicking it all away, walking into the bright day and just being herself. The hiding would be over.

Teo and LaRoyce rolled her through the section of the hall overlooking the main foyer downstairs. Iz glanced down.

And then—

She froze.

Her brain went numb.

Pat was looking straight up at her.

Chapter Thirty-One

Her brain started spurting out illogical ideas. *Had she summoned Pat somehow? Could she have really rearranged the universe by simply imagining it?*

Then, as awareness flowed into her brain and her limbs, she shot into panicked action.

"Let me down! Let me down!" She pushed at Teo and LaRoyce, scrambled off the skateboard.

"What's wrong?" Teo was saying.

"No, no," Iz snapped back, aware she wasn't making sense.

She took off running for her very survival, leaving his guitar and her backpack there on the floor. Everything was spilling out in her mind—all the terror and claustrophobia of That Place. All she knew was that she was trapped and she had to escape.

She careened into walls, shoving past kids walking in the hallway. She ignored Teo and LaRoyce calling after her.

At the end of the hall, there was a staircase. Panting, heaving great half sobs, she slid down the steps, until she got to the emergency exit. She shoved against the door with all her might. It swung open and a loud bell began to peal out.

She ran down the steps and into the remnants of snow, all slushy and splashing. Then she careened around the side of the building and exploded onto the sidewalk.

Students and teachers were beginning to spill into the street, forced there by the alarm. It was like The Métier School was turning itself inside out.

Iz scrambled past them all, took off down the sidewalk like she'd been shot out of a catapult. She did not know where to go. She turned down the first corner and then down another. At last, when her legs were going to give out, she gripped her knees and bent over panting, her lungs craving air.

A voice yelled from down the street, "Beaufort! What's going on?"

Teo was running toward her, his face red with cold. He didn't have a coat either.

"Go away!" she said.

She slid down the wall till she was squatting on the cold sidewalk. She pressed her face into her knees.

He stood there, unsure what to do. Then, after a minute, he bent down beside her.

Iz burst into tears.

"Beaufort!" he said. "Beaufort! Talk to me."

She shook her head. She couldn't bear to see how his face would change if he learned the truth.

"Are you in trouble?"

She shrugged. Then she nodded.

"Can I help?" Teo said.

"No," she whispered.

There was a long silence.

"Well, can we at least stop sitting here in the cold? And take this."

She looked up. He was holding out a Kleenex.

It was the second one she'd been offered today. The first had been from Dr. Perlinger, when she had been weeping happy tears.

Everything had changed in a matter of hours.

"Thanks." She took it, wiped her eyes, blew her nose.

He stood up, held out his hand. She finally took it and stood too.

They looked at each other.

"So what are we going to do now?" Teo said.

She shook her head helplessly.

"Okay," he said. "Let's just walk."

They started off together along the sidewalk.

Teo was silent at first. But, unsurprisingly, he could not pull it off for long. "Hey, did I tell you about how I used to squish the candles when I was a kid? We'd have these family dinners—well, we still do—and I'd have a slight bit of trouble sitting still. So I'd squish the wax and glob it on my fingers and wave it at my sisters and get it on everything. My mom would kick me out to my bedroom, everyone would yell. It was bad."

He grinned down at her, as if it was perfectly normal, them strolling together like this.

But there was an abyss inside Iz. He was on one side, and she was on the other.

Then Teo said, "Well, at least, I *thought* it was bad. But, I mean, you know ... later ... *after*, I would have given anything to get yelled at like that again."

They walked quietly.

"My point is, Beaufort, you can feel like something is really horrible, but maybe it's not as awful as you think, when you look at it a different way."

Iz whispered, "This is really, really bad."

"Did you kill someone?" he asked.

"No!"

"So it could be worse."

He was full of such goodwill.

Iz wrestled inside. It would feel like such a relief to tell someone at last, to lay down the heaviness of it. But she couldn't. That would be the end of everything.

Then her brain stirred like some despairing and lonely and feral thing.

It whispered, *This IS the end of everything.*

Suddenly she could feel the explosions erupting around her. Pieces blew apart everywhere and there was dust, smoke, flame. The old world was going, going, gone. In its place was a kind of empty middle ground that wasn't anything yet.

"I-I'm ..." She stared at him. Once she had said it, she would not be able to take it back. "Ahh, I've broken the law, like, a thousand times. I'm going to jail."

Her voice sounded like someone else's.

And then other words spilled out, like slugs from her mouth. They were poisoned and horrible. It hurt to say them out loud, to tell everything she'd done to get into Métier.

But as those words left her, she felt lighter, like space was opening up inside where before there had only been packed-in terror and guilt and shame weighing her down.

Teo's eyes widened as he listened.

When she had said it all, she just waited.

They walked in silence.

She glanced up at him. He was looking straight forward, like his eyes were headlights boring through what she had just told him.

Was he disgusted by her?

At last he said, "Well, Beaufort, this is a huge mess."

She nodded miserably.

"You have to go back. You can't keep running from it. There's nowhere to run *to*."

"I can't," she whispered.

"You can," he said. "I mean, if you can pull off all of this, you can definitely walk into Métier. It's easy. There's only a couple of steps."

He looked at her then. His eyes were cold, tough like they were not going to tolerate an argument.

All at once, she thought of him writing that song for his Nonna. She remembered him saying, *I would have walked her out of there.*

Chapter Thirty-Two

When they entered the foyer of Métier, people were standing around—Pat, Britnee, Iz's case worker Claudia, Dr. Perlinger, and some others she didn't recognize. Students were hovering nearby too. They all turned to look at her when she came in.

"Here we are!" Teo said heartily, as if he was used to bringing criminals to justice. "How's everyone?"

But his face was the opposite of his bright words. It looked like it was carved out of ice.

"Iz!" Claudia said, running over and grabbing Iz's arms. Iz flinched but stood there.

Claudia exclaimed, "What is this? What have you been doing?"

"I . . ." Iz said. "I just—"

Then she caught a glimpse of Dr. Perlinger's serious expression, and it completely undid her.

"I'm sorry," she whispered.

She burst into tears for the third time. Losing his good opinion—that was the most horrible feeling of all.

Everyone was blinking around at everyone else like there was no game plan for what you did when a foster kid scammed everyone and went to a totally different school for months.

Dr. Perlinger murmured to Claudia, "You could use my office if you'd like."

"Thank you, that would be great."

He led them along the familiar hallway Iz had walked through only a few hours earlier. As he unlocked his door, she couldn't help thinking that this moment was about as far removed from the joy and brilliance of their tutorial as was possible.

"I'll leave you to it," he said to Claudia. "Take your time. Buzz the office if you need anything from me."

He patted Iz on the shoulder.

She stared up at him gratefully, but his face was impassive.

Then he ushered Teo out and closed the door and left her in there with them.

They looked at each other blankly for a minute, before Claudia said, "Let's all have a seat."

They settled on his couch and in the armchairs. Claudia sat behind his desk. Uncomfortably, Iz perched on the edge of the windowsill.

"So!" Claudia said to Iz. "Do you want to start talking?"

Iz blew out her breath slowly. She did not want to start talking.

But when she glanced up, they were all waiting. So finally she whispered, "I just, you know, I wanted to go to this school. So I-I … auditioned and I got in."

Britnee stared at Pat in her pale-blue way. "She auditioned and she got in!"

"Well, why didn't you *tell* anyone?" Claudia said.

Iz looked directly at Pat and Britnee. Then she glanced away.

"I don't know."

They waited.

She muttered, "I didn't think anyone would take it seriously. So I just auditioned on my own. I figured I wouldn't get in anyway. But then I did."

Britnee said, "And how did you pull *that* off?"

A little rebellious thing rose up in Iz. "I performed songs from two time periods, and I figured out how to read music, and I learned arpeggios and scales and some theory."

Claudia was shaking her head. That went on for a long time.

Britnee clicked away on her phone. "Well, this says you need reference letters and transcripts. So how did that work?"

Iz shrugged. Finally she mumbled, "I … I made that part up."

"Pardon?" Britnee said.

"I made it up. I made up a school and teachers. I made a transcripts page."

Britnee raised her hands in utter disgust and disbelief.

Finally Iz whispered, "H-how did you find me?"

"Oh!" Pat said, sounding like her voice was barely working. "Baby, I went into the computer room to get one of the recipe books out of the closet. And there was a picture on the computer screen, then I realized it was the report card you showed me. But … but it was empty. So, I got Brit."

Iz's stomach flopped over. She had forgotten to shut down the laptop. If not for that, Pat would not have known about anything.

It was her own fault.

Britnee interrupted sternly. "Mom was an absolute wreck."

"So then we called the school," Pat whispered. "And they said you weren't a student there anymore."

Iz crossed her arms protectively.

"And … and I called Claudia. And Claudia came over, and we searched your room," Pat said, wringing her hands. "We went through the drawers, and the closets and everything, under the mattress—which, I mean, hon, we would never have done if we didn't have a good reason—"

"And then we looked in the guitar case," Britnee said sternly. "And we found all of this enrollment paperwork from The Métier School."

Iz's stomach felt like it was falling off a cliff.

She had been so careless.

"So," Claudia said. "The fees."

There was a long silence.

Iz started to shake. Then she groaned out loud and put her head in her hands.

"Whatever it is," Pat said, "it's okay, baby. We will sort it out. I promise." Her voice was kind and trusting, even in the midst of everything.

But it wouldn't be for long.

Iz could hardly get the words out while looking right at Pat.

She'd been able to justify stealing Pat's money by thinking about it in a kind of abstract way—about caregivers and foster children and expenses and what was fair. But now she realized it was the most personal thing in the world.

She whispered at last, "The first month, I went into my own bank account, for when I age out."

Everyone waited.

She felt like she was going to be sick.

"But then … I researched what foster parents make and what they are supposed to spend on foster kids." She squeezed fists on the sides of her head as if she could force history to change, make it not have happened. "And then I got your bank account number and I went into your online banking, and I just …"

She wrung her hands.

"You just what?" Britnee said, like a coiled snake.

Iz's face beat with shame. "I thought, maybe Pat wasn't spending as much of it on me as … as maybe she was supposed to."

The words hung nastily in the air.

She went on wretchedly, "So, I just arranged a money transfer. I only did it two times. And not the full fifteen hundred each time. The rest of it, I made singing on the street. And … and then, I got a job at this restaurant, Festa. I sing there in the evening, and I'm making enough now to be able to pay the fees on my own."

She added, dully, "But I guess I don't need it anymore."

There was an appalled silence as they all processed this.

Then Pat put her face in her hands and began to cry softly.

Iz stared at her in horror.

Suddenly, in Pat's devastated shaking shoulders, she *felt* the harm she had done.

She gasped aloud like someone had struck her in the face. "I'm sorry, I'm so sorry," she whispered.

"Mommy," Britnee said urgently. "We need to get into your bank account. Right now." She turned to Claudia. "And we need to call the police."

Chapter Thirty-Three

Everything happened very fast after that.

Claudia got on the phone and called the police department. Then she called Dominion Children's Care.

After that, everything was all jumbled up.

Handcuffs.

Walking out in front of people with blurred faces.

Sitting in a police car with wire in front of her so she couldn't attack the driver or something.

And fog curling over everything.

"Can you tell us everything again about how you pulled this off, Isabelle?"

She blinked. She was at the police station now, sitting with two officers, some lawyers, and Claudia.

Through the tumbling, roiling chaos inside her, she heard herself explaining it all piece by piece—how she falsified records, impersonated her social worker, syphoned Pat's money.

"It was actually easy," she said softly.

That was true. None of the things she'd done were very hard. They had just required a little thinking and planning. Like building up an argument.

"And nobody noticed?" one of the officers asked.

She shrugged. "They were getting ready for a wedding, so they weren't really paying attention."

The Dominion Children's Care lawyer got very involved at that point and everyone started arguing back and forth. Iz tuned them out. None of it mattered anyway.

"Isabelle. Did you hear me?"

She realized that the officer was talking to her again. "Oh! Sorry."

"You're coming with us now. We're going to Maplewood Youth Detention Centre tonight."

"Oh!" Iz said. Panic shot through the fog for a second. "Okay. But . . ."

"But what?"

"M-my guitar. It's at Pat's house."

Because obviously she wouldn't be going back there. And she had lost so many things over the years when Claudia or the people before Claudia had cleaned out her rooms. And she desperately needed her guitar, even though she didn't deserve it.

"I'll get everything," Claudia said. "Don't worry."

The officer added dryly, "I think that ship has sailed anyway. You know you're not going back to that school, kid."

As the police officer helped her to stand up and walked her out of the room, Iz tried to invite the fog back in.

To let it curl around her brain.

Placating.

Sedating.

Smoothing.

Because otherwise her heart was going to rip in half.

Métier—gone, all gone.

And Teo, staring at her with those cold, hard eyes.

Chapter Thirty-Four

She pled guilty.

Then there was a case conference.

They drove her to the courthouse, and she walked into a room where people were grouped all around a long table.

She was mostly looking down at her feet when she entered. But when she glanced up, she was startled to see Dr. Perlinger sitting quietly on the other side of the table. Next to him were Vito and Gisele. Vito glared stonily ahead, and Gisele had her hand on her mouth, eyes fixed down fiercely as if she was contemplating something violent. Pat perched on the edge of her seat, pale and blinking. Britnee sat beside her, rubbing her back.

"You can sit here, Isabelle." It was a woman speaking, not unkindly.

Iz fell into the chair where she was told.

They were all looking at her now. She felt trapped. Claustrophobia rose in her like bile. She dug her fingernails into her clasped hands, shut her eyes tight, tried to push That Place away.

Someone welcomed her to the case conference, thanked everyone for coming.

Then voices began to speak at different pitches. Vaguely, she knew that the people talking were from Dominion Children's Care, the school board, The Métier School. She knew the point of the case conference was to give everyone a chance to weigh in on what she had done—those who were victims, and those who could advocate for her—so the woman in charge could put together her report about Iz for the judge.

Iz ignored them. She stared at her knees. She counted in her head and wondered how high she would get before the case conference was finished. She turned everyone there into a cartoon figure.

But then, Pat's trembling voice pierced through the haze in Iz's head.

"I don't know, it was just such a shock when I saw that blank report card up there on the screen and I realized she'd filled it in herself. And then, when she started telling about breaking into my bank account—it just wasn't something I ever would have expected. It ... it was upsetting. It wasn't the amount that was the problem. It was more, I thought I had a safe space, and then it turns out I didn't."

"It's okay, Mama," Britnee said softly.

There was a silence while the woman was writing.

Then Vito cleared his throat, dragged back his chair, and stood up, glowering around at them all.

"Vito Santoro here. Iz was singing in the street in front of my restaurant when I first met her. Holes in her boots, no gloves till my wife knitted her some, she'd stand out there for hours. She was trying to earn money for her school. Night after night. You could set your clock by her."

Gisele stood up too. "And she was a hard worker. She always gave extra. She interacted beautifully with the guests. They loved her."

Vito rubbed his nose, eyebrows kickboxing. "Okay, obviously, she did a lot of things she shouldn't have. This stealing money and fraud or whatever it was ... you can't let that go. I'm just saying, I'd hate to see her get punished too hard. But obviously you can't just send her off with a slap on the wrist."

"No," Britnee said sharply. "You can't. Nobody at *our* house even knew she was working in your restaurant. It's been nothing but lies."

Vito levelled Britnee with a bearlike glance, rubbed his nose again, looked right at Iz. "You were there on time whenever you said you would be, and you gave it a hundred and fifty percent. I always had to kick you out at the end of your shift."

Gisele said fiercely, "You're a good kid, Iz."

She had to stifle a sudden ragged gasp. The joy of singing at Festa—it suddenly flowed back. And with that memory came an almost unbearable feeling of loss.

Someone handed her a Kleenex. Stonily, she swiped at her eyes.

Then she heard Dr. Perlinger's voice. "Could I also speak in support of Iz? Aaron Perlinger, from The Métier School."

He gave Iz a little salute down the table.

Her stomach twisted.

Dr. Perlinger said affably, "Well, Isabelle Beaufort was at Métier for only a few months but she was certainly one of the most interesting students I have ever worked with."

Was.

He put his hands behind his head, reminding her painfully of how he tended to slide down in his chair during their tutoring sessions while his brain churned a mile a minute.

"Her theory, history, technique, interpretation, they were all rudimentary when she auditioned. You must understand that it's highly unusual for someone to be admitted with such significant gaps. But we were all so excited at her natural ability as well as her extraordinary passion, that we offered her a place even without the usual prerequisites."

All gone now.

Iz covered her face.

Dr. Perlinger continued, evenly, "At the risk of being pedantic, I think it is worth pointing out an obvious parallel between Isabelle's audition and this case conference today. In both instances, she fell significantly short of what is generally considered minimally acceptable. And, of course, I should preface my remarks by saying that I am not advocating for delinquent activities of any kind. But Iz, here is what I *am* saying."

When Iz opened her eyes, he was staring directly at her. He was not smiling at all, as if what he had to say was too important for pleasantries.

"In the case of the audition, we believed that additional factors were crucial to consider in rendering our verdict. And now, indeed, we know how much dedication and how much drive was fuelling that extraordinary talent we glimpsed in the audition. A lonely road indeed. A rare child. And someone, a persevering soul, worth not abandoning, I do think."

There was a silence.

Dr. Perlinger said amiably to the woman who was writing, "The justice system must do what it must do in the end, of course. The law is the law and unquestionably many laws were broken here. People and institutions were harmed. But I might just suggest that this is not an ordinary young person and this is not an ordinary case."

Britnee's voice rose again. "So, what, you think if someone's supposedly talented they're above the law?"

Dr. Perlinger smiled at Britnee pleasantly. "Ahh, Miss Peters, what an interesting and complicated question! What do you think?"

Britnee shook back her honey-coloured hair and raised her chin. "I don't care how talented you are. You commit crimes and you face the consequences."

"No doubt that is absolutely right," Dr. Perlinger said politely. "And I would take it further. Societal crimes, *systemic* crimes—these things are not always so easy to prosecute, especially if they are embedded in law, but one could argue that they also should have consequences. There should be reparations. Victims of these crimes—even imperfect, problematic ones who don't fit easily into a compartment—should have a chance to be heard, be seen, and to reach their potential. I'm simply speaking in philosophical terms, you understand, for the sake of abstract argument."

He waited for her to answer, but Britnee just stared at him, like she did not understand Dr. Perlinger well enough to respond.

Finally, he turned to someone who was blocked from Iz's sight. "Would you care to say a few words?"

"Yes, I would."

She knew the voice. Where had she heard it before?

A chair scraped loudly back.

He stood up with that same gentle, careful movement she

remembered from the music store. Like he didn't want to harm anything. Like he was always aware of how he moved in the world.

"Iz," Jamaal said, looking right at her.

She flushed, trying to figure out how he could possibly be there.

"I never stopped wondering about you, you know. I really hoped you'd gotten into The Métier School. I'm glad you did."

He turned to the woman who was writing. "Jamaal Wickerson. I'm a PhD candidate in Composition at the university. I also perform with the Wickerson Trio. And a couple of nights a week, I work at Phil's Music Store. I am profoundly grateful that I was there when Iz came in. I caught her behind the bookshelf, trying to take photos of pages with her phone."

Iz heard Pat and Britnee suddenly whispering down the table.

"I talked her into playing and singing for me. I cannot describe for you the intelligence, the musicality, the *energy* of her piece. The polyphony between multiple voices. It was called 'Refugee.' It was remarkable. This is a girl with promise. And she was standing there shaking, like this meant more to her than anything in the world but a thousand things were standing in her way. And I couldn't just ignore that."

Iz's heart wouldn't stop pounding.

"So then we studied that audition list and we were surgical about it. One vocalise, and all the rest of it. We found exactly what she needed."

He shook his head, remembering.

"I'd play it and she'd have the melody right away, with the chords. Iz has a structural way of looking at a composition. Architectural. And it's completely innate."

He looked directly at Britnee. "And hey, I'm not here to suggest she's not *guilty*. I just want to tell about the whole person, that's all. To give a balanced picture of who I met and what I thought of her. So she's not just some statistic."

"Yes," Dr. Perlinger said down the table. "Exactly."

The woman was writing quickly.

Jamaal said softly, "When I was a kid, someone helped me, no strings attached. Meeting Iz, it was like coming full circle, like the universe saying, 'You experienced that same thing. So now, in this go-round, what are you going to do with that experience? How are you going to help? You have an obligation.' That's what I felt then."

Full circle. Well, she had come back around to face Jamaal again, but after everything she had done, after how many rules she had broken, she was nearly unrecognizable now.

Jamaal went on, "I've been remembering a song that Iz connected with that day. 'The Erlking' by Franz Schubert. The story is about a kid being pursued by a demon."

He rubbed his forehead like he was trying to find the best way to put it.

"And it has been gnawing at me that she's probably been dealing with her own demons, the best way she could. And I feel like we need to show compassion, to extend a hand to this girl who's been trying to negotiate her way."

The silence went on and on as the woman wrote down what Jamaal had said.

Chapter Thirty-Five

There was no trial because she'd admitted to everything.

So on the day of the sentencing, Iz stood at the front while the judge walked in. It was a closed courtroom, which meant that the only people in there were her, the judge, the director of Dominion Children's Care, lawyers, and the youth probation officer.

The judge read the charges out loud.

Iz stood there heavily and steadily while the list went on and on—falsifying documents, theft under five thousand dollars, larceny, fraud, identity theft. The judge outlined the seriousness of each of them. She spoke about the impact on the victims in the case—Pat, Claudia, The Métier School, the public school district.

Then the judge opened the file in front of her.

"So, Isabelle Beaufort has pled guilty to all charges before her. It therefore has fallen to me to decide upon a suitable sentence. In order to do that, I have needed to weigh a number of factors."

She riffled through the file, then lifted out a stapled set of papers.

"I have before me the report prepared by the youth parole officer, outlining the testimonies from the case conference. And I would like to highlight some mitigating themes I believe are important to consider."

Iz waited steadily, calmly, to hear about how her life had been distilled down into a few pages.

"First," the judge said. "We need to consider Isabelle's background as a foster youth in Dominion Children's Care, a for-profit agency. Twenty-six families. Fourteen different schools. This is surely not an optimal circumstance for any child. And it is doubly unfortunate for a child who might, in other circumstances, have been long-ago recognized as gifted and therefore have been provided educational programming to which an identified young person is entitled by law."

Iz blinked, surprised.

"Giftedness," the judge continued, "is rarely recognized in foster youth, according to studies referenced in this report. Instead, it is often treated as a behavioural or psychological issue to be fixed. But—"

She rummaged through a file, took out some new papers.

"But Isabelle Beaufort's giftedness is conclusively identified in this case. I have here the results of a battery of tests administered by the court psychologist, and Isabelle has consistently scored in the top percentile. This, I believe, is not surprising in light of the fact that she survived and even thrived in the elite atmosphere of The Métier School. Furthermore, she exploited multiple systems effectively in order to fulfill audition requirements, to facilitate transferring from one school to the other, and to find money to pay the monthly school fees."

She put the report down, looked up again.

"The fact that no one identified her giftedness is not Isabelle's fault. And it is an important consideration in light of the fact that Isabelle's actions were aimed at achieving an education appropriate for a gifted child."

She looked at the director of Dominion Children's Care. "It is my recommendation that a more transparent process be created in this agency to screen, identify, and support youth according to their unique needs, including giftedness. Adequate care, after all, is not limited to room and board or to helping students once they have fallen through the cracks."

Iz couldn't help peeking sideways to see how the director was taking this.

He showed no facial expression whatsoever.

"Second," the judge said, "we have to consider the character testimonies. They point to personal qualities we might ordinarily consider to be admirable outside of this particular context. Work ethic. Drive and focus. A hunger to learn. The ability to shoulder multiple responsibilities including full time school and a part-time job. All positives in another scenario."

She paused for a long time.

"And thirdly, we need to consider a number of serious questions about the decisions Isabelle made in order to achieve her goal. Why did she not simply express her wishes to her foster parent or her caseworker? Why did she not audition with their knowledge? Why did she not seek a scholarship? Why go through this truly entangled and seemingly incomprehensible collection of behaviours when there was assuredly a more reasonable and simple solution?"

She looked down at the report again.

"Twenty-six homes and fourteen schools. I believe that Isabelle had valid reasons to think that her voice carried little weight. To be of the opinion that her best interests were not necessarily at the forefront of decisions being made. To feel she was without power or recourse."

She spoke directly to Iz. "Did you know that you have the legal right, as a youth in foster care, to take part in decisions in your life? To have your thoughts and opinions and feelings taken into account before decisions are made? To ask for changes in situations that you are not happy with?"

Iz blinked and shook her head, unsure if she was supposed to answer or not.

The judge said, "You also have the basic legal right to *know* your legal rights. To have them clearly outlined for you. To have them referred to on a regular basis."

She then spoke directly to the director of Dominion Children's Care at some length, using words like *review of processes* and *reform*.

And meanwhile, Iz's brain was bouncing all over the place.

It was so weird, how the judge was separating Iz the person from Iz the criminal. How she had just made all that pain and hope and grief sound like a collection of recognizable, even predictable and explainable symptoms.

Work ethic.

Giftedness.

Admirable personal qualities.

Rights.

It was like the judge was genuinely trying to be fair. To take the time to weigh everything out. To see her.

It was the very opposite of what Iz had expected, maybe because she had been passing cruel judgment on herself for years.

"So, with these mitigating factors in hand, here are the questions that we have to consider now. Is Isabelle Beaufort an ongoing danger to society? Is she likely to reoffend? Can reparations be made to victims in this case?"

The judge paused.

"It is my belief that—if an appropriate education can be put in place—Isabelle is unlikely to reoffend and that punishment is unlikely to have a therapeutic or restorative effect. Therefore, my ruling is conditional discharge."

Iz gave a little cry. She nodded. She swayed and leaned against the table.

The judge was still talking. "I am mandating ongoing therapy with a licensed psychologist, and reparations to victims must be as follows."

Iz tuned out here. She had gone past the point of particularly caring what they were going to make her do. It was all deserved.

But she started listening again, when the judge said, "As to Isabelle's future at The Métier School, I have no jurisdiction over that. But whatever their decision, I would urge all parties to come to a consensus about how to move forward in a way that best supports her."

Then the judge looked right at Iz.

"Isabelle, if you meet these criteria, your record will be cleared in a year. And I do not expect to see you in my court again." She smiled thinly for the first time. "You're being given a second chance, so please do not waste it."

Iz was gasping, shocked. "I-I won't. Thank you."

Chapter Thirty-Six

After the sentencing was over, they took Iz to a small room next to the courtroom. There she sat with a policeman, waiting to find out what would happen next.

Claudia came bustling in. She threw all of her bags down on the table. Claudia always seemed to be in the middle of a rush.

"How are you? Feeling okay? You got the right judge, that's for sure," Claudia said. "You're lucky. They don't all give second chances, so you have to earn this one. You understand that, right?"

"Yes." After a minute, Iz added, "Where am I going tonight?"

"Pat Peters wants to take you back."

It took Iz a moment to process this. "*Pat does?* But I—"

But I stole from her and lied to her in almost every way imaginable.

"After the case conference, she reached out." Claudia was not quite meeting Iz's eyes. "She felt like you deserved a fresh start. And she's undergone some more training, and I'll be checking in pretty often. She really cares about you. It's going to be different."

Iz nodded awkwardly and somewhat anxiously.

"Your things are over there already," Claudia said.

Iz's insides turned over. "My guitars? My notebook?"

"Everything."

Then Iz and Claudia headed out of the courthouse. They drove to Pat's house.

When they got there, Pat opened the door right away, hands clasped, face red.

"Baby," she said awkwardly.

There was a horrible little pause as they stared at each other.

Iz was abruptly catapulted into a memory of entering the first foster home after That Place. She'd been shattered, flatlining in her foggy mind, a husk who had no idea who she was or how to act. All she'd dimly felt was that she had to be different—not herself.

"I'm so sorry," Iz said in a barely audible voice. Everything hurt in that moment. Pat had not deserved any of it. There was no malice in Pat at all.

"Oh, honey. I know. I know. You come on in."

Suddenly Pat had her arms around Iz, which was profoundly weird.

"Well!" Claudia said. "I'll leave you to it then." To Iz, she added, "Fresh start, right? Everything above board. When you need things, you're going to *ask*. Everyone is here to help."

To Pat she said, "I'll get on setting up the therapy. And if you could go over her rights—"

"I sure will, hon," Pat said.

Then Claudia bustled off into the night.

Pat closed the door.

It was just the two of them in the hallway.

"Thanks ... for taking me back," Iz said at last. "I don't deserve it."

The words rushed out of Pat then.

"Baby, I was so upset at first. I was." She twisted her hands together. "But I listened to everything those people said at the case conference. Oh, honey, it breaks my heart ..." Her voice trailed off and her usually placid face squished into sadness.

Iz shrugged and nodded and looked all around the hallway.

And she realized, with surprise, that it wasn't as horrible as she had expected—the pity. It could be managed.

"Everything is going to be fixed, and we're going to put the past behind us," Pat said, taking Iz's coat and hanging it up in the closet. "I just want to trust, Iz. I want to believe that you would never do *that* again, if we can help you get what you need."

"No! No," Iz said, in a muffled voice.

Britnee came into the hall then, and Iz tensed.

Britnee was smiling but her eyes were not. "Mama's putting on a brave face but this has been a nightmare for her."

"I'm sorry," Iz whispered.

"And I didn't think you should come back here. After what you did."

Iz nodded and shook her head at the same time. What Britnee was saying was utterly fair.

Pat said to Britnee, "But I just kept sitting there imagining, what if it was you? What if nobody saw your ... your *specialness*, and you had to fight for it?"

"Yes, I know, Mama. But I would never have broken the law like that. I wouldn't have stolen someone's money."

Iz breathed slowly and nodded and just accepted it all. And she tried not to think about how Britnee could not possibly know what she would or wouldn't have done in Iz's shoes. How could anyone judge anything when they had not lived in it?

But she also knew she did not have the right to judge the way that Britnee was judging. That was the thing about breaking the law. It removed you from any kind of moral high ground.

She said to Pat very quietly, "I will never do that again. I can't believe I did it in the first place. I ... I *hate* how I hurt you. I will do better. I will be better."

She said it from the very centre of everything inside her.

But Britnee's expression said that she sincerely doubted Iz meant it.

"Baby." Pat's face was wide open and kind and placid. "Why don't you go up to your room and get set up again? Then come down, and we'll have a snack, and I'll find those rights. We'll have a little talk about them together."

"And maybe," Britnee said, "we can have a little talk about the rights of foster families at the same time."

Iz nodded dully. She gathered up what she had brought with her and climbed the stairs.

The small room was almost exactly as she'd left it, like nothing had happened. Except, on the floor, by the desk, someone had neatly placed her two guitars, side by side.

Iz dropped onto her knees beside them. She'd been worried she would never see Teo's guitar again, since she'd left it at school.

Gently, she unfastened the lids and lifted the instruments out.

Placed them side by side on the floor.

Two languages.

You'll be bilingual, Beaufort.

Everything swept back in then, like some overwhelming tidal rush.

Talking with Dr. Nguyen about key changes and tonal colour and rhythm and the alphabets that lay all over the circle of fifths. Debating with Dr. Perlinger about the silent Beloved and what she might say or do if she could. Listening to those beautiful voices in Manifesto.

And Teo.

He would never want to talk to her again, not after what had happened. Not after he'd had to sit with the police and give a statement. Not after he'd learned how dishonest she'd been, how much she had kept from him. Not after he'd watched her be led away in handcuffs.

Iz erupted violently into broken sobs.

"Oh, baby," Pat said, in the doorway.

"It's all over. They won't take me back."

It was like waking up after a terrible, bone-crushing accident you'd caused yourself, and realizing that the new normal was going to be made up of pain and terrible regret. Always asking yourself, what if you'd made a different choice?

"We don't know that, baby. We have to wait and see."

Pat was sitting on the bed beside her now and rubbing her back. Iz's instinct was to edge away, but instead she sat there and just accepted Pat's hand, which was so much more tender than she deserved.

She said, after a while, "I think I'm tired."

"You could have a little nap, honey."

Iz nodded. She crawled into the bed like an animal burrowing underground for safety. Pat tucked the blankets in, tiptoed to the door, closed it behind her.

The next time Iz opened her eyes, late morning sun was shining through the little window over her desk, pooling on the bed. She'd slept all night.

She lay there and gazed at the demarcation between the part of the bed that was illuminated and the part that was not. If tiny creatures lived on that quilt, then those who lived in the sunlit part would imagine that the whole world was sunny, while those outside of that pool of light would think it was always dark. And what an arduous journey it might be to travel from one to the other.

Pat tapped on her door and popped her head around it.

"Iz? Are you awake?"

"Yes," Iz said, keeping her eyes closed.

"Hon, you've slept for over twelve hours! I'm making pancakes. Come on down."

After a while, Iz swung her legs over the side of the bed. She sat there for a long time, wondering if she could face sitting across from Pat and chatting like nothing had happened. But finally, she shuffled down the stairs to the kitchen.

"Sit down, baby."

Pat placed a heaping plate in front of her. There were pancakes and bacon, orange juice, and a cup of tea with milk and sugar.

"And so I printed off some information about your rights. Here it is, hon."

Pat slid the papers toward her anxiously.

"Uh, thanks."

Iz scanned the pages. There were headings like, *Good Care*, *Identity*, *Safety*, *Fairness*, *Your File*, and *Get Help*. And under each title she could see a list of many rights in that category:

You have a right to education that meets your needs.

You have a right to play sports, make art, and do other activities.

You have a right to be told how to appeal your placement if you are unhappy about where you live.

You have a right to have service providers respond to your complaint and try to solve it.

You have a right to not be hit as a punishment.

"Do you want me to read it to you?" Pat asked nervously.

"No." Iz couldn't take her eyes away. "Can I . . . can I have this?"

"You sure can, hon," Pat said. Then her mouth fell open. "I almost forgot, baby. The school called."

Iz looked up, her heart suddenly cold.

"The . . . The *Métier* School?"

"Yes."

"Who was it? What did they want?"

"Hmm," Pat said. "It was the man from the case conference. You know the one. Pearl or something."

"Dr. Perlinger!" She heard herself practically shouting.

"That's right," Pat said placidly. "He said they're having a meeting today with the board of directors. I guess maybe about if they're taking you back, baby?"

Iz swallowed painfully.

At that moment, Britnee walked into the kitchen and started to serve herself pancakes and bacon from the frying pan. "You're not going back. I mean, that's a given."

At the same time, Pat said offhandedly, "Oh, and Mr. and Mrs. Santoro are coming in a few minutes."

Iz practically jumped.

"Uh, here? They—how did they get this address?"

"Honey," Pat said. "We've all been in touch." Gently, she added, "You're going to have to see people again."

But Iz was now trembling uncontrollably. Vito was going to be so angry. And Gisele, who had knitted her mittens and given her dinners and talked Vito into paying union wages—she would see Iz completely differently now.

The doorbell rang.

"I have to go upstairs."

"Sit tight," Pat said. "You can do this, hon."

Iz heard her open the front door, and then the familiar rumble of Vito's voice. She willed herself not to cry.

"Can I take your coats?" Pat said. Then there was the sound of hangers and the closet door closing.

"Please have a seat, make yourself comfortable."

Vito and Gisele were in the living room now. If Iz shifted her chair slightly, she would see them.

"She here?" Vito said after a bit.

Pat said something so quietly Iz didn't hear it.

There were heavy footsteps.

"You planning to come into the living room anytime soon?" Vito said, leaning around the doorway.

"Ha!" Iz said. "Yes! I was just going to."

He pretended to cuff her around the ears as she scrambled to her feet. "Face the music, so to speak."

She stumbled into the room, awkwardly folded herself into the armchair. She couldn't look at anyone.

"I'll get coffee." Pat disappeared into the kitchen.

Vito said at last, "So!"

"So," Iz muttered, looking at her hands.

"I knew you were hiding something. I just didn't know what."

"Okay," Gisele said to him. "Back up." To Iz, she said, "How are you? You look thinner. And tired."

"I just slept, like fourteen hours or something last night."

Gisele nodded. "Not enough. When did you last eat?"

"Five minutes ago."

Iz thought suddenly of Teo's Nonna. Was Gisele anyone's Nonna? She would be excellent—still pretty young, filled with energy, organization, purpose. And she was superb at holding firm with Vito, but in a warm way. Gisele got things done.

What would Iz's life have been like if there had been a Gisele in it all the way through?

No point thinking about that.

Vito said, "I thought you were fifteen, sixteen, maybe even seventeen at least."

"I'll be fifteen in November," Iz said helpfully.

"Right now it's *May.*"

There was a silence.

"So," Gisele said. "What a time you've had, cara."

Iz drew her knees up onto the armchair like she was hiding behind some kind of fortress. She braced herself for the pity.

But Gisele's voice was rebellious, loyal. "You never caught a break. I couldn't believe it, hearing about all those homes, all those schools. And you were trying to take it all into your own hands."

She was like a small, grey, avenging angel. Iz imagined her storming into That Place and cleaning it out.

Gisele went on, "Maybe *I* should be going to jail for saying this, but there's crime and there's crime. When someone like that doctor at the school talks about you like that, about your talent, he's the expert. There's no question in anyone's mind where you belong. Maybe the real crime is that nobody noticed what was in you. Maybe you did exactly the right thing, just not the right way."

She waved her hand as if swiping the charges out of the room. "So as far as I'm concerned, you got a conditional discharge. You're paying back the money and fixing the other things and it's done. Clean slate."

Vito spoke now, gesturing at the kitchen. "So what's this one like? She's got to be some kind of clueless stolta, with you doing all that and her never noticing."

"Vito!" Gisele smacked him.

"Wedding of the century. Every time we talk to her."

Iz resisted the urge to laugh for the first time in ages.

Gisele put a restraining hand on Vito's arm. "So we wanted to tell you, nothing's changed. You sang beautifully before. You sing beautifully now."

"Gisele likes you. The customers like you," Vito said heavily.

Iz waited, holding her breath. She scarcely dared to hope. "You like me," she said when he didn't add that.

Vito waved his hand around. "You brought in business."

"We want you to come back, tesorina mia, if you want to. Where you belong." Gisele's voice was warm.

Iz was silent for a minute.

Then, without even planning to, she jumped out of her chair and flung her arms around them both.

"Well," said Vito. "Well, all right."

"Thank you! I'm going to bring you double the customers!"

"And Teo," Gisele said. "Bring him back too. Such a beautiful voice. A nice boy. They don't come along every day. He's welcome anytime."

"I-I will."

Except Métier was over.

And Teo was a frozen pair of eyes staring through her like she didn't exist.

Chapter Thirty-Seven

After Vito and Gisele left, Iz went upstairs and sat cross-legged on her bed with Teo's guitar. She worked on scales for the whole afternoon, up and down, over and over again. It was soothing, almost meditative, like pacing back and forth.

It helped her pretend that the board of directors was not meeting.

Late in the afternoon, the light in the room vanished. She looked up to discover that grey clouds had smothered the thin sun. Huge flakes were falling thickly and quickly in a final, freak late-spring snowstorm.

Iz dragged her chair in front of the window and leaned on the sill.

The flakes tumbled and lifted in an increasing stream of white. To the untrained eye, it looked like chaos. But Iz imagined that they were chasing each other, in some monumental and infinitely complicated game. Maybe chaos was what you called things you hadn't figured out yet. Then, once you'd learned how to see them, they were more like signposts.

At that moment, something caught her eye.

A car slowed, pulled into Pat's driveway. The lights turned off. Then someone stepped out—an outline of a person scribbled in with snow, pushing against the wind.

The figure began to slide up Pat's front sidewalk. Next, the doorbell pealed out. Voices echoed in the hall.

Pat called, "Iz? Can you come down here? There's someone to see you."

Iz's breath caught in her throat. She managed finally to croak, "C-coming."

She crept softly to the top of the stairs.

"Well, well, there you are!" Dr. Perlinger was looking up at her, shaking snow off his head.

"Huh!" Iz said. Her brain started racing.

Dr. Perlinger was standing in Pat's hallway.

Was that good or bad?

"Come on down, baby," Pat said gently. She took Dr. Perlinger's coat and hung it up in the closet.

Iz crept down the stairs, her limbs all shaky. Dr. Perlinger was smiling at her but something about that smile put every nerve in her on high alert. She had a terrible feeling of foreboding.

"So!" Dr. Perlinger said. "I thought I would come around to see you, to pass on how things went this afternoon."

Iz could hardly breathe. She nodded jerkily.

He said gently, "The board would like you to re-audition with real transcripts and real reference letters. The next round is in June. They also are strongly encouraging you to apply for a scholarship."

There was a silence.

"So—but in the meantime . . ." Iz said, her face going numb.

Even more gently, Dr. Perlinger said, "In the meantime, you will not be a student with us."

Iz stared. She could not think of a thing to say. Her heart felt like it was getting ripped up. Tears seeped into her eyes.

Dr. Perlinger saw it all.

He said, "I know. I am very, very sorry, Iz."

She couldn't answer. It was like she'd forgotten how to use words. She just shrugged and nodded and squished her hands together. She'd done this to herself. It was her own fault.

Pat looked stricken. "It's okay, baby. We can do that. We can order those transcripts. Claudia will organize that for us. And we can get some reference letters for sure."

"I wish I could be one of them," Dr. Perlinger said, in a very kind voice. "But unfortunately you won't be allowed to use any of your Métier teachers. We won't be able to be part of the audition committee either, and we can't coach you for it."

Iz actually felt like she was going to faint. Her legs and feet and fingers and arms were going numb.

"Maybe we could sit down," she heard Dr. Perlinger saying to Pat. And the next thing she knew, she was crouched on the sofa, and he was beside her.

And he was saying something else, something about applying for the scholarship.

"It means filming a concert in front of a live audience. You'll need repertoire from three different time periods and also some original writing. I'd strongly recommend you pursue your ideas about rewriting *Winterreise* from the perspective of the Beloved."

"Uh, what?" Nothing seemed to be going into her head.

"That wild girl who was trapped. Have you thought any more about writing her story?"

Dully, Iz shook her head.

"Well, let's have a look at your notes while I'm here. Go and get them if you want! Let's dig our teeth in and wrestle out some ideas."

He stayed for five hours. And when, at last, well into the evening, he put on his coat and boots to leave, he said kindly, "We will not lose hope, yes? The next auditions are a month away. That's plenty of time for you to write your song cycle, perfect your audition pieces, and plan your scholarship video. But first things first—get your references and transcripts organized."

He made it sound so breezy, so simple.

She whispered, "I don't . . . I don't know anyone who can write me a reference letter."

"Nonsense!" Dr. Perlinger looked appalled. "What about the two men from the case conference?"

"Vito and Jamaal?"

"Of course!"

That reminded her about the totally unexpected moment when Jamaal had suddenly stood up.

Dr. Perlinger grinned, as if he knew what she was thinking.

"You tipped me off to Jamaal Wickerson, by the way."

"I-I did?"

He nodded. "At the entrance audition, you said he was your teacher. Now, mind you, I wasn't sure whether that was true, but I reached out to the university just in case. And he remembered you immediately. He was extremely eager to help."

"Thank you," she whispered.

He half bowed. "Keep the faith, Iz Beaufort. I'll see you at your scholarship concert."

"Y-you're allowed to be there?"

Dr. Perlinger smiled. "Anyone can be an audience member, surely?"

Then he went out into the melting spring snow, and Iz had to close the door.

She gathered up all her notes and took them upstairs to her room. The great pain, that had been waiting until she was alone, erupted at last.

She sobbed into her pillow, with her knees drawn up.

Chapter Thirty-Eight

Two days later, Iz walked into the classroom at her old school.

It was one of the hardest things she had ever done. She crept to the seat Mr. Bains pointed out and slipped into it. She tried not to notice how everyone was staring at her.

Especially Audra Allen, who had a look of fascinated curiosity on her face.

Iz tried to force The Métier School out of her mind because she might lose it right here otherwise. But her brain kept whispering that, right now, she should have been in Guitar with Dr. Nguyen, working on the new Bach prelude they had begun. And after that, she'd have gone to Voice, exploring how to blend a classical sound with her own way of singing. And in her tutoring session with Dr. Perlinger, she'd have wrestled with her writing about the Beloved.

And there would have been Teo.

Those dancing eyes and that stellar grin lighting up a room—they burst into her memory like a supernova. She could picture him loping down the hallway, taller than everyone, hair bouncing everywhere, carrying on fifteen whirlwind conversations. She could hear him calling her *Beaufort* in that resonant voice that sounded like he really saw her or something.

Grief ripped through her all over again as she remembered his eyes looking blankly through her, like she had stopped existing for him.

Someone poked her hard.

Audra Allen said, "Where've *you* been?"

"I've been in jail." Her voice blasted into the air, channeling all her heartbreak into belligerence.

The whole room fell silent.

It was actually quite funny watching Audra Allen's face transform. First she looked astonished. Then, her eyes narrowed. "No you weren't."

"Yes, I was. For larceny and identity theft and theft under five thousand dollars and falsification of documents and a bunch of other stuff."

"I don't believe you."

"You want me to call the judge?"

"Okay, okay," Mr. Bains was saying.

Iz was shaking. Weirdly, it was like her old self was waking up, the one who couldn't handle frustrations except by shoving people, the one who disrupted stupid clubs by being as sarcastic as possible and slammed doors so hard they shattered.

That other, rude Iz began to take over.

She said, "But before I was in jail, I auditioned and I got into The Métier School. You know, because I'm so good at *humming.* Go tell your friends. We could meet at my locker later."

Mr. Bains said, standing right over them now, "Okay, girls, let's get ready!"

Iz took out her things and slammed them on her desk. Suddenly she didn't care at all how any of this would go. She didn't care if she got suspended again.

Then an uncanny thing happened. It was almost as if she heard Dr. Perlinger's voice.

Summon that terrific audition. You are a force.

Her heart felt like it flipped over.

She kept banging things around, but now she was imagining him looking at her, seeing the best in her. Expecting it.

And she was remembering that second day at Métier when she had sat with her knees drawn up outside his office, unable to knock. Everything had gone wrong. Her strings had been out of order. She had not known how to sing properly. She'd failed a theory placement test and bombed at Music History trivia.

Dr. Perlinger had sat down beside her. He'd smoothed it over. He'd told her how Schubert had fought to get into a music school. He'd pointed out that it was okay not to know yet how things were going to go.

What would Dr. Perlinger say to her right now if he were here?

Maybe he'd say, "You're just like Schubert. He went to jail too."

She had to stifle the laughter that barked out of her mouth.

Everyone was looking at her again.

"Sorry," Iz said. "Just had to cough."

She sat there then, picturing Schubert in the back of a police car wearing handcuffs. Going into a case conference. Getting sentenced.

It got funnier and funnier.

And Iz got giddier and giddier.

At last, she pulled out the tablet that Dr. Perlinger had forgotten to take back from her when he came to the house.

She typed in, "Schubert, jail."

Then the ragged laughter turned to astonishment.

"Holy—!" She heard a series of totally inappropriate things coming out of her mouth.

"Isabelle!" Mr. Bains' voice was louder but also a little anxious.

"Sorry, sorry," Iz said.

"If you can't be quiet, you'll have to head to the office. And I *really* don't want to send you there again. I want you here."

"I'll be quiet."

She slid down in her chair. She waited until Mr. Bains had gone on to something else.

Then she started to click on the hundreds of links about how Schubert had *actually been arrested.*

He'd been hanging out in a tavern with a group of young revolutionaries. They'd wanted to get rid of the harsh government of the day, the Metternich regime. They'd been determined to change the laws. Then the police had raided the place, rounded everyone up, and thrown them in prison.

Iz was blowing out breath slowly, shaking her head with astonishment.

Nobody knew for sure if he had been working with those young revolutionaries. Maybe he'd just been socializing with them for the day.

But maybe—just maybe—he hadn't been happy accepting the way things were. Maybe he'd raged against unfairness while keeping it a secret. Maybe he'd had a lot of secrets—even a double life, like Iz.

She wished Dr. Perlinger was here so she could talk to him about it.

No, more than that. She wished she could *reach out* and Dr. Perlinger and Schubert could reach back. She imagined their hands gripping in a unified trio.

While the class got ready for math, Iz opened a new, blank document on her tablet. She slouched down in her seat like Dr. Perlinger.

It was time to write the rest of her song cycle.

Chapter Thirty-Nine

By the time she left school, she had finished the second song, "Waking."

When she got home, she sat in her room plucking out the terse melody, experimenting with an accompaniment that—like the Beloved—was hardly even there at the beginning of the song. Iz plucked out scattered notes that were like the faltering breath of someone who had nearly given up. Then she started to pile musical lines on top of each other, like resentment growing. Finally, she built the accompaniment to a howling roar as the Beloved decided she wasn't going to live like this anymore.

As she wrote, Iz tried to tune out the arguing voices downstairs that bumped and groaned. Britnee was trying to get Vance to settle on glassware while Pat anxiously interrupted. Same old, same old.

After dinner, Pat drove her to Festa.

On the way, she said, "Oh, hon, Claudia called. She's set up the therapy. Third Friday of June is the first one."

"Oh! Great!" Iz stammered.

She sat there absolutely quietly, like it was nothing.

But a kind of cold dread fingered its way through her. She'd been trying not to think about the psychologist. She'd been hoping they wouldn't make her go there after all. Because the psychologist would figure out in about two minutes just how messed up Iz was. And who knew what would happen after that?

Pat pulled up in front of Festa.

"Thanks," Iz said, her voice mostly steady.

"No problem, baby. I'll be here at nine."

She climbed out of the car and waved as Pat drove off. Then she stood alone outside the restaurant, trying to calm the panic.

"Well, well, look what the wind blew in." Vito was holding the door open for her.

"Thanks," she said awkwardly, walking inside.

"Don't mention it." He was frowning down at her. "Gisele made acqua pazza. Come into the kitchen."

"What's acqua pazza?"

He looked at her sidelong. "Crazy water."

"Huh," Iz said.

With a guitar in each hand, she followed him across the still-empty restaurant and through the swinging doors at the back into the large kitchen where the sous chefs were busy and Gisele was peering into a huge steaming pot.

"Cara!" she said, when she saw Iz. "Sit down, sit down."

"I hear you're making crazy water," Iz said. She sat at the long wooden table.

"Haha! Crazy!" Gisele said.

"Like some kids I know." Vito seated himself heavily across from Iz.

Here it came.

"Imagine if you took that brain and actually used it for something good. Not breaking the law, stealing, lying."

"Yes," she said humbly. There was no point in arguing.

"Nobody taught her right from wrong," Vito told Gisele accusingly.

Iz muttered, "Well, that's not *quite* true. I'm not, you know, some rabid animal."

"Could have fooled me," Vito growled. "Tell me something you've learned through all this."

She blinked at him. "I learned that Schubert got arrested."

Vito let out a long, exasperated breath. "You and me, we're going to be working on a few moral lessons."

Gisele spooned something into a bowl and brought it over to her.

Iz peered down into it. "It doesn't look so crazy to me."

There were pieces of fish, with carrots and celery, peppers, olives, and tomatoes. It looked and smelled delicious, actually.

Gisele said, "Fishermen in the old days, they used to poach fish in salt water from the Mediterranean Sea, because salt was so expensive. Which turned that ordinary old seawater into a beautiful broth. Here, bread to do scarpetta."

She brought a bowl for Vito too, and one for herself. Then the three sat down and had soup together. They wiped the bowls with the bread.

It felt natural, like they were all linked together.

Iz said finally, "I wanted to tell you something."

"Oh, Jesus, what now?" Vito said.

She was squeezing her hands so hard they hurt. "Métier kicked me out. I have to re-audition."

Gisele reached out and took her hand. "We know."

Iz didn't bother to ask how they knew. The unseen network of information was clearly alive and well.

She said, "I need two letters of reference. And ... and Dr. Perlinger said I should ask if you might be willing to be one of them. I need it by next Friday."

"Hmm," Vito said.

Seeing his grim face, she began to babble. "I also have to apply for a scholarship. I have to make a recording of at least twenty minutes of me performing in front of an audience. Dr. P wants me to write something original, so I'm doing a song cycle, but I don't have a name for it yet ..."

Finally she wound down under Vito's intimidating glower.

"You finished?" he said.

Iz drooped. "I'm finished."

Vito rubbed his chin and grimaced up at the ceiling. "We can write the letter, no problem."

Relief flooded her.

"But where are you going to do this concert?"

"Well," said Iz, "I don't know yet."

Gisele said, "You could do it here."

"Oh!" She gaped in astonishment. "No, I—"

Vito growled, "All the regulars, they'd come. And your friends, anyone else you want. We could make it a real event."

"We could have a special menu," Gisele said. "Think about it."

Vito got up abruptly and walked out of the kitchen. A minute later, he returned with a big book, slammed it on the table, muttered to himself, turned the pages. "You don't have to submit the scholarship video at the audition, right? You can do it, say, a week later?"

She blinked, completely overwhelmed, unable to process any of it. "Uh, I think so."

"Your audition is the third Saturday in June. So how about the scholarship concert is a week later? Say, the following Sunday afternoon?"

"Uh yes, I think that's ... that's good."

"Done," Vito said. "Now, get out there and do some singing."

Out in the main restaurant, there was her old stool set up for her. A few customers had arrived now, and some of them recognized her.

"Iz! Where've you been?"

She said shyly, "It's a long story. I'm just glad to be back."

Then she lifted up her guitar, let out a long, slow, cleansing breath. She looked around the familiar restaurant, tried to push all the darker, paralyzing thoughts out of her head.

She began to play.

Then Teo Russo walked in the door.

Chapter Forty

Iz stared down at her guitar immediately. She kept playing. She did not have the nerve to glance up again.

His sneakers came into her line of sight. She heard the scrape of a chair. Then he sat down. After a minute, he poked his shoe against hers. Instinctively, she moved her foot away.

A long silence went by while she kept plucking tunes.

Softly, finally, he said, "Hey!"

"Hey," Iz said, still looking down.

Then Vito appeared out of nowhere. "Look at this, the two troublemakers together again! Here, Gisele made you this."

Iz couldn't help peeking up. Vito placed a little plate of sfogliatelle on the table.

He had known Teo was coming.

Teo held the plate out to her. "Want one?"

"I'm playing right now," she said tightly, hardly able to get the words out of her anxious throat.

He laughed out loud, startling her. "Beaufort, I absolutely do not want to interrupt your performance."

She kept on playing, trying to ignore the fact that he was sitting right there beside her. But after several minutes, it started to get a little weird. Finally she fashioned a lingering cadence and let her hands drop.

People in the restaurant clapped.

Iz nodded around at them, smiling a little.

"Now?" Teo said. He held out the plate again.

Iz sighed. Finally she took one of the little shell-like pastries with ricotta cheese and dried fruit inside. She looked at it for a minute and at last bit into the flaky crust. It tasted like Christmas morning or something. They sat there together and munched in silence.

"How are you?" Teo said at last.

"Fabulous," Iz said tensely.

As he waited, she added, "Well, actually, things are a little up in the air right now."

"Yeah, I know."

Iz shivered slightly.

She waited for him to tell her how he couldn't forgive her for what she had done. How he saw her differently now. How he was just here to basically let her know how worthless she was.

But instead he said, "I'm ... I'm sorry, Beaufort."

Iz blinked. "What are *you* sorry about?"

Teo's rich voice rose slightly. "I mean ..." He started tossing the last piece of the sfogliatelle in his hand up in the air and catching it again. "You must have been so scared all the time trying to make everything work."

"Well, yes," Iz said. "That's what happens when you're committing crimes."

Teo went on like he didn't hear her. "And it kills me, thinking about how you were in foster homes and getting moved around and stuff. I mean, I keep wishing I could have been there, just ... watching out or something. Helping."

Then, he straightened up awkwardly, as if he felt he'd gone too far. "As your student mentor, obviously."

Iz digested these words. "Obviously," she said, at a loss.

He was skirting so close to That Place. It was like he could sense it there, that dark thing that couldn't be translated into words. Not yet, anyway.

Finally she whispered, "I thought you hated me."

"Hated you?" His voice sounded confused.

"That day. When I told you everything. And then we walked back to Métier."

"I didn't hate you!"

"Your face did."

Tears sprang into her eyes. She blinked and squeezed them shut, willing them to stop.

"Ah, Beaufort," Teo said softly.

There was a silence while she wiped her eyes with her forearm.

At last he said, "I just wanted to get you back there in one piece. I was just focused on that. And I was slightly in shock, I guess. I'm sorry."

She shrugged and nodded.

Then he added, "But let's talk about the elephant in the room. Why are you constantly judging my face, Beaufort? The eye thing or whatever. You have a problem, seriously."

She looked right at him then, to see if he was angry. But his eyes were full of laughter.

So she said, "*You're* the one with the problem. Shining your teeth at everyone like they're lightbulbs."

"So now my *teeth?*" He burst out laughing with that toffee voice. "What wattage of lightbulb are we talking exactly?"

"A thousand."

He shook his head at her with a wry grin. "Beaufort, welcome back. I've missed the constant insults."

Then they were both suddenly quiet, thinking about why she had not been there insulting him. About courts and crimes and judges.

And after awhile, Teo said, "So what happened, you know, after they . . .?"

Her stomach clenched, as she remembered walking past him in handcuffs.

"Uh . . . well, you know, I went to this Maplewood Youth Detention Centre place at first, because they didn't have any space for me anywhere with Dominion Children's Care. And then later they found a spot in a group home while I was awaiting sentencing. I basically had a lock on my door, and I had school at the kitchen table. And now I'm back with Pat, because she wanted me even after everything. And I still am not quite sure why. I think she wants a do-over or something." She winced then, hearing the callousness in her voice. "I mean, she is pretty kind too. So it's okay. Better than a lot of places. It's basically good. They're checking up on us a lot."

She paused.

"And if I make everything right, then I get my record cleared in a year."

"Okay then," Teo said softly, "You'll make everything right."

She couldn't resist seeing what his face was doing. But he was just gazing back at her with those confident, tawny eyes. Like he had faith in her, despite everything.

He went on, "And in the meantime, you're re-auditioning. And you're doing a scholarship concert. And you're going to write a song cycle about the Beloved from *Winterreise*."

"Wow. Everybody knows everything."

He was smiling now. "If you wanted to keep a low profile, you should probably have gone about things a little differently."

"Yeah, probably."

Weird joy erupted in her for the first time in ages. The day might have begun with horrible Audra Allen, but it was ending with Teo Russo, and miraculously he didn't hate her after all. The two sides of her life were now aware of each other, and the world had not ended.

Just then, Teo straightened and waved cheerfully. "Hey! Over here!"

Iz turned to look at who he was talking to.

Her mouth dropped open.

Jasleen and LaRoyce and Bijan had just come strolling in the front door.

Jasleen ran over, leaned down, and wrapped Iz in an actual hug. Iz found, to her surprise, that she didn't mind so very much.

Jasleen said warmly, "I have been thinking about you so much. Worrying about where you were. I'm so glad to see you."

Iz flushed. She thought about how angry she'd been when she saw Teo fall into Jasleen's lap and their silly banter after. Now she saw how generous Jasleen was.

"Thank you," she whispered.

Then Ahmed and Will and Kwame walked in, with Rina and Becky coming in behind them. They looked around, saw Teo waving, and jogged over too. Kwame squatted down beside her so he could look her in the face. "Hey. You good? We missed you."

"We're set up in the back room. Follow me." Vito was striding toward them through the restaurant, hand up to acknowledge them all.

Iz frowned up at Teo. "What exactly is going on here?"

"We're going to the back room," he said. "Follow Vito. Bring all your stuff."

Then he picked up most of it himself—her guitar case and tablet and notebook—and began walking after the rest of them. After a minute of utter confusion, Iz gripped her guitar and followed.

She'd never actually been in the back room. It was for private parties. Sometimes people celebrated a birthday in there or a confirmation or an anniversary or a christening.

When she walked in, Gisele was bustling around putting snacks everywhere. And everyone was sitting down around a large rectangular table.

Iz stared, completely confused. What was going on? Why were they all here?

"Are you going to join us?" Teo said. His eyes were dancing.

"Not till you tell me what's happening."

They all looked at each other, grinning.

Bijan said, "Dr. P mentioned you were going to be writing a song cycle for the scholarship concert."

Rina added, "So we wanted to know if you wanted a sounding board."

"We're good listeners." Kwame smiled at her.

"Do you have anything written yet?" Jasleen asked.

Iz gaped. Her brain felt like it was running to catch up.

"We promise not to be all banal and complimentary," Rina said. "If it's bad, we'll rip it to shreds."

"That's comforting," Iz said.

They all burst out laughing.

Dr. Perlinger's words shot into her memory then, what he'd said about Manifesto. *None of us operates alone. We inspire each other. We look after each other. We encourage each other. We are all interconnected.*

She said shyly, "I just finished the second song. It … it's called 'Waking.'"

Their eyes lit up generously.

"Can we hear it?"

Iz found herself fumbling in her guitar case for her notebook. She put it on the table, opened to the right page. "It's just rough."

She could not look at them as, blushing furiously, she began to pick out the heartbroken opening notes.

In the village
The dogs are barking
Daring me to fight off the fog of sleep

I cover up my ears and eyes
But still their barking pierces through
Makes me long to explode the skies
Shatter the sun
Turn and run
Leave the rich man at the altar
And slam the door

My limbs are burning
My heart's untamed
Like a chain snapping
Like a leaf ripping free

Bark away, you watchdogs!
I am awake
Dreaming done
And so—
I will go!

When she had smashed out those last, harsh chords, she put her hands down. There was a short silence.

Then Manifesto erupted with supportive excitement.

"The imagery, the way you've woven parts of *Winterreise* into it—"

"The dogs in the village—"

"Burning limbs—"

"I am done with dreaming—"

"The leaf on the branch—"

"Apocalyptic," Bijan declared. "The end of the world. Destruction of the old earth. Ushering in a new era with new ways."

Iz gaped. "That's exactly what Dr. P said!"

Jasleen's voice rang out then. "But to put it over the top, you may want to come up with a more complex arrangement. Not just guitar and solo voice."

"Uh, like what?"

"Choral parts? Maybe orchestration?" She looked around the table. "I mean, what instruments do *we* play?"

Everyone started talking at once. It turned out that they played a lot of instruments.

"If you need us—"

"We'd be happy to support by performing orchestral parts—"

"We could *sing*—like, provide splashes of homophony and polyphony against the melody—"

"Only if you want—"

Iz was overwhelmed, thinking about the possibilities. They were right. It would make her song cycle really huge, competitive, hard to ignore. Even the most hardened member of the scholarship committee would have to pay attention.

But first she had to admit something out loud to the members of Manifesto sitting there.

"I-I—my music education is pretty nonexistent. I don't know how to play any instruments except my own guitar, pretty much. And I play it totally wrong. Also, I barely know how to read music."

Jasleen grabbed some manuscript paper. "So let's talk about how to write a score. Then you can start thinking about if you would want to use different combinations of instruments or voices to create different effects."

They all leaned in, taking turns sharing about their oboe, flute, violin, cello and everything else they played.

And after awhile, Iz's brain began racing.

Brass, Woodwind, String, Percussion.

What if you added voices for rocks, trees, graveyards—

Instrumental voices, human voices—the world beginning to speak—?

There must be some kind of an app that would allow her to hear different instruments together while she was at home writing. A clarinet and a violin, for example. How was that different from an oboe and a flute? And what if you combined them all and you added in a double bass and a French horn?

Perhaps at first only her own voice would be heard, maybe fumbling out a thin duet with an oboe. But then she would bring in other orchestral colours and textures. Strings, maybe warm horns. Definitely guitar, acoustic and electric. A shower of barely brushed percussion.

Everything—everyone—included. No one left outside looking in.

She imagined Dr. Perlinger smiling with satisfaction.

Chapter Forty-One

The next morning, Iz took her guitar to school. When lunchtime came, she waited until everyone had finished eating and was walking outside. Then she snuck the guitar out of her locker and slipped into an empty classroom.

She sat cross-legged on one of the desks, working through the second song, thinking about some of Manifesto's ideas.

"What are you doing?"

A group of girls was peering in at the door. Audra Allen was at the front.

"None of your business," Iz said.

"You're going to get in trouble."

Iz didn't answer. Instead she put her fingers in position, gazed at them all standing there. Then she started ripping out the wildest, loudest chords she could.

She was *done.* She was going to perform a scholarship concert with Manifesto. The world had entirely changed in a day.

A voice called, "Everyone outside! The bell rang."

The girls all turned to look down the hall.

"Then *she* has to go too," Audra called back, gesturing at Iz.

Heels clacked closer. A teacher appeared in the doorway. She was frowning.

But when she saw Iz sitting there, her face changed, got cautious and careful, like she'd been warned about her. Like Iz was a bomb waiting to go off. Which made sense. After all, Iz had been suspended from this school twice and she'd been kicked out of Métier. And then there was obviously the whole court thing, which the teachers probably all knew about. She was an unpredictable, damaged, scarred foster kid.

Iz sat there glaring back. She did not feel like going anywhere.

Audra Allen and the rest waited with interest for what would come next.

"Hey," the teacher said. "That sounded amazing."

Iz blinked. She shrugged. She didn't trust the teacher's friendly words for even a minute. This was some kind of ploy, like enticing an animal into a crate.

"Would you play me something else?" the teacher said.

"Yeah, no, I don't think I feel like it."

The girls were waiting for Iz to get yelled at for being rude. But instead, the teacher came all the way into the room and sat down at a desk nearby.

"Please?" she said.

Iz frowned.

Finally she decided to call the teacher's bluff.

She ambushed the strings. She pounded, scraped, detonated the classroom. It was the second song, "Waking."

When she was done, she let her hands fall at last. She scowled up at them all.

Audra's mouth was hanging open.

After a long silence, the teacher said quietly, "Thank you for playing that. What is it from?"

"Uh, I wrote it."

The teacher looked astonished. "You wrote it?"

Iz shrugged.

"What's it about?"

Iz frowned. She was tempted to say it was none of the teacher's business, but something in her decided to answer. And as she began to talk, the teacher looked so interested that she kept going. Gradually, everything came out. Manifesto. Schubert. Dr. Perlinger. Rewriting *Winterreise.*

When she was done, she just sat there.

She'd just told them exactly who she was, and she didn't actually care what they thought. It was a slightly weird feeling.

The teacher said at last, "I have an idea. Something that might interest you."

Iz stiffened.

She said sharply, "I'm not going back to the Great Expectations Club."

"No, no, not that!" the teacher said. She looked over Iz's head like she was seeing something that wasn't there anymore. "The music program here is a shadow of what it was. Cutbacks. I remember when we had four choirs and a band and an orchestra."

"Okay," Iz said, after awhile.

"I know there are a bunch of guitars in storage somewhere. They haven't been used in years. If I organized everything, would you consider teaching a few of the kids?"

Iz's eyes widened.

"Me?"

"They'd love it. I'd love it. I'd supervise. I'm Ms. Walters by the way."

Iz looked down at her guitar. "Um, I'm just starting to learn the proper way to play."

"It sounded pretty proper to me," said Ms. Walters.

"Yeah, well, it's not. This guitar has strings in the wrong places. I made it up. It's like my own language."

Then she thought about Teo. She thought about Dr. Perlinger. She thought about Jamaal.

They would probably all tell her to do it.

"I … I have another guitar though." She paused awkwardly. "I'm just a beginner on it."

"They'd be beginners too," Ms. Walters said.

Iz stared down at her hands.

"I don't know. Maybe," she said.

"Come with me," said Ms. Walters. "Let's go find them. And the rest of you girls head outside."

So Iz and the teacher ended up walking along the corridor together, till they arrived at a dusty room filled with bins and boxes.

Ms. Walters began lifting things out of the way. "They're in here somewhere."

At last, behind mounds of old math textbooks, there they were, all squished up against the wall like prisoners. Iz imagined them waiting patiently for years, hoping someone might come along, trying not to lose faith.

"Here," said Ms. Walters, passing her one. "What do you think?"

Iz sat down on a green bin. She unclasped the case and lifted out the little guitar inside.

She plucked a string. It was woefully out of tune, like a kind of metallic groan.

"Ha!" Iz said to it. "Poor you."

She bent her head and listened to the right pitches in her head. Gradually, painstakingly, she turned the tuning pegs and plucked gently, until the strings came back to themselves.

Then she played a G chord gently.

It filled the storage room like a sigh.

Like exhaling at last.

Chapter Forty-Two

After school, Iz walked over to Phil's Music Store. The little bell jingled as she opened the door and stepped over the threshold.

It was weird to be here. She hadn't ever expected to return.

Jamaal was at the cash register with a customer. He glanced up, saw Iz, and his face transformed into a grin. He raised his index finger to say she should give him one minute.

She nodded and half waved back.

Then she wandered behind the shelves where he'd caught her six months ago. Gazing at the titles, she thought about what an uphill battle it had been to learn those vocalises and songs and scales and arpeggios. She remembered how the intense desire for Métier, for Manifesto, had been straining inside her like a victim trying to break free from bonds.

"Iz! What a wonderful surprise."

He was there then, as gentle and warm and open as that first day. He held his arms out to her, and after a minute, she actually reached out too, and they hugged.

She said, haltingly, "I never came back. I-I'm sorry."

"But better late than never, right?"

They headed over to the bench by the gleaming racks of guitars, where they had sat on that other day.

"Tell me everything. Tell me about Métier," he said.

So she did. Rehearsals and classes—and tutoring sessions with Dr. Perlinger.

Jamaal said enthusiastically, "Aaron Perlinger gets written up in journals because of this amazing stuff he's doing with his students. You landed in a good place."

"I know," Iz said, feeling a rush of gratitude. "And you helped me get there. I never really thanked you, so I wanted to thank you now." She glanced sideways at him, kind of scared to be so frank and honest. "And to thank you for being there at, you know, the case conference."

He shook his head. "Nothing to thank."

There was a short pause.

Iz said softly, "Métier kicked me out."

He was nodding. "But you'll get back."

"I don't know. I feel like they will be expecting a lot more this time."

"And you can give them a lot more," Jamaal said. "If you want help, I'm here."

Unexpectedly, she found grateful tears rushing into her eyes. She wiped them away. "Ah, this is what happened last time. I'm such an idiot."

He fished out a tissue and passed it over. "It's like the heart revealing itself, you know? The right person gets it. Soul to soul communication."

Iz nodded and snuffled, thinking about how this was exactly right. "I-I was wondering if you would be one of my references?"

He looked at her as if she were crazy. "Already written. Just tell me where to submit it and we're good."

Iz shook her head. She should have known.

"Do you know about my song cycle too?" she asked. "The one I'm writing for the scholarship concert?"

"I heard there might be one in the works. Sing me part of it?"

So Iz drew out her beloved old guitar and tuned it in her idiosyncratic way. She caught Jamaal grinning at her as she did it.

She said, "You *knew* my strings were all wrong. You didn't say anything!"

"Yeah, but I also knew your musicality was going to speak for itself. Everything else is convention anyway. Convention needs to get shaken up every once in a while."

His eyes softened.

"Like the song you sang me that day, 'Refugee.' Deciding to be homeless rather than bound to something that doesn't work. 'I will not walk the roads you choose for me. I'm running from you, and I am a joyful refugee.'"

She was amazed. "How did you remember that?"

"Because I loved it."

She sucked in her breath.

That was Jamaal's gift, she decided. He was totally unafraid of speaking from his heart. Soul to soul communication, that was him.

"I was so lucky you were here that day," she said.

"*We* were so lucky, kid."

She ran her fingers over the strings then.

"So this is the third song. It's called 'Destruction.'"

I explode the bars
Blast out the walls
And then I stand in the frozen air
See the frost smothering everywhere
Holding the river prisoner
And shackling the trees in frost

Well, this prisoner shall be unbound
So I tear the mantle of heaven down
Carve my name on the anchoring ice
Hurl my two eyes into the skies
Then three suns burn the frozen ground
And with their triple heat and rage
Force the ice to drown

The old world melts and starts to flow
Water's weeping through the snow

Frost gives way to fledgling green
The gash of glaciers slowly heals
Old world smashed
New world being born
Future is unseen

When she was finished, she put her hands down at her side and just waited.

Jamaal was quiet for a minute. Then he said, "It's you, right? This is about everything that's happened."

She frowned. "Well, it's about the Beloved, from *Winterreise.* How she got trapped in what society expected for her but then refused to accept it. And she fought to escape, so she could be free on her own terms. And she created a disaster in the process. An apocalypse. But then, it paved the way for a new beginning."

He smiled at her, his head tilted to one side. "Yeah, okay. The Beloved."

He made them tea in the back. Then they chatted companionably for over two hours, alternating between sitting on the couch and at one of the pianos. Every so often, Jamaal jumped up to serve a customer, before bounding back and settling down again.

They talked about writing, about Jamaal's studies at the university, about his band the Wickerson Trio, about songs he thought she would like. They sang and played, he on the piano and Iz on her guitar. They improvised around each other, and it was brilliant to go back and forth with someone who could string notes together like she did. He invited her to come and perform with him at one of his gigs.

At last, the light outside began to transform into early evening.

"I've got to get home," Iz said regretfully. "Pat'll have dinner ready."

At the doorway, she added softly, "Thanks again. Actually, I think I'll just keep saying it over and over, because it's never going to be enough."

His eyes were warm. "Just do some good writing. And be open, you know? Soak in every experience. Pass it on. Build someone. That's it."

Then she was off and running through the soft spring evening, guitar slung over her back, feeling like anything was possible.

But when she entered Pat's house, she could tell right away that something was wrong.

"Hon, it completely throws off the seating in the church. And I have to redo all the table assignments." Britnee's voice was rasping with emotion. "Honestly, I think it's actually really rude of them. Like, how can a *single one* not be coming?"

Then Pat's voice quavered out. "Now, now, we can solve this. We don't need bride's and groom's sides in the church. It would be nice and friendly to just sit wherever."

Her words ran down to silence.

Then Iz heard Britnee croak in a shattered halftone, "And *you*—you won't even *talk* about anything. You just sit there like a lump. And I try and I try—"

There was a silence.

Britnee shouted, "Say something!"

Iz's hands were fists pounding on the sides of her head, trying to shut it out.

She ran up the stairs to her room.

The fighting and the wrangling and Pat bleating at everyone—she was so tired of it.

Chapter Forty-Three

As the days passed, Iz completed the application for her audition, Claudia organized the transcripts, and Vito and Jamaal submitted their reference letters.

Then Iz started practising again for that moment when she would walk into the big old room and stand before that jury. She and Jamaal had decided she'd perform the same pieces as before but include things she'd learned in the last six months—like adding some German in "The Erlking," and incorporating Dr. Henderson's techniques while singing. As well, she'd add in the Bach prelude that she and Dr. Nguyen had been working on right before everything had come tumbling down. She would use Teo's guitar for that.

She also wrote furiously.

And she met with Manifesto several more times in the back room at Festa. While they munched on arancini or bruschetta, she gained the confidence to ask them question after question. Every time they answered, it felt like her brain stretched a bit more.

On the day that her whole song cycle was finished, she handed out musical scores to everyone. They moved the table back, set up their instruments, and waited.

But her courage failed her as she looked at them all.

Who was she to conduct Manifesto?

"Huh," she said, her face going numb. "I don't—I'm not sure—maybe this isn't—"

Teo's voice rang out. "Beaufort, you've got this."

She gulped, nodded, tried to absorb a little of his confidence. "Okay. I . . . I will sing the opening line, and then at bar sixteen we'll bring in first sopranos."

After that, weirdly, it was like a lot of the trappings fell away and it was just a bunch of minds all focused on the same music.

"Iz, at bar sixty-four, do you want the oboe to come in stronger if it's picking up the melody there?"

"With the reprise of the wandering motif, what tempo do you want?"

"I was wondering if you want a pause in the violins after the third iteration of the graveyard theme before you go into the transition to 'Waking'?"

She was even more amazed at how confidently she answered, how much she felt in control of her writing, how easily and passionately she could converse about it with people who were as invested in getting it right as she was—and how much better the music was after they had all talked it through.

They were all involved in the planning of the concert too.

It started one late-May evening, when Teo came strolling in the door of Festa, wind blown and all cheerful high energy. He strode over to her stool, where she was gently playing a version of "Torna a Surriento."

"Hey, Beaufort." He slung his coat over the back of a chair. "Don't let anyone steal it. See you in a minute."

"Where are you going?" she said.

"Talk to Vito."

"What for?"

"Concert logistics."

"Shouldn't I be in on that?"

"No," Teo said teasingly. "Leave it to the professionals."

"Um, it's *my concert*."

He laughed out loud. "Vito just wanted to know what equipment we'd be bringing. So I was talking to everyone and I think we've got access to a soundboard and a couple of mics, and LaRoyce's dad might be able to loan us some lights from the university. And Becky's going to bring her keyboard. That's all."

She was frowning at him.

He raised his eyebrows at her.

"I do not," said Iz, "like people making decisions without me."

"Not even about a mic stand?"

"No."

When he saw that she was serious, he nodded. "Okay. Understood. Hey, should we have a committee then? Concert planning kind of thing."

"That," Iz said, "would be acceptable."

So Teo put out a call for anyone interested. A couple days later, they arranged a meeting at Festa after school.

Once everyone had arrived, Gisele drew out a paper.

"Here's the menu I'm thinking of. Four courses." She passed it around. "But it's optional of course. People can just come and listen for free too. We'll set up chairs. And we'll have a special arrangement for Métier students."

Vito was writing in a notebook.

"We'll advertise there will be, what, a one o'clock seating for food, followed by recording the concert at say two-thirty. People can reserve their spot in advance, either for the meal and concert or just the concert. And let's say we set it at forty each for the meal, beverages extra, which is a bargain." He loomed at Iz suddenly. "We'll split it down the middle, you get half. Pay back what you owe. Fill up those bank accounts you stole from."

It got silent for a minute.

"Technically, I only stole from one of them," Iz said in a tiny voice.

Vito glowered around the table at everyone. "Next?"

LaRoyce and Bijan looked at each other. They started talking more or less at the same time.

"We've been thinking it would be cool to do kind of a social media campaign—"

"Twitter, Instagram—"

"—Link it to Iz's website and Festa's website and people could reserve their place online. They could pay in advance for the meal—"

"—And we'd make some short videos of rehearsals, interview different people, record some clips, kind of show the process of getting it ready—"

"—Post them on YouTube, websites about upcoming events—"

She sat and watched it all, feeling completely overwhelmed. It was too much. After everything she had done, all the lies and the sneaking around, they should have rejected her. But instead they were all here trying to make her scholarship concert as perfect as it could be.

Bijan was gazing at her quietly. He caught her eye and smiled. "You know what this is? This is a Schubertiade."

"What's that?" Iz said.

"Schubert's friends used to organize special parties for him, Schubertiaden, where people would pay to listen to him perform his latest works."

"Well," Iz said. "I'm definitely not Schubert."

"No," he said gently. "But we *are* your friends."

"Oh, that reminds me," Teo said. "My Nonna wants you to come over for dinner."

Iz jumped, utterly startled.

"What for?"

Teo's eyes were dancing. "I played her some videos from your website. She says you have the voice of an angel. I think she wants us to sing duets for her."

"Why would you even do that?"

Vito was looking from one to the other. "Sure. She can go," he said. "I'll drive her."

Iz spread her arms in protestation and shook her head at Teo, who was laughing outright.

It was like getting ambushed. Like she was being moulded into some new version of herself.

And it was happening at the public school too.

Ms. Walters went ahead with planning the guitar club. She made some announcements over the PA system, reserved space in the library, and organized kids to put up posters advertising it. And after Ms. Walters and the special education teacher and Mr. Bains all talked together, Mr. Bains started giving her some regular class time to research guitar pedagogy and figure out how she was going to go about teaching the concepts.

Iz said to Ms. Walters anxiously, "I might not be here that long. I mean, if I get back in to Métier. Although I probably won't . . ."

Ms. Walters smiled reassuringly. "You've inspired me to get out my old guitar too. If this thing catches on, I will take up your mantle and keep it going."

Then the day came when Iz took Teo's guitar to school. She walked into the library, where chairs were already set up in a circle. She sat down, ran her fingers across the beautiful instrument he had given her.

One by one, kids came walking in the door. Ms. Walters handed a freshly-tuned guitar to each, ushered them to chairs, and went around helping everyone get settled.

When they were all ready, it got quiet.

And Iz had a sudden flashback to her first lesson with Dr. Nguyen. It seemed like a thousand years ago.

She said shyly, "So, let's meet the strings. E, A, D, G, B, E."

Something moved in the corner of her vision. She turned to see what it was. Her eyes widened in disbelief.

Because Audra Allen stood in the doorway, looking untrusting and like she wasn't sure if she was going to enter the room all the way.

Their eyes met.

There was a weird, tense push-pull, like two magnets fighting with each other.

"So are you going to join us or not?" Iz said.

For a minute, she didn't think that the other girl was going to move.

But then Audra raised her chin and walked in.

Chapter Forty-Four

On the morning of the audition, Iz was a bundle of nerves.

She sat in her room right up until it was time for Pat to drive her to The Métier School. She couldn't stop practising the scales and arpeggios, or going over the phrasing in "Where'er you walk."

If she did not do her audition perfectly, then there would be no reason why they should let her into the school again. After all, other parts of her application were not nearly as good as they'd been the first time. Her transcripts were horrible. And then there was all the lying and stealing and hiding and cheating that hung over everything.

At last, she and Pat headed out in the car. As Iz sat there watching the green spring world racing past the window, she felt more and more like she was going to pass out. Meanwhile, Pat was looking extremely thin-lipped and upset about something.

When they arrived at The Métier School, Pat said tensely, "It's so crowded. I'll wait in the car, hon."

So Iz climbed the steps alone, which was fine with her. It was the only way she knew how to enter Métier anyway.

She reached for the handle. But before she could grab it, the door swung open. Teo held it for her, beaming like a mischievous sun. "Saw you coming through the window."

"What are you doing here?" Iz burst out.

"Did you notice I didn't knock you down this time?"

They walked together to the counter, as they had done on the first day of classes, six months before. Only now, everything felt different.

Teo said to Mrs. Harvey, "I'd like to introduce you to Iz Beaufort. She's auditioning. But I should warn you, she's kind of lippy."

Iz smacked him.

Mrs. Harvey smiled. "Iz Beaufort, I have been so looking forward to seeing you again. How are you?"

"Nervous," Iz said frankly.

"You'll be fine!"

When Iz had finished with the paperwork, she and Teo walked over to a couple of empty chairs in the waiting area. Iz tuned her guitars with trembling hands. She wasn't sure if she had the nerve to walk back in there—to face everything. Because it wasn't just going to be a chance to show how well she could play and sing. She had to try to wipe the slate clean. To show them that she could be different now. To try to make amends.

Teo's voice broke through her thoughts. "You're up!"

Startled, she looked around. Mrs. Harvey was waving at her from across the room.

"Ha! This is it," she said, standing up shakily.

She gazed down at him, where he was sprawled in his chair and grinning encouragingly up at her. She couldn't remember now why she had hated him so much.

"Th-thanks for coming to wait with me."

He shrugged. "Someone had to make sure you went through with it."

Clutching both guitars, Iz stumbled along the familiar hallway to the audition room.

Suddenly the judge's words came into her head. *You're being given a second chance. Don't waste it.*

Mrs. Harvey pushed open that big, carved wooden door and held it for her. Iz tried to conjure up the bravery to walk forward. But her feet felt like they each weighed a million pounds.

"Come in!"

It was a voice Iz did not recognize. She didn't actually know anyone sitting at the table, although she had seen some of them passing in the halls. She tried not to think about how they probably had all kinds of horrible opinions of her.

"H-hi," she said. "Uh ... here's my form."

As they passed it down the line, she added, "Do you want to start with technique or theory or my pieces? Or do you want to talk about Classical and Romantic history first?"

The lady at the head of the table smiled gently. "Before we begin—how are you?"

"Me? Fine," Iz said, heart beating so fast she thought it would explode out of her.

"You've been back at your old school," someone else said. "What has that been like?"

There was kindness in his voice.

"Huh," Iz said. "Okay, I guess." She tried to think of something they would find interesting. "I've been working hard on my audition. I've been writing a song cycle. Oh, and I kind of started a guitar club."

Then she wanted to kick herself. Who cared about the stupid guitar club?

But the first lady leaned forward, looking interested. "You did? Tell us about that."

Iz shuffled her feet. "It's not that exciting. This teacher talked me into it. I didn't think it would go too well, because, I mean, I'm still such a beginner on guitars that are actually strung the *right* way. But the kids are all beginners too, so it's ... it's pretty good."

The lady said gently, "Maybe someone there will pursue music because of you."

Awkwardly, Iz said, "Maybe."

Someone else added, "What a good use of your time."

Their encouraging words were almost more than she could handle. Her eyes welled up yet again.

And everything started spilling out.

"I-I felt horrible the first week. I actually thought about just giving up. And it was all the worse because it was totally my own fault. I deserved *everything.*"

She watched their faces transform.

"But I thought about Dr. Perlinger. I thought about how he would want me to keep going. I tried to picture him there with me."

Someone breathed in sharply.

"And," Iz said wretchedly, "I am so, so sorry I let you down. I let everyone down. If I could do it again, I would try to be honest right from the beginning. I would let Dominion Children's Care know I was auditioning. I would be up front with you that I've been in twenty-six homes and fourteen schools. I would give you my real transcripts—which, as you know by now, are not pretty. I would tell you, I have no musical training whatsoever and I have a history of being a little difficult and it takes me a long time to warm up to anyone. And I'm possibly a little, you know, unhinged or whatever."

She stopped to grab a breath.

"And I'd say that I kind of, like, stopped caring about anything for a long time, but then I saw Manifesto perform, and there was this *chord.* And it got right inside me, and it was like some kind of alarm clock. And I woke up right there in the concert, and I felt like I was looking at myself on the stage. And I took out my guitar for the first time in, like, *forever*, and I just sat there with it and I hugged it. And then I wrote this song, 'Refugee.' It was about how all I wanted was to be able to make my own path. It's kind of like my *theme song.* I don't know, like, it's my fist in the air or something."

There was a silence.

It went on and on.

"Anyway," Iz said, starting to feel stricken as they all just sat there. "Uh, I guess I should stop talking. I guess we should get started. There are a lot of kids waiting."

The lady spoke quietly. "At your last audition, you played Dr. Perlinger an original song. Maybe you would indulge me this time by playing 'Refugee'?"

Iz gaped. "I, uh, I haven't practised it. I've been spending all my time on the vocalise and 'Where'er you walk' and 'The Erlking' and arpeggios—"

The lady waved her hand. "I understand. But as the director of this school, I would absolutely love it if you might consider indulging me." She smiled. "Since it's your *theme song.*"

Iz drew in breath sharply.

Then, impossibly, she picked up her guitar and found herself conjuring an introduction that was all staccato, like galloping hooves. Only this time they were outrunning the demon.

***

When she stumbled back out of the audition room, she had no idea what to think. The examiners had all been incredibly humane. But she also had messed up a scale she had done okay on last time. And she still had breathed in one wrong place in the vocalise, and she'd totally forgotten the date when "Where'er you walk" had been written.

Teo jumped out of his chair. "So?"

Her heart swelled to see him there.

"I don't know. They were nice. But I made a bunch of mistakes. Ahh, they aren't going to let me back in."

"Beaufort, breathe," Teo said. "And think about how delicious all that food is going to be."

But that only made Iz panic even more.

Because tonight she was going to Teo's house for dinner. And she was even more scared of that than she'd been of the audition. She would be meeting the famous Nonna. And Nonna would no doubt spend the whole time glaring at Iz because Iz was a criminal and a liar.

Teo walked her to the car. Pat was on the phone when they got there. Her face was all squished up.

"Hey, hon," she said distractedly. "Come on in."

"See you tonight, Beaufort," said Teo. "Come hungry."

"Okay. Th-thanks for, you know, being here today."

"No problem." He grinned warmly at her.

Then Iz and Pat rode tensely home.

"Is … is everything okay?" Iz asked at last.

"Oh, hon, I didn't want to upset you before your audition."

Iz froze. Her mind started to race over scenarios, each worse than the last.

Pat said, in a quivering voice, "Baby, Brit and Vance broke up this morning."

"Ohhhh! I'm so sorry."

Pat's voice was teary and disbelieving. "And he didn't even give an explanation. After all she has been doing to make this wedding happen. He hasn't lifted a finger but he has the nerve to tell her he just doesn't think it's working. He was always one to keep everything to himself."

When they entered the hallway, Iz could hear Britnee on the phone in the kitchen.

"But babe, it was for *both* of us—"

There was a long period of silence.

Britnee said, "Yes, hon, but—"

She stopped again.

"Well, we could make changes if it means that much—"

Her voice dipped down low. "I miss you … do you miss me?"

There was more quiet, and then husky, rasping sobs. Her next words were hardly spoken aloud: "Baby, I can be different. If you give me a chance."

Pat raced out of her shoes and coat. She scrambled into the kitchen.

Iz thought about going into the kitchen too. But instead, she climbed the stairs up to her room and shut the door.

Chapter Forty-Five

A few hours later, she stood there in the front hallway all hunched over, waiting for Vito to pick her up to take her to Teo's house. And the whole time, she was panicking inside her head.

When Vito's old truck finally rumbled into the driveway, she called out tentatively to the tense kitchen, "Bye! See you later!"

"Bye, baby," Pat responded in a subdued voice.

Iz ran down the sidewalk and opened the passenger door. She jumped into the front seat beside Vito.

"Hi! Thanks for picking me up!" She added tartly, "Though I would like to point out that none of this was my idea. I'm not even sure why I'm going."

"Ah, calm down. He's a nice kid," Vito said, backing out of the driveway. "You could do worse."

"What are you even talking about?" Iz said.

"Nothing, nothing," Vito said, in a kind of huff of laughter.

Teo's house was located in a part of the city with old brick buildings, tall trees, and narrow roads. In the June evening, pale-green leaves had popped out on the trees. Soon they would mature into a canopy of green, and then shade and light would dance everywhere.

It didn't make the dread in her stomach go away.

Vito pulled into Teo's driveway and came to a stop. He turned the car off and opened the door.

"Are you coming in too?" Iz said, surprised.

"I'm going to say hello. I'm not just leaving you at some house."

When they rang the doorbell, a tall man opened the door. Iz thought Teo might look exactly like that about thirty years down the road.

"Iz? A pleasure to meet you. Joe Russo. Come on in. I'm glad you could join us." He shouted into the hallway, "Teo!"

Iz stepped into Teo's house.

Vito walked in behind her. He held out his hand. "Vito Santoro. Your son's a nice kid."

"We like him on a good day," Mr. Russo said.

"Iz here is a nice kid too. Talented. Special."

"My mother loved the recording on your website, Iz." Mr. Russo gleamed at her with a dazzling smile she recognized, but it made her nervous too. Because Teo's father surely must also be suspicious of her after everything.

He added, "Would you like to come in for a while, Vito?"

"No, no, I can't."

But he wasn't exactly leaving either.

"Hey! You made it!" Teo came striding into the hallway, even taller than his dad.

"Both of us!" Iz said.

Teo grinned at Vito. "Want to stay for dinner, Mr. Santoro?"

"No, no, I'm heading out." Vito finally stepped through the doorway onto the porch. "What time should I pick her up?"

"We can run her home," Mr. Russo said.

"Not necessary, thank you. I'll be picking her up."

It was like he was some overly involved border collie and she was a sheep he had to guard at all costs.

"How about … eight o'clock?"

"That'll be fine."

After Mr. Russo closed the door, Teo said, "That gives us two hours and fifty-eight minutes. Come on! Hurry up!"

He hung her coat in the closet and then led her through a living room dominated by a grand piano. Iz stared at it, eyes wide. They walked through the dining room, where the table was already crowded with casserole dishes covered in tin foil.

"Yeah, Nonna's been doing a little light cooking for you," Teo said, his mouth twisting with barely-contained laughter as Iz's eyes ran disbelievingly across all that food. "Come and meet her."

Iz steeled herself, stomach suddenly tightening.

They entered the warm kitchen, where a tall woman with grey and black hair crouched over the stove, humming sonorously, and doing things with pots. The smells hanging in the air made Iz's stomach growl.

"Nonna!" Teo said loudly, draping himself over her from behind in a huge hug. "I want you to meet Iz."

The woman turned around. Her eyes fell on Iz, who stared back. After what felt like forever, Nonna smiled, then reached for Iz's hands. She began speaking to Iz with warmth and affection, but Iz did not recognize anything she was saying.

Teo was talking at the same time.

"Nonna mostly speaks Italian. She understands a lot of English, but she hardly ever says anything in English. Right, Nonna? I can translate though."

"It is very nice to meet you," Iz said, half forgetting to be scared because Nonna's smile was so massive.

"She wants me to say that you have the voice of an angel. I already told you that before though."

"Wow. Not really. Thank you."

Nonna took Iz over to the wall in the hallway and gestured to a painting of a beautiful woman with sculpted brows, a fine nose, and a brilliant mouth that seemed to be on the verge of laughing. She looked dazzling in a long, burgundy gown.

"That's her," Teo said. "When she was young. She sang in opera houses. But then she got married and she had to stop singing, and my dad was born, and they left Italy. And the rest is history, as you know."

Iz gazed into Nonna's striking light-brown eyes, so similar to

Teo's. Hers were folded over with wrinkles but still powerful. "I wish I could have heard you."

Then Nonna put a hand to Iz's face and spoke to her.

"She says after dinner maybe we can sing together," Teo said, mouth curving into amusement. "See, I told you she had an ulterior motive."

Dinner was served exclusively by Nonna, who carried in pasta, meat, and cheese dishes with ceremony and placed them in the few remaining places on the table. Iz tried to help, but Teo's grandmother insisted she sit beside Teo and be served as if she was a treasured guest.

"Don't argue with her," Teo's dad said. "You're not going to win. Just enjoy."

"You've gone to such trouble," Iz said to Nonna.

Teo burst out laughing. "She does this every Sunday when everyone comes over. In fact, she does it whenever people set foot in here, which is, like, nearly all the time." He narrowed his eyebrows fiendishly. "Except tonight. Because I said I'd hurt anyone who showed up."

"That's very violent," Iz told him.

Then Nonna was encouraging her to eat, and she lost herself in the food. And somehow it gave her the confidence to speak up, buoyed by Teo's teasing and Nonna's delight in how Iz was devouring everything.

"That's a beautiful piano in the living room," she said to Teo's father.

"Ah, thanks! We kids got together and bought it for my mom. There are six of us, four boys and two girls."

"Wow," Iz said.

"And seven thousand cousins," Teo added.

"It's an old instrument but it has a beautiful tone." Mr. Russo half smiled. "It was a thank you for, well, a lot of things."

"She taught me how to play on it," Teo said.

"She did." Mr. Russo's voice was light. "Maybe Teo told you about all of that, how Nonna came to live with us. Eight years ago now."

"He did. I'm so sorry," Iz said.

She looked at the three of them, picturing that time. Nonna must surely have been like a miracle then, like a nail holding together fragments by sheer will. If anyone deserved a piano, it was her.

She said to Teo, "Nonna introduced you to opera, right?"

Teo said something in a questioning tone to Nonna. Nonna spoke back to him.

"*La Bohème* was the first," Teo said. "Puccini in general. Then Verdi. She told me the stories and sang the parts. And looking back, it was like being ganged up on by Mimi and Rodolfo and Violetta and everyone. Right, Nonna? It wasn't a fair fight. I didn't stand a chance."

Then Teo and Nonna and his dad were laughing, but Iz bet that it had taken them a long time to get to that point.

Nonna reached over and put her hand on Iz's. She spoke to her seriously then, frowning a little.

Iz panicked. She was sure that Nonna was talking about the court and stealing and lying. Nonna was asking her to explain herself.

Teo was watching Iz closely. "She wants you to know—"

"I'm sorry," Iz said, looking down at her plate.

But Teo was still talking. "She just was saying, she feels like she understands your story."

Iz looked up then into Nonna's face, which was solemn and somehow searching at the same time. Like Nonna could tell what was inside Iz.

"She does?"

"Yeah. I hope it's okay I mentioned it."

"Uh." Iz was blushing furiously now. "I guess."

Nonna said some more. Then she patted Iz's hand.

"She's saying she understands not being able to do something you love and how it's like your soul being eaten away. And she wants to tell you that even though sometimes it feels like you're lost, you have to always be like the earth. You have to keep spinning through the dark toward the sunrise." Teo leaned over to his grandmother. "Nonna, that's cool. Is it from something?"

Nonna answered.

"It's from Nonna," Teo said, grinning. "And she says it's for you."

Nonna spoke again and put a hand on Teo's face while he gazed back at her with such undisguised love that Iz was blushing to see the two of them.

"She says she found the sunrise when she gained a little partner. She says she went from never singing again to never singing alone. Aww, Nonna." He leaned over and kissed her on the cheek.

But gaining a partner surely wasn't the same, Iz thought, as being allowed to sing *yourself.*

She said softly, hoping it wasn't too rude, "I wish, though, that you'd never had to stop."

Nonna spoke at length then, her Teo-eyes on Iz's face all the while.

Teo said, "She wishes it too. She wishes she had fought harder. She sometimes even wishes she'd walked out on Nonno—no way, Nonna! *Seriously?*"

Mr. Russo said to Nonna, "He was awful to you sometimes. I was scared of him too."

A stark look passed over Nonna's face, so fleetingly it was like the shadow of a cloud on a windy day. Maybe everyone who had survived such a thing carried it forever after embedded in their skin.

It made Iz feel brave suddenly, audacious. She said softly to Nonna, "I understand that. Being scared of . . . of people, I mean."

That Place.

She wasn't ready to tell Teo or Nonna about it. But maybe one day she would.

Nonna reached over and took Iz's hand as if it was very special. Held it in communion.

After dinner, she felt so full that she could barely stand. But before she knew it, Nonna was guiding her out to the living room.

Teo sat down at the keyboard; ran his long fingers reflectively through some chords. She stood by his right side, mentally translating what he was playing into notes on her own familiar instrument.

"I wish I'd brought my guitar tonight."

"That's okay. I can accompany us."

His hands continued to meander through a variety of progressions, then resolved into an introduction to "Santa Lucia." He smiled as she recognized it. Nonna sat down in the armchair opposite, moving her head gently as if she were agreeing with them.

Teo said to Iz, "Jump in."

"What? Oh, no. Not in front of Nonna. I have zero technique. I'm not very good."

"I'm just going to keep riffing till you start." He smirked at her and played the same thing over and over. "Are you getting bored yet?"

Iz rolled her eyes finally. "Okay."

She waited till it felt right.

Then she jumped off the shore, hoping she could swim.

When she began to sing, she heard Teo's piano chords supporting her voice, answering it, giving it meaning. Then suddenly, his beautiful, rich, buttery voice joined with hers.

After another minute or so, Nonna was singing with them too.

Iz got the courage to open her eyes, look at them both. Teo's dad sat and sipped a glass of wine, listening.

At the end of the song, Teo kept playing, one cadence dissolving into another.

Nonna called from her chair to Teo, who broke out laughing.

"She wants me to tell you I'm a good grandson. Which, you know, I don't really *need* to tell you because you can see that just by looking at me. I embody greatness." Teo continued to play softly, smiling down at the keys.

And Iz intended to say something obnoxious in return, but somehow it never came out.

The evening seemed to pass quickly in that little living room. Before she knew it, the time had come for Vito to arrive. Teo got Iz's coat and then they stood on the front porch together, waiting for Vito to pick her up.

Teo said, "Hey, thanks for coming. It meant a lot to Nonna."

"Thanks for inviting me." She kicked at a pebble, sent it tumbling over the step.

Side by side, they gazed out at the dark street. The only light came from street lamps and muted windows. Teo shoved his hands in his pockets. "I never," he said, "really noticed how tall street lamps were before."

"Is that right?" Iz said, laughing. "You thought they were shorter?"

"I thought," Teo said, "they were so much shorter."

All at once they were staring at each other, and the laughter was gone, and Iz was feeling slightly hypnotized by Teo's tawny eyes locked on her own.

Then Vito's truck rattled into the driveway.

Chapter Forty-Six

After that, the final week began. It was filled with rehearsals and the guitar club.

That was the good part.

The bad part was the horrible thing looming on Friday.

Therapy.

Iz tried to pretend it wasn't coming. But the days passed anyway. And suddenly she was sitting with Pat in the car on the way to her first session, feeling like she was going to throw up.

She said in a tiny voice, "I might be getting sick. My legs are kind of weird. I think we should reschedule."

Pat fixed her childlike eyes on Iz and simply said, "You can do it, hon," as if her flimsy words could somehow calm the churning in Iz's stomach.

They pulled into the parking lot of the place.

Pat's phone rang.

She rummaged in her purse and pulled it out. "It's Brit, hon. I have to take this. Are you okay to go in on your own?"

"Sure," Iz said dully.

She walked the thousand miles to the front door, knowing how much this was the opposite of a good idea. Her whole insides were curling up as if she were a dying insect. Soon she'd be dissected and pinned and judged.

Audra Allen's voice shot into her memory. *You're not normal. Not balanced.*

Once inside, she followed the signs until she came to a horrible frosted door that said, *Meredith Danes, Individual and Family Therapy.*

Iz crossed her arms protectively over her chest. She stood there for a while, unable to imagine opening the door. Finally, though, she reached out a trembling hand, turned the knob, and pushed.

"Isabelle!"

A woman poked her head out of a room at the back. Her hair was barely contained in various combs. She was smiling in a kind of chaotic, open way.

"Uh, hi," Iz said, standing there anxiously.

"I'll be right with you. I'm Meredith. Just have a seat anywhere."

So Iz sat down on an overstuffed couch and gazed guardedly around the little office. Took in the plants and the seashells and the framed pictures. The fish in the little bowl on the desk. The coffee table that had sand and pebbles under the glass, all zen-like.

None of it made her feel the least bit relaxed.

"Sorry for the delay! Come on in. Sit wherever you want."

Meredith was ushering Iz into the little room. Iz stood up jerkily, stumbled through the doorway. She looked at the various chairs scattered around. Finally she sat on the one that was farthest from Meredith's little desk against one wall. She picked up one of the pillows and clutched it in front of her.

The fog was curling around the edges of the room, waiting.

Meredith sat down opposite. All of her busy energy seemed to suck back into her, like she was becoming completely focused on Iz.

"How are you doing today, Isabelle?"

"Good," Iz said. "You . . . you can call me Iz."

"Iz." Meredith nodded and wrote something down on her notepad. "Have you ever attended therapy before?"

"Not really." She clutched the pillow harder.

"Then you are probably feeling completely nervous and cautious, and that is perfectly normal. So let me take the pressure off for a few minutes, and I'll tell you a little bit about me. And you can feel free to interrupt at any moment."

Iz nodded, kind of feeling like she was outside herself.

Then Meredith talked for quite a while about her background as a psychologist and how she was married and had a dog named Buster, and how her favourite colour was green because it was like growing things and lots of other information. Then she explained that she was there to be a support to Iz, to help her to try to make sense of things, to unravel what might feel tangled up. She said her role was to walk beside Iz, to figure it all out together.

And Iz was struck by that, because she was suddenly remembering Dr. Perlinger saying the same thing about Manifesto. How he walked beside them and helped bring out of them what was already there.

Then Meredith said, "If you want to, you could tell me some stuff about you. If you feel comfortable enough. And if not, we can talk about something else completely! Or nothing. I'm totally open."

Iz put her chin down on the pillow.

She waited a couple of minutes.

And then she heard her voice unexpectedly saying, "Yeah, so I guess I'm here because I think I'm obviously kind of totally messed up."

She waited for Meredith to agree.

But after a long time, Meredith said, "Totally messed up. Those feel like heavy words to carry around."

Iz laughed a little half bark.

"Well, I mean, you're going to find out that my brain doesn't work right at all. So anyway . . ."

Meredith said curiously, "How do you think a brain should work?"

Iz clutched the pillow further. "Ha! Not like *mine.*"

Meredith just waited.

Finally Iz went on, mostly to fill up the silence. "It's . . . it's kind of like I don't exist, you know? I mean, I've been a lot of different people in a lot of different places, good places and . . . and pretty bad places. And sometimes I'm not sure which me is actually real."

And her eyes widened because she had never said the words out loud before and she hadn't been planning to say them now. But they seemed to have been waiting under the surface for exactly this minute, and they were bubbling out now like water forcing itself through the crust of a frozen stream.

After awhile, Meredith said gently, "You exist. You're a human on planet earth. Just like me. Just like everyone else."

"Well, I mean, I know I am *physically* here."

Meredith waited.

"But inside my head, I'm all kind of . . . fragmented."

A silence went on.

And Iz was thinking about That Place.

Tears began to edge out of her eyes. She smudged at them miserably.

Meredith held out the tissues that were sitting beside her. Iz wiped her eyes and blew her nose.

Meredith said gently, "That sounds really hard."

Iz shrugged.

Meredith went on, "Tough experiences—traumatic experiences—can have an effect on us. We figure out how to cope with them in a lot of different ways. And afterward, even when the traumatic thing is gone, those coping mechanisms can stay with us. They can change how we respond to just about everything."

Iz thought about that.

She whispered finally, "Like you're looking through a fog."

Meredith nodded. "Sometimes people respond to danger by running or by fighting. And sometimes they freeze."

Iz blinked.

Freeze.

Like the Beloved—completely stuck in ice at the beginning, not knowing who she was, bound all around, until she made the decision to smash everything.

Which was fine in a song cycle. In real life, it wasn't that easy.

She muttered, "How are you supposed to fix that?"

Meredith smiled. "Maybe we can explore it together." She paused. "You're a writer, correct?"

Iz was startled. "Well, you know, I write *songs*."

"Exactly. You're a writer. And a beautiful musician, I hear." Meredith's face was kind.

"I guess. I don't know."

"Tell me this," Meredith said softly. "In your writing, what kind of voice would you say is there?"

"Uh," Iz said. "What do you mean?"

"What are you writing about? What are you passionate about? What are you saying? What is your *voice*?"

Is thought about that for a while. "I . . . I think I'm angry."

"Good," Meredith said, encouragingly.

"I think I'm not just angry for myself. I'm angry for . . . for people who are trapped. For kids who are, you know, under the power of adults who don't know how to look after them or-or who shouldn't be allowed anywhere near them. I guess I'm calling it out in my songs. I'm shining a spotlight on it and saying it's wrong."

Her voice had risen during this. When she stopped talking, it felt like it was still ringing in the air.

Meredith said after a minute, "What would you call that voice?"

Iz frowned. "I don't know."

She thought for a while.

"A . . . a fierce voice, maybe. I guess."

Meredith exhaled softly and nodded. "A fierce voice." She smiled. "And that's powerful, don't you think? That's someone who exists."

Iz blinked.

She squinted directly at Meredith for the first time.

Thought of all those songs, of the little girl who had written them.

"Maybe," Meredith said, after awhile, "we need to follow that fierce voice and see where it takes us."

Iz winced, without meaning to.

"It might—" she said.

Meredith waited.

"It might take us somewhere kind of—"

Iz drew up her knees and hugged them.

She couldn't figure out how to finish the sentence. So they sat there quietly for a long time while she examined her kneecaps.

Eventually, Meredith said, "Well, art does kind of take us through everything, doesn't it? Some things are pretty and some, not so pretty. Some are downright *yucky.*"

Iz nodded, all confused inside.

Then she whispered, "Yeah, some of my songs—I mean, *a lot* of my songs—"

She swallowed.

Could she?

"There was—"

She took a deep breath.

"There was this one place."

She was shaking now. She hadn't intended to tell Meredith any of this. But now she couldn't stop.

"And, I mean, I asked my social worker to get me out of there, like *twice,* and nothing ever happened. Then, when it got to the point where I couldn't stand it, I kind of went postal."

She flushed with shame.

"And, like, then they finally let me go. And they didn't press charges. But—"

She breathed out slowly.

"I kind of feel like I never left. Like I'm still stuck there and I'm still begging people to help get me out, and nobody's listening. Which is actually a violation of my *rights*, I recently found out. And why didn't anyone ever talk to me about my rights before?"

There was a long silence while the fury simmered up in her. The stillness kept going on and on.

Finally Meredith said in the kindest voice Iz had ever heard, "I'm so sorry that happened. You didn't deserve it. You weren't to blame. It wasn't fair."

Iz's eyes blurred and she swiped at them.

"Yeah, no," she said thickly.

Meredith said softly, "Anger. Acting out. Those big feelings. We tend to consider them to be bad things. But sometimes they are the healthiest response to an unhealthy situation. You didn't get swallowed alive. You got yourself out of there. You survived."

Iz let out air slowly. "I guess so."

"Fierce voice," Meredith said.

Iz thought about that for a while.

She said tightly, "I've got a lot of songs. I basically started writing them when I was seven."

Then she stiffened, wondering if Meredith would think she was bragging.

But Meredith was just smiling at her, like she was actually interested. Like she would welcome anything Iz wanted to share.

And totally unexpectedly, Iz heard herself saying, "So, I mean, I ... I guess I could bring my guitar some time."

"I'd be honoured," Meredith said.

"Huh," Iz said. "Uh ... okay."

This was not at all how she'd thought the therapy session would go.

Chapter Forty-Seven

When Iz and Pat got home, Britnee was in a fetal position in the living room. Pat rushed in and draped over her like some kind of blanket.

"Baby," Pat said, like a bell tolling. "Baby."

Britnee's voice was half gone with crying. She rasped, "I still don't get it. He says I never listened. But he never spoke."

She turned to Iz, with swollen eyes.

"I mean," Britnee said huskily, "Iz, did you ever hear him once say *anything*?"

Iz looked from Pat to Britnee. She thought about Meredith. She thought about being a fierce voice.

She realized she was tired of accommodating Britnee's point of view all the time.

"Um. I-I—maybe he was scared of saying something wrong."

"What exactly does *that* mean?" Britnee's voice went cold.

Iz's heart was racing, but somehow she couldn't stop talking. "Well, remember the vows? He tried to write them. You didn't like what he wrote. You rewrote everything."

Britnee looked like a steaming pot on a stove. "So what?"

"Like, *vows.* They're the ultimate thing a person has to say, if you think about it." She paused. "And you told him his words were no good."

Britnee was glaring at Iz now, hair poofing around her head like a martyr's halo. "You don't know anything about it. He was stuck. He didn't know what to write."

"Oh, baby," Pat said to Britnee. "That's for sure. You were just helping."

Britnee suddenly shouted at Iz, "I was just trying to help him get his thoughts out! And to be honest, you don't know anything about it. I don't even know why I'm talking with you about this. Like *you're* the authority on doing the right thing."

Iz winced and flinched at Britnee's fury.

Her fingers went numb.

"Okay," she said.

Then she turned and hurried out of the living room. She took the stairs two at a time.

Behind her, she could hear Britnee saying, "Where does she *get off*—?"

Iz stayed up there in her room for the rest of the night. She ate some of the food she kept under the bed for emergencies. Finally, she crept under the covers and fell into an anxious sleep.

But in the middle of the night, she was wakened by Britnee screaming on the phone, like an emergency signal going off.

Then Pat was screeching, "Oh, baby! Baby!"

Iz peered at the alarm clock, terrified.

It was two fifteen in the morning.

Not long afterward, the doorbell rang. Britnee yelled and pounded to the front door, and then a new voice growled, a bass line under Britnee's spurts of strained alto.

Iz heard Britnee say, "Baby, I've never listened to you. Not really *listened.* Like with the vows. I had to have it my way. And I don't need everything to be pretty and perfect. I just need *you.*"

Iz's eyes widened.

Vance's voice rumbled thickly. "Yeah, I don't know. You don't understand. My childhood, it wasn't . . . like yours."

Britnee said fervently, "I want to hear everything."

That was when Iz put a pillow over her head. She tried to dive deep, deep down into a murky place where there was only dark sleep. Where Britnee was nowhere to be found.

She only woke up when Pat tapped at the door, all crackling energy.

Sunshine was streaming in.

"Baby, amazing news. Brit and Vance are back together!"

"No way," Iz said sleepily.

"It's true! They're both downstairs having breakfast. We've had such a night! You have no idea."

"Wow, that's great."

"Hurry down," Pat said warmly. "I've got bacon and eggs and pancakes."

Iz struggled to a sitting position, swung her legs over the bed, and sat there for a long time. Finally she shrugged into some clothes.

When she entered the kitchen, Britnee and Vance were sitting at the table, and Pat was frying things.

"Iz!" Britnee squealed when she came shuffling in. Like she was Iz's best friend. Like they hadn't had a brutal showdown the night before.

"Hey," Iz mumbled, guardedly.

Britnee put an arm around Vance. "Did Mama tell you our good news?"

"Uh, yeah," Iz said. "I'm really happy for you both!"

"Aw, that's so sweet of you. We're really happy too. Everything's going to be different now. Right, Vance?"

Vance nodded. Like an engine trying to start up, he said, "New beginning."

Iz slipped into a place at the table, and Pat set a full plate in front of her. Doggedly, she began to eat while Britnee chattered away.

"Yeah, we're paring down the wedding a lot because Vance finds all the details kind of stressful. And mama may not come on the honeymoon after all. Then, afterward, we're going to try to save some money toward a house, so we might be living here together for a while."

"Oh!" Iz said. "That's wonderful."

She forced her face to stay neutral, but her brain started gasping and spluttering like it was being drowned. *She couldn't do it.* She couldn't live with the three of them, crammed into Pat's house and tiptoeing around the drama of everything. Just the thought of it made her feel bone-weary.

As soon as she was finished eating, she pushed back her chair abruptly. "Uh, I should probably get ready for the tech rehearsal. Vito'll be here soon."

"Oh, that's right, your concert's tomorrow! What's it for again?" Britnee spoke brightly.

"We're recording my scholarship audition."

Britnee lit up with the sudden generosity of someone who had reclaimed her top position in the world. "Mama's phone is the best one out there! It has four different cameras. You should use that to record your concert!"

Iz flushed. She couldn't tell if Britnee was genuinely offering, or somehow needling her some more about stealing Pat's phone. "Uh ... no, that's okay."

"Seriously!" Britnee turned to Pat. "Can't she use it?"

"Sure, baby, of course," Pat said placidly. "Anything she wants."

"You were such an amazing help getting us back together," Britnee said, her eyes flat and blue. "I think you're turning a corner, Iz, I really do."

Chapter Forty-Eight

The back of Vito's truck was filled with microphones, a sound board, music stands, speakers, and lights that he had been driving around collecting from everyone's homes.

"All this stuff isn't even going to fit in the restaurant," Iz said, climbing into the passenger seat.

"Of course it'll fit in the restaurant."

She fastened her seatbelt, hugged her knees, then was silent on the drive from Pat's house to the restaurant.

Vito said at last, "Butterflies?"

"Huge massive killer moths."

He barked a short laugh.

"I don't think I can do this," Iz said frankly. "I think I'm going to throw up instead."

"You sing in front of people all the time."

"Yeah, but this is different. This is my own composition, you know? And there's a lot of money riding on it. And I have to show that I've gained massive amounts of knowledge since coming to Métier ... but at this moment I don't remember anything anyone's ever even said to me there."

Saying the words out loud made it all feel nearly unsurpassable.

Forget having a fierce voice. She was more like festering laryngitis.

"Slow down, slow down." Vito waved at her while keeping his eyes on the road. "First of all, you've sung lots of your own songs.

Second of all, every time you sing in Festa it's for money. Third of all, I don't even know anything about music and I can tell you deserve a scholarship."

"Yeah, but The Métier School has standards."

"What, are you saying I don't have standards?"

"No, no, that's not what I—"

But he was laughing at her now, and they were pulling up at the back of Festa.

"Relax, cara," he said. "You've got this."

When Iz and Vito walked into the restaurant, everyone from Manifesto was already there. They helped to bring the equipment inside, and Teo began to direct where to set up the keyboards and music stands the way they'd discussed. LaRoyce and Bijan started to put the lights where they wanted them. Ahmed was concentrating on the sound board. Kwame and Will took Pat's phone and connected it to the tripod and speakers.

Becky appeared in front of Iz, holding a microphone stand. "Do you want this in the centre or on the right?"

"Uh ... I don't know. I don't know," Iz said helplessly.

Everything was suddenly too big.

Then Teo came vaulting over a keyboard—which Dr. Perlinger would not have approved of at all—and Iz found herself blushing, which she'd been doing pretty much since that dinner at his place.

"Hey, Beaufort. Why don't you go off and practise or something?"

The next thing she knew, he'd maneuvered her into the kitchen and she was sitting there with her guitars and her music, all alone except for the busy sous chefs.

"Sit! Stay!" Teo said, as if she were a dog.

"I should help."

"Frankly, you're no help whatsoever, Beaufort. Just chill and do some deep breathing or something. Meditate. Think about nothingness."

Then he was flashing his teeth at her and heading back out into the restaurant.

She closed her eyes and leaned back in the chair and thought about nothingness to the best of her ability. But her brain was full of far too much to be able to empty itself. It kept trying to make lists of things to remember in the *Winterreise* songs, kept searching out particular moments for intonation and expression in the Lágrima. And of course, it wound round and round the score for her song cycle, all of the vocal and instrumental parts.

Not to mention the words!

She had written far too many words. She was going to forget them all. In fact, she *had* forgotten them.

Iz groaned out loud, just as Gisele came down the stairs from the apartment up above.

"Iz, are you nervous? It'll be okay!" Gisele sat down at the table and patted Iz's hand.

"This is a mistake," Iz said tightly. "All this." She waved her other hand at the air. The more she thought about it, the more she knew that none of it should be happening. "I'm not good enough. They've just been, you know, humouring me up till now. I don't know nearly as much as everyone else."

Gisele put an arm around Iz. "It seems to me that you were born to do exactly this."

Iz was silent.

"All those homes, and all those schools and yet somehow, you are here today. Isn't that something?" Gisele squeezed her.

Gisele meant well. But in Iz's current state, she didn't find Gisele's words particularly comforting. They seemed to highlight the precariousness of everything that was happening at Pat's house right now.

"Somehow," she repeated in a little flat voice. "I'm here today. But every morning, you know, it's always at the back of my mind that they'll show up at the door and tell me to get my stuff. Or maybe they'll come to Métier with my things already packed, maybe half of it left behind, and take me to a new place. And I keep thinking, what happens if I leave a guitar at home that day and they don't bring it to me? Or what if they don't see my notebook sitting on the box by the bed and it gets thrown out? And what if I have to fight with them to allow me to keep going to Métier or ... or to *here?*"

Gisele looked a little stricken.

Iz felt immediately guilty. "I'm sorry. Never mind. Chalk it up to nerves."

"Okay," Gisele said.

She stood up and went out through the swinging doors. And Iz sat there, fuzzy, trying to figure out what had just happened.

Should she run after Gisele and apologize?

Here they were offering their restaurant and making a lovely meal and giving her half of the money, and she was complaining about things they were certainly not to blame for. Stupid, self-pitying, today of all days.

She was getting out of her chair to go find Gisele and beg her not to be offended. She would thank Gisele, over and over and over, for everything.

But just then the doors swung open, and Vito walked in followed by Gisele. They looked serious.

Iz stared at them, open-mouthed. Were they going to cancel the concert?

"Sit down," Vito said to her grimly.

Iz sank into her chair again.

"I'm sorry," she said in a tiny voice.

Vito was frowning at her. "What for?"

She waved her hand. "Complaining. I didn't mean to. It's horrible. I'm horrible. Please forgive me. I won't do it again."

And she was gripping the chair with her hands so she wouldn't cry. She was so, so tired of crying. Everyone else was tired of it too. Why couldn't she keep it together like other people?

Gisele slid into the chair beside her while Vito walked around the table and sat down. He leaned his arms heavily on the table, regarded her with no expression whatsoever on his face.

"Am I . . . fired?" she said in almost no voice at all.

"Fired? What are you talking about?"

"Cara, we were going to speak to you about this after. But maybe now isn't such a bad time." Gisele's voice was very quiet.

"Speak about what?"

Every nerve was firing now.

"Gisele and me, we were talking," Vito said. "I mean, we're not exactly young. She's younger than me but that's not saying much."

Gisele was smiling at Vito then, as if he was the most adorably idiotic person she knew.

Vito began to speak somewhat confusedly, looking off at the ceiling. "But we're not so old that we're over the hill. And I know we're not the most interesting people around, or the most cultured. We do what we do. We run a nice restaurant. But we love beautiful music. We don't know much about it, mind you. This Bach or Schubert or whoever. But now Verdi, I know *Verdi.*"

Iz was trying to follow this.

Gisele said, "Can I step in here? What Vito's saying is, we've been talking. And we can offer a stable home, good food, walking distance to The Métier School. But it's up to you. If you want. Give us the word, and we'd start the training sessions to become foster parents. And then, you know, there's this thing called foster to adopt—"

Iz's eyes flew open. "Whaaa—?"

Foster parents?

Adopt?

"Only if you want," Gisele said hastily. "It's just an option. Just an offer. You could try it out, see what you thought—decide if you wanted to make it permanent—"

"You'd have your own room. That's one of the rules . . ." Vito's voice trailed away.

Gisele said at last, "Just think about it. No pressure."

"You don't have to," Vito said at the same moment.

They were both gazing at her with great hope all the same. Like she was some rare, cherished thing in their eyes.

"Oh!" said Iz.

She blinked.

It was like when she'd burned herself on a stove top, years before. The sensation had taken a minute to register in her brain. Now she stared blankly back at Vito and Gisele, wondering how you were supposed to respond to finding out someone actually *wanted you there* and you actually *wanted them there* too. Were you supposed to jump up and down and scream? Did you shake their hands, or burst into tears? What?

Out of her half-numb mouth, a word scratched out. "Well . . ."

They waited.

Her brain responded at last, pictured being three altogether.

Like . . . like a kind of *family* or something.

And a weird joyful feeling erupted in her.

"Yes . . . yes. *Yes.*"

Chapter Forty-Nine

When Iz opened her eyes on Sunday morning, she was immediately buzzing with equal amounts of excitement and terror and happiness.

It was *the day!*

She spent some time lying in bed before getting up. Her mind cast back over everything in the past year, almost as if this was her birthday. In a way it was. She was being born all over again, this time on her own terms.

Pat drove her to Festa midmorning. She parked, then handed Iz the phone. "You're going to be careful with this today, right, baby? With so many people milling around."

"I will be so careful," Iz said, taking it gently in her hands.

"I know you will, hon. I'll see you at the lunch. Vance and Brit are coming too."

"Oh, good!" Iz said.

She waved as Pat drove off. Then she took in a deep breath, let it out slowly, as the late-June breeze curled around her face.

She pushed open the door of Festa.

Vito was telling waiters where to move tables. When he saw Iz, he said, "Here's trouble." Then he waved for her to follow him over to the bar.

Iz hopped up on a bar stool.

"Gisele," Vito roared.

She came out of the kitchen, wiping her hands, her face red. They were cooking like crazy in there, Iz guessed.

"Are you excited? Here we are, after everything!" Gisele enveloped Iz in a hug.

Vito leaned down, opened the bar fridge, lifted out a small box. He put it on the bar.

Gisele said, "Vito chose it."

"This is for me?"

"It's not for me," Vito said.

Under the eyes of Vito and Gisele, Iz opened the lid. Nestled inside was a purple flower and some smaller pink and white blossoms. They were on a long pearl-headed pin that was wrapped round with ribbons.

She leaned in and inhaled deeply. It smelled like deep summertime.

"It's *beautiful,*" she said.

"Yeah? Okay."

Gisele added, "He's been fretting about it. Had to be just right for Iz."

Vito waved a hand as if to swipe away her words. "Let's put it on."

"You put it on?"

"It's a *corsage.*" He sounded gruff, but the grimace on his face had a softness to it.

Iz had no idea what a corsage was, but she stood still while Gisele gently pinned the bundle of flowers onto the dress that Pat had bought her for today.

"Go see yourself," Gisele said gently.

Iz went over to one of the mirrors. She turned one way and the other. The little flowers picked up the rich sheen of the dress. It was perfect.

She turned to them and said softly, "Thank you."

Vito loudly cleared his throat and started cleaning the bar.

Just then, Becky and Jasleen came pushing through the front door, laughing and talking.

Iz's stomach immediately tensed right up.

It was starting. No going back now.

Jasleen came over, hugged Iz. "Okay if we warm up?"

"Of course!"

They sat at the front on the chairs and music stands that had been set up in a semi-circle. Becky took out the three pieces of her oboe and twisted them together while soaking the reed in her mouth. Jasleen opened the cello case and lifted out the heavy instrument. She tightened the bow and slid rosin up and down it. Then she adjusted the endpin, leaned the cello against herself, and put her head down as if she needed to see each vibration up close. She drew the bow across the string. A nearly human voice sang out, long and low.

Next, Ahmed and Will and Kwame burst in together, loud and high energy. They waved and went to set up too. Before long, everyone was improvising together.

By late morning, Manifesto had all arrived except for Teo. Iz kept waiting to see him come swaggering in the door. She was going to ask if he had wanted to make some big entrance by being late. But there was no sign of him.

Meanwhile, the place grew ear-woundingly loud.

"Okay, okay." Vito went around clapping his hands at twelve-thirty. "Everyone upstairs. We've got snacks up there. Clear the space. Guests are coming in a minute."

Everyone clomped through the kitchen and up the back stairs. Iz remained with Vito and Gisele, though, ready to greet people as they arrived.

Where was Teo?

She was starting to worry.

The first people walked in, diners she recognized from many previous nights. She smiled and welcomed them while everyone talked about how much they were looking forward to the afternoon.

The waiters showed people to their reserved tables and began to take drink orders.

Gradually, almost everyone arrived.

Directly in front of the stage, at table five, there was Dr. Perlinger, his wife and his two little wild-haired and lovely daughters. Dr. Perlinger was engaged in animated conversation with the smaller one, who was energetically waving her arms and explaining something important. His wife, Celeste, fixed the straw in her older daughter's glass and held the cup so it wouldn't spill.

Dr. Nguyen and his wife were sitting in a large group of several couples at table three. There was a lot of laughter happening over there. Dr. Nguyen was bent over guffawing.

At table nine, Dr. Henderson and her wife held hands across the table. They were talking about something so intently that they seemed not even to be aware of the noise and movement around them. Dr. Henderson was as festooned with wraps and scarves as her wife was not.

Then Jamaal came walking in the door, tall and easy and comfortable. It was so weird to see him here.

"Iz! You look great."

"Thanks! We have this table for you," she said, leading him to the right of the stage.

"It's perfect."

"Do you need anything? I could get you some water."

He laughed. "I'm all set."

Pat, Vance, and Britnee were sitting at table seven together. Britnee was sipping champagne and Vance had his arm around her. Whatever they had talked about in the middle of the night had seemingly changed everything because they were gazing at each other like they were the same person. It felt like the period after a storm when the world was gradually figuring itself out.

Iz was staring at them when a voice broke into her thoughts.

"Hey, Beaufort."

She jumped, flew around. "You're late!"

"No, I'm not. We just came later so Nonna wouldn't have to sit as long. Concert's not for another hour and a half." His eyes crinkled at her. "Were you worried I wasn't going to show?"

"No."

"Yeah, you were. I'm going upstairs. *Relax.* You look like you're in the middle of a war."

"You'll be in the middle of a war in a minute," Iz said.

Nonna had just been seated with Teo's dad. She waved at Iz from their table.

Iz walked awkwardly over in the heels Pat had bought her and leaned down. "Hi, Nonna! Hi, Mr. Russo! Thank you so much for coming!"

Nonna kissed her on both cheeks and spoke at length.

Mr. Russo said, "She says you look beautiful, Iz. She's right. She wants to know where you got the lovely corsage."

"Oh! Uh, thank you!" Iz touched the fragrant purple flower. "Vito and Gisele—Mr. and Mrs. Santoro—gave it to me."

Nonna spoke again.

"She says go easy on Teo in that beautiful dress."

"What?"

Iz stumbled in the heels, almost fell over. She had the definite feeling that Mr. Russo was laughing at her. He was as bad as his son.

She started fidgeting away. "Well, have a great afternoon."

At one o'clock, the lunch began. First the waiters brought out the antipasti—a choice of insalata mista, calamari, or arancini. Accompanying the antipasti were grilled tomato crostini, bruschetta, olives, and focaccia bread.

The restaurant soon filled with beautiful aromas. It felt weird to just stand and watch everyone eating without playing something lovely and atmospheric on her guitar.

Next was the primi. Gisele had prepared a choice of two different pastas as well as a risotto dish with mushrooms. Cutlery clattered and voices were raised, wine sipped. It came to feel closer and closer to the Festa in which Iz was safe and comfortable.

The secondi, with its chicken and veal and fish and fagioli, seemed to pass quickly. All at once, everyone was on the dolci.

At that point, Iz retreated upstairs.

When she entered Vito and Gisele's apartment, Manifesto students were lounging in the living room, leaning against the counters in the kitchen, sitting cross-legged against the walls in the front hallway.

She looked around to see where Teo was.

Not surprisingly, he was at the centre of an outburst of laughter. Bijan, Becky, Jasleen, and Ahmed were clustered with him around the couch.

Teo looked up, saw her. "Beaufort!"

He leapt over the arm of the sofa and bounded over.

"It's almost time," she said lightly. She felt tingly and cold.

"It's going to be great. Really. How could it not be? I mean, you get to sing a duet with *me*."

It was true. At the end of the last song, the great throng of voices would dwindle away bit by bit until there were only Teo and Iz singing. Then, finally, it would be Iz's voice by itself.

"I'm totally proud of you," Teo said, looking down at her.

She could feel her face beating red. Abruptly, she needed to get away. "I-I have to tune my guitars."

Flustered, she stumbled down the hallway, past the kitchen and toward three bedrooms.

You'd have your own room. That's one of the rules.

Her own room—her own *home*—that was a joy she couldn't really look at yet. It would either be the icing on the cake or a great consolation prize, depending on whether the concert was a success or an utter disaster.

She plunked herself down cross-legged at the very end of the hall. She drew Teo's guitar onto her lap to tune it, leaning close and listening in her head to what the notes should be.

LaRoyce sat down beside her, holding the piano score he'd be playing while she sang the four songs from *Winterreise*. He was unusually muted for him.

"How're you doing?" he said, looking at her sideways. "You ready?"

She shook her head.

"Iz, Iz, Iz. Have faith. It is going to be sublime."

"I have no faith in anything, including myself. Except you. I have faith in you. Thank you again for accompanying me."

"If I can give you your cues, that's all I ask."

At that moment, Iz heard the rumble of Teo's voice followed by a screech of laughter from the living room.

It brought an unexpected smile to her face.

He was such an idiot.

Chapter Fifty

The waiters cleared away dessert plates and poured coffee for people. Meanwhile, Will and Kwame were doing final adjustments to Pat's phone at the back, playing with the tripod and quietly testing the microphones that were attached.

Vito gusted around like a bossy wind. "Please and thank you, everything off and away. Nobody records this. No exceptions. You can access the official video later." Then there was the rustle of everyone obediently putting their phones into purses and pockets, settling into a comfortable position.

Bijan and Teo were to be the masters of ceremony.

They stepped at last into the small spotlight, Teo so much taller than Bijan. Teo glanced at Iz, who was hugging herself offstage and trying not to run away. He gave her a half smile and a tiny fraction of a wink, so fast she nearly missed it.

Then his resonant voice echoed out over the audience. "We would like to welcome you to Isabelle Beaufort's scholarship concert."

Everyone applauded and Iz felt her stomach turning somersaults as if she was in an elevator going very fast in fourteen directions at once.

Bijan said, "We will be recording it for her submission, so I ask you to be mindful of remaining very quiet during the performances. Applause in between, though, is most welcome!"

"Our concert is in three sections," Teo continued smoothly. "The first focuses on guitar. Iz will perform the Bourrée from Bach's Suite in E minor, from the Baroque period, followed by Lágrima, by Fransisco Tárrega, from the Romantic period."

He spoke so calmly, sounded so self-possessed. It was like he had always been standing on a stage in front of people.

"We would like," Bijan said, "to welcome Isabelle to the stage."

He gestured, smiling, for her to come forward.

In the sudden silence, she settled herself on the stool she had used at Festa so many times. She lifted Teo's guitar onto her lap and found homes for her fingers.

She blinked, breathed in.

And then she began to play.

As she travelled over the strings, part of her mind was thinking about bringing out the voices, having the correct intonation, finding the arc of each phrase.

The other part was remembering again what Teo had said when he gave her the guitar.

You'll be bilingual.

Tonight, she bent into this new language, her fingers producing the music in whole new positions on the strings. She felt profoundly grateful. She made the gratitude come out through the vibrations in the strings, imbued every note with it.

In the silence after the second song, she finally lifted her head.

Clapping burst out of the darkness beyond the lights that Manifesto had set up for her.

She stood up, bowed as Dr. Henderson had taught her to do.

Becky was suddenly there, smiling and taking Teo's guitar from her hands.

Then LaRoyce settled behind the keyboard, stretched his fingers and feet into position. He looked to Bijan and Teo, who had stepped back out into the little spotlight.

Bijan said, "Our next section is devoted to works by Franz Schubert, from the Romantic period. Isabelle is going to perform four songs from the great song cycle *Winterreise*, which is based on a series of poems by Wilhelm Müller. The songs are, 'The Weathervane,' 'In the Village,' 'Flood,' and 'The Hurdy Gurdy Man.' You'll find English translations for each of them on the back of your menu."

Then LaRoyce's eyes were locked on her, waiting for her signal.

It was just the two of them.

She closed her own eyes for a minute, breathed.

Think about nothingness, Beaufort.

Opened them again.

Nodded.

All through the *Winterreise* songs, she didn't stop looking at LaRoyce. He, for the most part, glanced up and down from music to fingers, and occasionally at Iz. But the two of them were completely connected by the way they were *speaking in sound* to each other—picking up each other's ideas and agreeing, building, saying, *I was thinking about this,* and *Yes, and consider this.*

When the songs came to an end, she took a short break. She gulped water, hands shaking. Waiters moved around discreetly, delivering cups and glasses. Gisele hugged her and Jasleen got her a chair.

A short time later—too soon, too soon—Manifesto students filed through the kitchen doors and came to stand around the ring of the restaurant.

Then the rustling and whispering stopped. Silence fell.

Bijan and Teo resumed their places at the front.

Teo smiled around at the audience, his eyes lighting on hers in passing.

"We're all very excited about the next performance. It's an original song cycle written by Isabelle. As such, it represents the Modern period."

Bijan added, "This song cycle is like a twin to *Winterreise.* Iz repurposed symbols and images from the original, to create an alternate winter journey."

Teo continued, "In Schubert's version, the hero descends into despair because his Beloved is betrothed to someone else. In Iz's version, the Beloved refuses to accept her fate of being married off to a rich man. She leaves home in search of who she was before she was confined by societal rules. She enters a kind of alternative reality in which she smashes the frozen status quo and finally melts it, revealing a new world."

Bijan said softly, "And in that new dream world, she meets another person—maybe her own missing younger self. As the song cycle ends, they join voices together."

Manifesto began to wind onto the stage, taking their place in front of chairs. They picked up their instruments and stood waiting.

Bijan said, "And now, Isabelle, will you come and join us onstage for the premiere performance of *Meltdown*?"

Meltdown.

A meltdown could be a tantrum. The Beloved melted down when she had hit her limit, when she could not take things as they were anymore. A meltdown could also be the transformation of a frozen world into life-giving water. Together—tantrum and transformation—they were like the apocalypse Dr. Perlinger and Bijan had talked about. They were at once the destruction of the world and the renewal of it.

Fierce voice.

Iz felt strangely calm.

Then a weird flicker happened—like this moment was suddenly sliding against other moments, and all times were happening at once. She was in the middle of that concert at Dennison Hall. She was auditioning for Métier. She was attending her first lessons, and she was singing on all of those nights at Festa. She was longing to be part of Manifesto and also standing with them at this very minute. *Right now* was always *right now*, in every story.

It was like a message from someone, somewhere, not seen but felt.

You are exactly where you were intended to be.

Chapter Fifty-One

After the storm
After the melt
The rivers are running
And I'm breathing at last
Freed from the ice
That held me fast

I'm broken and I'm singing
New life is springing
And it doesn't look the same
Because I'm not the same

And I'm wandering now
And I don't know where
Then I come on a figure
Standing there
She's playing a song
And she's all alone
No one to listen
But she doesn't care

I know the song
It used to be mine

Back when I wasn't scared to sing
When my heart wasn't
Broken with everything

When a soul gets ripped in two
Can the pieces join anew?
I hope it's true
For here I am
And there I am
And I'm half-dead with fog and pain
Just longing to be whole again
After the storm
After the melt
New world
New choice
My voice

At the very end, it dwindled down to just Iz's voice singing alone.

Then she fell silent too.

And the silence was like a spell. People waited, not wanting to break it.

But suddenly shouts of "Bravo!" rang out. Everyone started to stand up, clapping.

The confused shock travelled up her nervous system to her brain.

They are cheering for me.

Then Bijan, LaRoyce, Teo, and Becky were beckoning. She stared at them, hardly sure what they wanted. Becky put an arm around her shoulders and walked her to the front of the stage.

Iz stared out at everyone.

"I—" Her voice sounded so thin. She gathered herself.

"Thank you, thank you for coming. Dr. Perlinger, Dr. Henderson, Dr. Nguyen. And Pat and Britnee and Vance. Ah, and Vito and Gisele, who offered their beautiful restaurant this afternoon and created this delicious menu, and who have made this place like a home for me. And Jamaal."

He smiled at her all the way up to his eyes and raised a hand.

Frantic whispering erupted behind her.

"That's Jamaal Wickerson!"

She went on. "And Manifesto. I couldn't have written any of this without you."

She was absolutely not going to cry this time.

"You stood by me when there was no good reason to do it. You worked to make every single thing here happen, from helping me figure out the ideas, to teaching me how to create an orchestral score, to organizing the space at Festa, and the lights and the . . . the"—she looked around wildly—"music stands and the microphones and the sound board and the—"

"We get the idea," LaRoyce said, his expressive face one huge grin.

She nodded rapidly. "I've been thinking a lot about song cycles. How they're made up of all these separate pieces. And how the pieces kind of gain meaning in their *relationship* to one another. No song really stands by itself. It needs the others to make sense. Same with keys—majors, minors, they are related to each other. Nothing alone."

For a fleeting minute, her eyes locked with Teo's.

"And that's what I feel like this year has been for me. Like I began as a single rough melody line but started collecting all of you along the way. And you filled out the harmonies and the instrumentation. And now I'm completely changed because we are somehow all *connected* now."

She looked at Jamaal then.

She said softly, "Soul to soul."

He nodded and smiled.

She wondered if she should say more. She didn't know how to put it any better. But it didn't matter, because everyone started clapping again.

When the lights came up, she was swarmed. She shook hands, thanked people over and over, and squatted down to chat with Dr. Perlinger's little girls, who were awestruck at meeting her. Vito steered her around the room to chat with some of the regulars.

Meanwhile, Jamaal was mobbed by several members of Manifesto, who all seemed to know exactly who he was.

"I read about you in *Motif Magazine* this month! Thirty most promising jazz musicians under thirty."

"I have both of your recordings. They're amazing. If I'd known you were going to be here, I would have brought them."

When she had spoken to nearly everyone, the crowd began to thin out. Soon it was mostly the Métier students, Dr. Perlinger and his family, Pat, and Britnee and Vance.

Finally Iz could take a breath, to allow herself to savour what had just taken place.

Then someone cleared his throat behind her. "Uh, Iz?"

She whirled around. Vance stood there.

Iz stammered, "V-Vance! Thanks for coming!" She had never actually talked to him one-on-one before. She had no idea what to say.

"It was good," he said, in that thick voice that seemed to have to work hard to come out of him.

"Thanks."

"If you haven't gone through it, you don't understand." He waved at the stage.

Iz turned to look, not sure what Vance was talking about. "Gone through ... what?"

"Huh," said Vance heavily.

Iz let out her breath slowly. She started thinking back to the baby pictures he didn't have, to a childhood that wasn't there.

"Were you ... in care too?" she asked.

He shook his head. "But I should have been."

Then he was staring at her as if he could see through to That Place, just like Nonna had. They all carried the mark somehow, those who had gone through such a thing.

"It's hard," she said softly, "to figure out who you are."

He nodded.

"Babe! Iz!" Britnee's husky voice broke into their conversation. She was still holding her champagne glass. She beamed at Iz. "That was incredible, hon. I mean, I can't believe you were doing all of this up in that little bedroom. You have such a bright future ahead of you."

"Thanks," Iz said.

Britnee turned her attention to Vance. "I was thinking, maybe we should have our honeymoon somewhere that has a lot of music. Like, Mexico, maybe."

"Uh, yeah," Vance said, looking claustrophobic, like he was cornered.

Iz knew that feeling far too well.

Controlled. Trapped.

Britnee kept going. "Gotta be on the beach, Margaritas, mariachi bands. We should start looking into that soon if we're going to—"

Vance sighed loudly, raggedly.

Britnee stopped dead. Two little red dots appeared on her cheeks. Weakly, she said, "Okay. Right. We're keeping it small."

Vance closed his eyes. He took a deep breath. "Maybe . . . maybe I want to just elope."

Britnee sucked in a shocked breath.

She opened her mouth and shut it again.

In a small voice, finally, she said, "Okay. If that's what it takes. Bottom line, I want to be with *you*, Mr. Vance Whitney."

Iz almost choked then.

Britnee Whitney.

And Vance burst out laughing. "Ha! Like *you'd* be happy eloping!"

Britnee pushed him. "You're bad!"

Iz started trying to figure out how she could tactfully get away from them. She said, "Well, I should probably—"

Panicked voices interrupted her from across the room.

"No! Oh, no! *No, no, no, no.*"

Iz whipped around to see Kwame, Will, Bijan and Teo all staring at Pat's phone with horror.

Something flipped over inside her.

Then she was scrambling across the room toward them.

"What is it? What's wrong?" Her voice sounded all high and thin, like a violin screaming.

Teo looked up at her blankly, for once with nothing to say.

Bijan said softly, "The power drained somehow. It didn't record."

Chapter Fifty-Two

Everything seemed to be happening through a waterfall. She stumbled against Teo, who was standing beside her now.

"I don't understand," LaRoyce was saying. "It was full before the concert."

Pat came racing up. "Is my phone okay?"

"Your phone is just fine, but it ran out of power," Bijan was saying patiently. "Maybe you put on a new app or something? They can drain the battery sometimes, depending on how big they are."

"I do not," Pat said, flustered, "put on apps. Brit, where are you?"

Then Britnee was there.

"They say I put on an app," Pat said to her anxiously.

Britnee frowned and blinked.

"Well, I downloaded a new Wedding Registry Organizer on there yesterday, because you said you would coordinate the gifts. It does everything, communicates with all the stores. It gets amazing reviews." Britnee looked around at everyone, frowning. "What's the problem?"

When they explained, her eyes widened so the mascara ringed them into nearly perfect Os.

"No!"

Nobody answered.

Britnee's voice was shaking, not its usual drawl. "Oh, I'm so stupid. Iz, hon, I'm so sorry! I didn't know it would do that!"

Everything in Iz was suddenly writhing, furious, dark-dark-dark.

All she wanted to do was shout at Britnee, *Yes, you are stupid! You have taken something that was so precious and mattered so much and you have so easily destroyed it!*

But instead other words staggered weakly out. "It's ... it's okay."

"It's not okay!" Vito's voice spewed out like enraged lava. "Do you know the work that went into this concert?"

"Vito," Gisele said warningly.

"No, this one here, it's all about her and this stupido matrimonio. Has to make sure she gets her wedding gifts—" He was sounding really dangerous and a little unhinged.

"*Basta!*" Gisele's voice made it clear she wasn't going to tolerate another minute.

Britnee's eyes were filled with tears.

"I'll make it up to you, baby, I promise," she said.

"I'm not a baby," Iz found herself muttering. She said it louder. "I'm not a baby."

"I know you're not. Oh, Iz, I know that!"

"You don't actually know anything about me—"

She had more to say, but all at once she felt Teo's hand on her back. That surprised her so much, she stopped mid-sentence.

She took a deep breath. "It was a mistake. You didn't mean to." Then, fiercely dismissive, she turned away. "I'll see you at home."

Britnee was blinking at Iz's tone. "Well, bab—Iz, if there's anything I can do ..."

Pat said in a chastened voice, "What time should I pick you up, hon?"

"Don't worry. I'll get a ride. Everything's fine." She took a deep breath. "Thank you for coming."

It was like she was standing outside herself and witnessing it all.

"Oh, hon," Pat was saying softly.

Iz muttered, "It's okay. It's okay."

If she said it enough times, maybe it would be true.

She watched as the three of them said their final good nights, gathered their things, and made their way out. Watched as they *escaped* and left her there with the aftermath.

Iz could hardly meet anyone's eyes. She couldn't stand to see the pity.

Jasleen spoke up then, her voice soft but clear, like the ocean calming itself.

"We could do it again." She looked around at everyone for agreement. "I know some of the audience is gone but maybe those who are left wouldn't mind sitting through it one more time. Who has something to record it?"

Then everyone was pulling out the phones they'd been forced to put away during the concert.

"But can Iz's voice hold up if we do the whole thing again? With *Winterreise* and *Meltdown*, it's a marathon." Teo looked worried. "We don't want to blow out her vocal cords."

They began to argue among themselves.

Iz felt a tap on her shoulder.

"Ahem," said Dr. Perlinger.

He had his phone out too.

Seeing him, Iz burst into tears. Soon the full magnitude of what had just been lost would flower grotesquely in her mind, but right now she just felt like she was in horrible shock.

He said in her ear, "No, no. See this."

He held up his phone and she saw students filing onstage to take their places at the beginning of *Meltdown.*

It took her a moment to realize what she was looking at.

"You recorded it?"

"Ssh," said Dr. Perlinger. "I have the whole concert."

Iz stared. She said, numbly, "What—how?"

Dr. Perlinger shrugged, smirking a little. "Occasionally, I operate outside the law."

LaRoyce shouted, "Dr. Perlinger made an illegal video!"

Everyone erupted at this. Dr. Perlinger rode it out quite gamely, smiling around. Then he said, "I think, in view of the surprise ending to our evening, I can buck the rules a bit and submit this on behalf of Iz."

Then they were cheering and leaping around.

Amid the uproar, Dr. Perlinger said softly to Iz, "It was an excellent concert."

"Thank you."

Then she could not help asking the big question in her mind. "Do you—is there—have they—?"

Dr. Perlinger said gently, "The official audition results go out tomorrow."

Then his face was filled with a kind of compassion. And she felt her own face draining of blood, because people who made that expression were usually planning to soften a blow.

"It's agony waiting, isn't it?" he said very quietly.

She nodded, every muscle tight now. "If I didn't get in, could you just tell me? I don't think I can handle another night if it's going to be a no."

Dr. Perlinger took a deep breath, looking like he was trying to weigh something out.

Finally he said, "Well, let's put it this way. I've been chatting with Dr. Starling, our director ... and I *think* it may be worth the wait."

Iz had her hands to her face then, stifling whatever raw sound was trying to come out.

"Ssh," said Dr. Perlinger. "I did not say anything. I am also not saying—based on this extraordinary concert—that you *might* have a good chance at a full scholarship. Because none of it is in my hands, you understand—"

He was interrupted by the smash of something metallic at the back of the room.

Shadowy people were hurling themselves around back there, freed from the intensity of performing. Ahmed and Will seemed to be throwing buns while whipping each other with napkins. Bijan was trying to lunge up and touch the ceiling. And Dr. Perlinger's younger daughter was standing on one of the tables, gesturing wildly at Jasleen and Becky, who were laughing at whatever she was saying.

"Ah," Dr. Perlinger said. "This may well be my cue to leave."

He and his wife, Celeste, made their way to the back of the room and collected their daughters. Dr. Perlinger said something mild to everyone that made them calm down. Then he and Celeste wrestled their children into coats.

At the door of the restaurant, Dr. Perlinger turned, and waved at everyone.

Iz suddenly ran forward and threw her arms around him.

"Well!" Dr. Perlinger said, in a surprised and delighted way.

"All of this," she said, lacking the words to adequately convey her meaning. "Thank you. Our lessons. Talking together. You … you changed my life. You have no idea."

He smiled at her with great kindness. "And you, mine, Iz Beaufort. What a joy it has been to watch you blossom."

Then his eyes widened. "I almost forgot! Silly me."

He paused. Regarded her.

"You missed the May round of Manifesto auditions."

Iz's breath caught in her throat.

Dr. Perlinger continued, "If you are interested, that is, if it might appeal to you …"

She waited.

"We *might* consider this evening's performance to be, I don't know, a sort of makeup audition, perhaps …"

"What?"

Her mouth was hanging open.

Hoping. Hardly daring to—

He spoke solemnly. "In which case, under the circumstances—"

"You are killing me, Dr. P," Iz said.

He laughed out loud.

Then he whispered, "Iz Beaufort, welcome to Manifesto."

Iz threw back her head in amazement and ferocious joy. She yelled so loud, she half wondered if that long-ago Iz at Dennison Hall might hear it.

Everyone came running, looking alarmed.

All she could stammer, inarticulately, was, "Manifesto! I'm in Manifesto!"

"Ah! Beaufort!" Teo shouted.

"Not officially!" Dr. Perlinger was saying helplessly, but it was too late. Iz was at the centre of a warm and jostling circle of laughing and screaming friends.

When she was free again, she grabbed Vito and Gisele, drew them forward.

"Dr. P, before you go, I would like you to meet Vito and Gisele. They're—" She looked at them both. "They're the best people in the world. And they're going to be my new foster parents. Foster to adopt, I mean."

Dr. Perlinger's eyes lit up. "A pleasure!" Warmly, he shook each of their hands.

"The pleasure is all ours," Gisele said, blushing. "Thank you for taking her on."

He bowed his head to her. "No thanks needed. It's been a joy dealing with this wunderkind."

"You speak German?" Gisele said. "My mother spoke German."

"German," said Dr. Perlinger. "French, Russian, this and that." He eyed Iz. "We'll have to get you started on other languages soon."

"You teach Italian?" Vito asked abruptly.

"Italian," said Dr. Perlinger, "will be absolutely *essential.*"

Vito regarded Dr. Perlinger with approval. "Good."

After Dr. Perlinger had finally herded his family out the door, the Métier students pushed six tables together and threw themselves around it. They looked like they were about to have some kind of out-of-control Thanksgiving feast. The waiters put down enormous pitchers of water, juice, and iced tea. Then platters started arriving, filled with the pastas, meats, and appetizers that had been served early in the afternoon. It turned into a party.

As she approached, everyone looked up and roared, "Iz!"

Teo had saved a spot for her beside him. She slid into it gratefully.

"Hey, Beaufort," he said. "Look at this."

"What am I looking at?"

"Total awe," he said, grinning at her.

She blushed hugely. Before she could think twice about it, she leaned over and kissed him on the cheek.

Then she pulled back, appalled. "I'm sorry!"

But Teo gazed at her with some kind of steadfastness and warmth. He put out his arms and wrapped them around her, hugging her tightly, like he was a stronghold. And suddenly it felt exactly right. Suddenly she just wanted him to be there forever, with that gleaming, teasing grin and tossing hair and gigantic heart. He felt like he was *hers.*

"Sfogliatelle," Vito said loudly, placing it down in front of Teo.

At his voice, they shot apart guiltily.

"Thanks," Teo said, actually reddening for once.

"You're welcome," Vito said grimly.

When Vito had walked away, Iz peeked sideways at Teo. He was staring with stunned amazement, like a mirror of her own overflowing self.

He smiled slowly.

Seeing her.

Iz smiled back, seeing him too.

Then she realized that everyone along the table was watching them.

"Nice," Bijan said to LaRoyce.

"Finally," LaRoyce said.

Teo picked up a roll and whipped it down the table. Amazingly, it ricocheted off Bijan's head and across the table at exactly the right angle to bounce off LaRoyce.

"Yesss!" Teo said. "You saw that, right?"

"I saw that," Iz said, rolling her eyes.

"Because you know that was a million to one shot."

Will threw the roll back, and Iz reached up and caught it. She stared at it.

Million to one shot.

That was her.

That was this moment.

Then she gazed around at them all. She watched Ahmed twisting napkins through the handles of an army of empty espresso cups, saw LaRoyce mutter something that made Bijan laugh uncontrollably. Kwame was hanging spoons off his face. Jasleen sat beside Becky and talked quietly with her, but then caught Iz's eye and smiled, putting a hand on her heart.

Iz couldn't contain the exultation welling up inside.

Her voice rang out, fierce and wild and joyful.

"I love you all. I can't wait for the beginning of next term."

They all cheered. Cheered for her.

Acknowledgements

I am so grateful to Common Deer Press for giving Iz a home and a voice. Thank you to my editor, Emily Stewart, who guided this process with such insight and sensitivity. Thank you also to Debbie Greenburg for proofreading the manuscript, and to David Moratto for the typesetting. Finally, I must express my gratitude to the uber-talented Bex Glendining for their gorgeous cover art. It continues to take my breath away.

I am also thankful for the many people who gave input into the story. First on the list must surely be my husband John, who has read all versions of this novel and unfailingly given me a perspective on what was working and what wasn't (a very tall feat, accomplished uncomplainingly over seven years). My parents, Jean and Martin Terry, both read an earlier version of the manuscript and gave thoughtful feedback. My friend Dana Lynne Endersby offered the invaluable and sensitive insight of a caring foster parent who adopted three of her foster children. Susan E. Powell read some early chapters and supplied an extremely helpful lawyer's perspective on possible ways in which Iz's case could transpire. And lastly, I must thank my friend and colleague, Heather Cooke, who has set aside a shelf in her home for the eight binders of previous versions of this story that she's read. I'm grateful for her passionate empathy for Iz, her fierce defence of characters when I wasn't sure about their place in the story, and her unending enthusiasm for—and loyalty toward—all things

Métier. When I worried that this book would always be my favourite piece of writing that was never published, she never wavered in her conviction that the wandering Iz would find a home and a voice. Everyone should have such a friend.

I also owe a debt to the academics whose perspectives on Franz Schubert and *Winterreise* helped to inform this story. In particular, the great tenor Ian Bostridge's book, *Schubert's Winter Journey*, unquestionably influenced my thinking and informed the conversations between Iz and Dr. Perlinger. Barry Mitchell's book, *Schubert's Wanderers,* contains the translation of *Winterreise* that I'm referencing in this manuscript.

Thank you also to the Office of the Ombudsman of Ontario, which very graciously gave permission for me to quote portions of their brochure, "Know Your Rights in Care."

I also need to acknowledge the role that my own background has played in this story.

As an adopted person who spent my first weeks in foster care, I understand Iz's feelings of not casting a shadow or quite existing in three dimensions. I did not know my own Indigenous background (Cayuga Nation) until I found a biological aunt, Bev Hazzard. And I did not know about the existence of a biological brother who had also been adopted, until I applied as an adult for my redacted records from Children's Aid. Getting to unite with the wonderful and big-hearted Rob Herlick (a complicated and creative process, due to the fact that CAS would only connect siblings if there was a medical emergency) was like suddenly standing on the earth like a real person. Rob and I missed out on the first half of our lives together, but we're making the very best out of the second half. It feels like the triumph of humanity over bureaucracy.

My experiences as a teacher have also informed this story. I've taught several foster children whose educations had been disrupted due to multiple moves and whose files bulged with paperwork that referenced behavioural issues. And yet, many of these children blossomed when given a chance. One little girl in particular entered my room with fury and belligerence but—like Iz—melted at the first sign of music. That year, she learned to read through an improvisational and totally experimental mashup of letters, melodies, and rhythms. Her musicality exploded along with her literacy—until the day she was unceremoniously and without notice transferred to a new foster home outside of our school boundaries. This novel is, in part, a love letter to her and all of the other promising little souls out there who deserve a better chance.

Lastly, I must express my tremendous gratitude toward everyone who nurtures children in the arts, whether it be in the public school system, in private venues, in community groups, or in any other mentoring capacity. Unquestionably, exposure to the arts helps to craft young people's development as whole humans. The world is a better place for it. In an era of cuts to programs deemed non-essential by governments whose priorities lie elsewhere, we must all fight for the arts to remain available to children everywhere.